The Regent Mysteries Continue

While Captain Jack Dryden would lay down his life for the Regent, he draws the line at endangering his wife in the dark alleyways of Cairo—the place where the Regent's friend and procurer of antiquities has gone missing.

But Lady Daphne Dryden will not be denied the opportunity to see swaying palms, crumbling pillars, and soaring pyramids in exotic Egypt. She even insists on bringing her youngest sister, Rosemary, who's enamored of all things Egyptian. The Regent insists on sending Stanton Maxwell, England's most imminent expert on Egyptology, as their interpreter and his own soldiers as their protectors.

Some of the praise for Cheryl Bolen's writing:

"One of the best authors in the Regency romance field today." – *Huntress Reviews*

"Bolen's writing has a certain elegance that lends itself to the era and creates the perfect atmosphere for her enchanting romances." – *RT Book Reviews*

Lady By Chance (House of Haverstock, Book 1)
Cheryl Bolen has done it again with another sparkling Regency romance. . .Highly recommended – *Happily Ever After*

The Bride Wore Blue (Brides of Bath, Book 1)
Cheryl Bolen returns to the Regency England she knows so well. . .If you love a steamy Regency with a fast pace, be sure to pick up *The Bride Wore Blue*. – *Happily Ever After*

With His Ring (Brides of Bath, Book 2)
"Cheryl Bolen does it again! There is laughter, and the interaction of the characters pulls you right into the book. I look forward to the next in this series." – *RT Book Reviews*

The Bride's Secret (Brides of Bath, Book 3)
*(*originally titled *A Fallen Woman)*
"*W*hat we all want from a love story...Don't miss it!"
– *In Print*

To Take This Lord (Brides of Bath, Book 4)
*(*originally titled *An Improper Proposal)*
"Bolen does a wonderful job building simmering sexual tension between her opinionated, outspoken heroine and deliciously tortured, conflicted hero." – *Booklist of the American Library Association*

My Lord Wicked
Winner, International Digital Award for Best Historical Novel of 2011.

With His Lady's Assistance (Regent Mysteries, Book 1)
"A delightful Regency romance with a clever and personable heroine matched with a humble, but intelligent hero. The mystery is nicely done, the romance is enchanting and the secondary characters are enjoyable." – *RT Book Reviews*

Finalist for International Digital Award for Best Historical Novel of 2011.

A Duke Deceived
"*A Duke Deceived* is a gem. If you're a Georgette Heyer fan, if you enjoy the Regency period, if you like a genuinely sensuous love story, pick up this first novel by Cheryl Bolen." – *Happily Ever After*

One Golden Ring
"*One Golden Ring*...has got to be the most PERFECT Regency Romance I've read this year." – *Huntress Reviews*

Holt Medallion winner for Best Historical, 2006

The Counterfeit Countess
Daphne du Maurier award finalist for Best Historical Mystery

"This story is full of romance and suspense. . . No one can resist a novel written by Cheryl Bolen. Her writing talents charm all readers. Highly recommended reading! 5 stars!" – *Huntress Reviews*

"Bolen pens a sparkling tale, and readers will adore her feisty heroine, the arrogant, honorable Warwick and a wonderful cast of supporting characters." – *RT Book Reviews*

Cheryl Bolen's Books

Regency Historical Romance:

The Brides of Bath Series
The Bride Wore Blue
With His Ring
The Bride's Secret
To Take This Lord
Love In The Library
A Christmas in Bath

House of Haverstock Series
Lady by Chance
Duchess by Mistake
Countess by Coincidence
Ex-Spinster by Christmas

Brazen Brides Series
Counterfeit Countess
His Golden Ring
Oh What A (Wedding) Night
Miss Hastings' Excellent London Adventure
A Birmingham Family Christmas

The Regent Mysteries Series
With His Lady's Assistance
A Most Discreet Inquiry
The Theft Before Christmas
An Egyptian Affair

The Earl's Bargain
My Lord Wicked
His Lordship's Vow
Christmas Brides (Three Regency Novellas)
Marriage of Inconvenience
A Duke Deceived

Romantic Suspense:
Falling For Frederick

Texas Heroines in Peril Series
   Protecting Britannia
   Murder at Veranda House
   A Cry In The Night
   Capitol Offense

World War II Romance:
It Had to Be You

American Historical Romance:
A Summer To Remember (3 American Romances)

AN EGYPTIAN AFFAIR

(The Regent Mysteries, Book 4)

Cheryl Bolen

DEDICATION

For Kay Hudson, a gifted writer, who for the past two decades has read every book I've written and has supported me as reviewer and "corrector" extraordinaire

Forward

Throughout this book I have used the words *Orientology, Orientalist,* or *Orientalism* for what present-day readers consider *Egyptology.* The scholarly study of Egyptology did not come about until at least 30 years after my story takes place. All study of Arab cultures was then known as Orientalism. The days of Egypt's great archaeological expeditions were also decades away.

I have also spelled the place we now know as *Giza* in the way it was spelled in the early nineteenth century, *Gizeh.*

My story takes place a decade and a half after the 1798 French defeat by Lord Nelson at Abukir. Four months before that British naval victory, the Egyptians had been conquered by the Napoleon-led French. Both countries were interested in the Suez Canal to shorten routes to India and the Orient. The British were not interested in ruling Egypt—as Napoleon had been. At the time of my story, there were few English in Egypt besides a diplomatic consul. There were more Frenchmen in Egypt, and their consul was a more powerful force than the British.—*Cheryl Bolen*

$\mathcal{P}$rologue

Lady Daphne, whose preference to be known as Mrs. Dryden was largely ignored, sincerely hoped the Prince Regent had summoned her and Jack here today to seek their assistance in one of those investigations the Drydens had proven to be so capable of solving. Poor Jack had been rather restless of late. It was such a pity that in order to stay in the Capital with his wife he had to forgo the adventures he had enjoyed as Wellington's most successful spy.

How disappointed she and Jack would be if their sovereign had asked them to Carlton House merely to see one of his new (and massively expensive) pieces of art. As fond as she was of their rotund ruler, she concurred with the general populace which deplored the manner in which he squandered the excessively generous funds granted him each year in the Civil List.

As she and Jack progressed up the Regent's staircase that mirrored an identical one opposite, she eyed every painting and statue they passed. In this, the wealthiest city in the world, there was no greater display of impeccable taste--and bottomless pockets--than the Regent's ever-evolving and expanding Carlton House in the most fashionable part of London.

They came to the marble octagon and passed through it and two more anterooms before reaching the throne room. She could not readily see the Regent's throne because two well-dressed gentlemen stood before him, but he quickly dismissed them and welcomed Jack and her. Daphne's first thought was that he must have shed at least ten stone. Then as they moved closer, she was convinced he'd gotten a wider throne. Which was actually quite clever of him. The last time she'd been in this chamber she kept thinking how much the Regent reminded her of Mr. Tom trying to squeeze his furry feline body into one of Papa's shoes.

"So very, very good of you to come today, my lady," he said to Daphne. Then he turned to Jack and nodded. "Captain Dryden." She had not seen the prince looking so robust in a long time. And he really did look much slimmer in his fine black jacket and the expertly tied cravat that concealed the rolls of flab beneath his chin. For the first time, she could understand how he had long ago been referred to as the handsome young prince.

As soon as he had addressed them, he rang for a servant, and when that footman appeared almost immediately, he said, "Procure chairs for Lady Daphne and Captain Dryden."

Other than the throne, there hadn't been a single chair in the chamber. Monarchs were not accustomed to their subjects sitting beside them. But their dear Regent always treated Daphne and Jack almost as he would his dozen siblings.

A moment later, a pair of armless gilt chairs were placed facing the prince. He peered at Daphne. "I beg that you take a seat, and you too, Captain."

After they sat before him, he drew in a deep breath. "I have asked you here today because I am faced with a most perplexing problem." This was punctuated with another sigh. "In the past you two have been able to satisfactorily resolve every distressing situation with which I've presented you." He frowned. "I fear, though, that no one can help me this time."

"Your Royal Highness," Jack said, "I cannot at present speak for my wife--not knowing the nature of your difficulties--but I shall always be happy to offer myself in service to the Crown."

Offer himself? Daphne did not at all like the sound of that. Offer his life? She might just have something to say about that.

The Regent held up a pudgy hand. "Allow me to tell you the nature of my difficulties." It was a moment before he continued. "Do you know what a mummy is?" His gaze shifted from Jack to Daphne.

"As in Egyptian?" she asked.

He nodded solemnly, as did Jack.

"Good. Let us begin at the beginning. Last year. For some years now I have been interested in Orientology."

She and Jack both nodded. One had only to see his pavilion in Brighton to understand how thoroughly enamored His Royal Highness was over Oriental architecture and decor. The Royal Pavilion looked like an Indian palace designed by a Chinaman in an opium stupor.

"I have had a great many dealings with an Indian, Prince Edward Duleep Singh, who has procured nearly priceless works of art for me from throughout the Orient. Last year he showed me a painting of a highly ornamental mummy's mask with jewels set in solid gold. It came from the coffin of the pharaoh Amun-re. He offered to sell it to me for a very great sum."

For their spendthrift Regent to consider it a very great sum, it must be a fortune.

"Of course, I had to possess it. I managed to sell a few statues and come up with enough money for the purchase. He left last August and told me that once he'd procured it for me, he would send it to London by specially armed couriers as he's always done so readily and reliably in the past."

Jack quirked a brow. "I take it you've not yet received it even though nearly a year has passed?"

"What's more," the Regent added, "*no* one has seen the prince since he arrived in Cairo last winter. I've been in communication with several British officers who've returned from Egypt. They know many of the men with whom Singh associated, and none has seen Singh."

"Has it struck your Highness that the man may have been murdered?" Jack asked.

The Prince Regent winced, then nodded solemnly. "Especially since he carried with him so many gold sovereigns."

"The international currency," Daphne mumbled.

"The surprising thing is that Prince Singh went nowhere without a veritable army of men who were sworn to protect him. He was never careless, always cautious. I've been dealing with him for two decades--you must see some of the vases he procured for me from the Chinese Ming Dynasty. They're at the Pavilion."

Jack looked grave. "I don't have to point out to Your Majesty that the trail will be exceedingly cold by the time I could undertake the voyage to Egypt?"

Voyage to Egypt? I and not we? She'd certainly

have something to say about that.

"Yes, but I have great confidence in your investigative powers, Captain."

Daphne could not help but to wonder which distressed His Royal Highness the most: his failure to take ownership of the mummy's mask or the suspected murder of his old procurer.

The Prince answered her question. "I feel I've been doubly wronged. While I am disappointed I won't take possession of the mask and while I lament the loss of ten thousand guineas, I'm more upset that someone may have murdered my old friend. I feel responsible for placing his life in danger."

"You did not endanger him," Jack said. "The very nature of his dealings jeopardized him."

Daphne could not dispel the notion that Prince Singh might have come into possession of the mummy's mask through disreputable means.

"Nevertheless, I feel responsible."

"I will undertake a journey to Egypt to investigate this for you," Jack said.

"We." Daphne glared at her husband.

Jack turned to her, returning her glare. "It's entirely too dangerous. Besides, you're incapable of taking a sea voyage."

There was that. Her stomach became queasy at the very memory of her wedding night spent jostling about on a man o' war. She hadn't realized when she'd accepted Jack's hand in matrimony it would be holding her spewing basin. Much to her eternal embarrassment.

The Prince directed a sympathetic look at her. "Poor Lady Daphne. The ship's captain informed me of your great distress during the crossing, and I have since discussed the situation with my excellent physician. He has a concoction – ginger is one of the ingredients – that he swears will dispel the most pronounced propensity to sea sickness. He also recommends chambers in the center of the ship."

He paused, his gaze moving to Jack. "I have taken the liberty of procuring a fleet packet boat for your passage. With your consent, I will assign ten of my own House Guards to protect you, and I have secured the services of our country's foremost expert upon Orientology. Mr. Maxwell can serve not only as your advisor but also as interpreter. He is fluent in Arabic.

Maxwell? Why was the name so familiar to her? Then she remembered her sister Rosemary—a young lady enamored of all things Oriental—was reading a book titled *Travels Through the Levant.* "Do you refer to Stanton Maxwell?" she inquired.

"Indeed I do. Have you read his travels?"

She shook her head. "Not yet, though it is precisely the kind of book I should love to read." Daphne could hardly contain her excitement over the prospect of travel to exotic lands. How she had always longed to see the crumbling pillars of ancient temples, to hear Calls to Prayer ringing from centuries-old Persian minarets, to ride a camel across vast deserts beneath an unfailing sun. "We shall be delighted to undertake such a commission for Your Royal Highness."

Jack gave her The Glare. "I don't think the Orient is quite the place for a lady."

"Together, each of you is stronger," the Prince Regent said. "I was in hopes the pair of you would consider going."

She knew that as good as Jack was at inquiries, he was better with her.

"Rest assured," the Regent continued, "I would never ask if I believed either of you would be in mortal danger."

Not only was this the most exciting prospect in her entire life, but she also truly believed it was just the kind of assignment that would utilize her husband's many talents. He was as adept at understanding maps (a talent she most profoundly lacked) as he was at picking up foreign languages. He commanded respect from all the soldiers serving under him. He was possessed of a very fine, analytical mind.   And no one was braver. Get him to Egypt, and he would not only locate the missing mummy's mask, he would find Prince Singh--or find Singh's killer.

She gave her husband an imploring look. "Oh, please, Jack. And Rosemary must come with us. She adores anything to do with the Orient."

He held up both hands. "Then you be the one to tell your father I'm removing his eldest and youngest daughters from the comfort and safety of London to exotic lands in search of a possible murderer."

She pouted. "The Regent said he would never ask us to do this if he thought we would be in mortal danger. Didn't you, Your Highness?"

The Prince Regent nodded, eyeing Jack. "I'll speak with Lord Sidworth myself. I would never jeopardize his daughters. I have a daughter myself."

Jack turned to face the man on the throne, stood, and bowed. "We are yours to command."

$\mathcal{C}$hapter 1

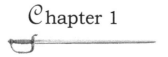

Two months later . . .

Jack ducked to keep from hitting his head on the ship's entry as he came onto the deck. He eyed Maxwell, who stood at the ship's bow, staring into the horizon. No doubt he was watching for a glimmer of land to break the monotony of the endless blue sea. Maxwell shot Jack a recognizing glance. "We should reach Alexandria today."

Stanton Maxwell, the Arabic scholar the Regent had engaged to join them, had been tutoring Jack in Arabic throughout the long voyage. In spite of the vast differences between the two men, they had developed an easy camaraderie during these weeks of confinement aboard the small ship. For so learned a man, Maxwell was exceedingly quiet. Jack was grateful the lessons had somewhat helped the man shed his timidity.

Moving toward the other man, Jack nodded, his glance whisking over the younger man's very modest, very English woolen clothing. Jack tried to imagine the slender man dressed as an Arab. From reading Maxwell's *Travels Through the Levant*, Jack knew the man had done so, but it was bloody difficult to picture the unprepossessing man with a full dark beard, flowing headdress, and . . . the spectacles the man always wore.

Jack welcomed the salty air and strong winds

after the stuffiness in their tiny cabin. Both men solemnly watched the sparkling sea in hopes of glimpsing the Orient. Jack's thoughts were not on the Orient or on the missing Indian prince or on the ancient mummy's mask of solid gold. His thoughts were on Daphne. He'd been uneasy about her throughout the journey, fearful her former malady would return. It sickened him to remember the times when ships landed, and bodies of those not strong enough for the voyage were carried off. If they had not been buried at sea.

He thanked God his wife had held up throughout the journey. He must tell the Regent how well his physician's elixir helped to alleviate Daphne's suffering. She had not avoided sickness altogether, but she had been considerably more robust than she'd been on their previous journey.

"Where are the ladies?" Maxwell asked. "I thought Lady Rosemary's eagerness to behold the Orient would have made sleep impossible."

"Oh, she awakened early, but my dear sir, you must be incredibly ignorant of women if you know not how long it takes them to fashion themselves presentable." Most women. Not his Daphne. She cared not a fig what she looked like. And Jack loved her exactly as she was.

Which was opposite of her sister. In many ways Lady Rosemary was mature. Next to Daphne, she certainly was the most intelligent of Lord Sidworth's six daughters. But she acted like a giddy school girl when she launched into a catalogue of all the fine attributes of one Captain Cooper of His Majesty's Dragoons.

Jack had thought she must be promised to the Captain, but Daphne disavowed him of that notion. To the same degree that Lady Rosemary sang the officer's praises, Daphne disparaged him. But Daphne's impugnment could go only so far, for she would never hurt Rosemary. Daphne always stopped short of reminding her sister that the Captain had demonstrated no more attachment to Rosemary than to any other young lady.

"Look, Dryden!" Maxwell pointed to the one o'clock position. "There. You can see the huge dome of the Pasha's seraglio."

Jack had vowed he was not going to go into raptures over the Orient as the ladies were sure to do, but the sight of an Oriental dome was no everyday occurrence for a lad from a farm in Sussex (unless one was at the Prince Regent's hideous Pavilion in Brighton). Jack watched with fascination as the dome that dominated the horizon grew larger and larger.

By the time the ladies joined them, other sights peculiar to Persian countries could be seen. "I declare," Rosemary shrieked, "do you see those camels? Could anything be more thrilling?" She whirled at Jack. "Oh, do say we will be permitted to ride a camel."

He rolled his eyes. "We shall see."

As their boat came into the harbor at Alexandria, Daphne, with hand at her brow to shield her eyes from the sun, continued to take in the scene before them. "Pray, Mr. Maxwell, what is the name of that mosque?" She pointed to the domed building that had dominated the city's outline.

"That's the seraglio of the Pasha. Were it a mosque, it would have minarets on its perimeter. The great Blue Mosque at Constantinople has six minarets, but I've never heard of another with that many."

Daphne's brows quirked. "Seraglio? You mean the place where the harem is kept?"

"That is so," Maxwell answered, avoiding eye contact with the ladies.

Rosemary, who had never stepped foot on soil that was not English, nodded with authority. "The seraglio was built in the 11th century."

Maxwell turned admiring eyes upon the young woman but was too reserved to comment.

"You see, Mr. Maxwell," Daphne said, "I told you my sister fancies herself an expert on Egypt even though she's never been here."

"I daresay one can learn much from books," the bespectacled man said.

"I enjoyed your book immensely," Rosemary said, not really looking at the scholar because she could not remove her gaze from the sights of the busy port city. "And that was before I ever met you." Now she deigned to look up at him. "I thought you'd be a much older man."

"How old?" he asked.

She shrugged. "At least fifty."

Maxwell frowned. "I am attempting to determine if it's a good thing or bad that I'm younger."

Rosemary shrugged. "I suppose it's good. You must be very clever. I suspect too you were an awfully clever boy."

"I am sure he was," Daphne interjected. "His papa was also a noted Orientologist at Cambridge."

Maxwell cleared his throat. "Is. My father's still alive. Not that I'm saying my father was noted. I shouldn't like to boast."

"I would wager the father is not so terribly old."
Jack glanced at Maxwell. "How old are you?"

"Six and twenty."

Rosemary's mouth dropped open. "That's
terribly young to have done all the things you've
done."

"My father taught me Arabic at the same time
as I learned English, so I had a leg up, so to
speak, in my studies of Orientology." His gaze
went back to the quay. Arabs in flowing white
robes, bare-chested Negroes hauling grain sacks,
donkeys, and bored-looking camels all contributed
to the oddly discordant chorus.

Jack noted that most of the men's heads were
crowned with turbans. Somehow, he'd thought
they would be wearing the head-dress of the
Syrians and other Arabs, a few of which could be
seen among the throngs.

What stood out the most was the noise. Such
wailing and shrieking he'd never before heard.
How different were people in the Orient than those
in Europe! If one person in any European city
made such a shattering noise as one of these
people made, residents would be running from
their homes to see what caused such a
commotion.

Some Arab men were smoking at hosed pipes of
considerable size. That was one more thing he'd
have to ask Maxwell about.

As they disembarked the boat, they were met
by a smiling middle-aged Englishman, whose
clothing was of excellent quality. "Captain
Dryden?" he said to Jack.

"Yes." Jack's hand settled at Daphne's waist.
"And this is my wife, Lady Daphne."

The man effected a bow. "I am Ralph

Arbuthnot, attaché to the Consul in Cairo. The Regent has requested that we see to all your needs whilst you're in Egypt."

"That is so very dear of the Regent," Daphne said.

"Pray, Lady Daphne," the attaché said, "are you the daughter of Lord Sidworth?"

"Yes, and this is also Lord Sidworth's daughter, my sister, Lady Rosemary."

He bowed again. "I am your servant, ladies. My father was at Eton with your father."

"Your father is?" Daphne asked.

"Sir Robert Arbuthnot."

Daphne nodded, then introduced Mr. Arbuthnot to Mr. Maxwell before members of the Regent's House Guards joined them, after which they departed.

"I have taken the liberty of engaging a dragoman to assist you." Arbuthnot indicated a small, dark-skinned man whose youthful head was swathed in a dingy turban while his lower torso was clad in something that looked like a short skirt. He was likely in his mid-twenties and was clean shaven, save for a thick black mustache. "Habeeb will put all your things on a donkey and take them to the hotel. There's another dragoman to serve the soldiers." He eyed Jack. "It's my understanding you desire to spend just one night in Alexandria before traveling to Cairo?"

"That's correct," Jack said.

"You'll be wanting to eat. Decent European food can be procured at the hotel where you'll be staying, but I daresay that while you're in Egypt, you'll learn to eat some of the native food."

"I cannot wait," Rosemary said.

"My sister fancies herself enamored of all things Oriental," Daphne explained.

"I wish you'd join us for dinner," Jack said to Arbuthnot. "I am curious about several matters which I am sure you will be able to satisfy," Jack said.

"It will be my pleasure."

* * *

"This may be your last meal for a while in which you sit at table," Mr. Arbuthnot said as the five of them sat down to their evening meal.

Finally, the reticent Mr. Maxwell spoke. "Yes, you will become accustomed to sitting on cushions and eating with your fingers—only on the right hand."

Daphne noticed that Rosemary turned up her nose at the notion of eating with her fingers. Perhaps her sister would learn that not all things in the Orient were as lovely as their exotic silks.

Once the boiled mutton was served, Jack began to query Mr. Arbuthnot. "Have you been apprised of the nature of our visit?"

Daphne, who normally wasn't given to taking notice of clothing, observed that Mr. Arbuthnot's clothing was very fine. Though, sadly, it mattered not what the gentleman wore. The finest clothing ever constructed could not make the balding man handsome. He must be fifty, but she had learned he'd never married. It was such a pity that appearances played so heavy a role in courtship. (Except with dearest Jack, who cared not that she was no beauty.)

She found herself wondering why anyone in this infernally hot climate would persist in dressing in fashionable English clothing. She would be most happy to shed her attire in favor of the skimpy costume of the Arabian dancing girls she'd seen in pictures. Even if great expanses of her flesh showed.

"I have some idea," Mr. Arbuthnot said. "I believe the Regent outlined the situation to the Consul. That would be Mr. Briggs. I seem to recall something about a missing artifact and some missing Indian prince, I believe."

Her brows lowered. "Then you don't know Prince Edward Duleep Singh?"

"No, I don't."

"Do you think the Consul knew him?"

"That I couldn't say." He gobbled down a handful of fresh fruit and made no effort to wipe his hands after he devoured the juicy offerings.

English table manners were apparently tossed aside whilst living on foreign soil, Daphne decided. Still, it would be very difficult for her to ever eat with her hands. Too fresh was the memory of her governess rapping at Daphne's fingers whenever she did not hold a fork properly. "I would advise you to withhold the information that you are in Egypt to recover valuable antiquities," Mr. Arbuthnot said to Jack. "It would be far better to portray yourselves as tourists—or," he turned to face Mr. Maxwell, "Orientologists."

"Why?" Jack asked.

"If it's known you're on a mission for the Prince Regent, people will assume you have come with a lot of money. And . . ." He lowered his voice. "There are many men in Cairo who would slit your throat for five guineas."

"That settles it," Jack thundered, glaring at Daphne. "I hadn't wanted to bring my wife and her sister in the first place. I'll not put them at risk." He glared at Daphne. "We will not disclose the nature of our investigation to anyone. Is that clear?"

She nodded somberly.

His gaze swung to Rosemary, who also nodded.

"Tell me, Mr. Arbuthnot," Daphne said, "do you conduct your duties in Alexandria or in Cairo?"

"Cairo's where I make my home, but I am frequently summoned to be rather a tour guide for important British citizens. Many times I've travelled along the Nile and have journeyed as far as the first cataract."

"Pray, sir, what is a cataract?" Daphne asked, brows hiked in query.

"A cataract is a place in the river where huge rocks disrupt the peaceful flow of water," Mr. Arbuthnot said. "There are said to be six on the Nile, but as you know, the Nile is the longest river in the world."

"The first cataract is even farther from here than Thebes." Rosemary directed a beseeching look at Jack. "I do hope we'll be able to go to Thebes and the Valley of the Kings—dead kings."

Daphne shuddered. "I fail to see why anyone would want to see a valley of dead people."

Mr. Maxwell chuckled, then begged Daphne's forgiveness. "It's not what you think, my lady. Were you to go to the Valley of the Kings, it is unlikely you would see a single dead body. The valley is ringed with mountains, and in these mountains are many caves. It was these caves that served as royal burial chambers for four-hundred years. Pharaohs were secretly buried there beginning more than three-thousand years ago."

Jack looked sternly upon Rosemary. "Despite that we'll be identifying ourselves as tourists, we have come here for one purpose and one purpose only."

His sister-in-law nodded meekly.

Daphne sighed. Jack was always so stodgy, so inflexible, so single-minded. But one way or another she was going to see to it that before they returned to England, Rosemary would get to see Thebes. And that blasted Valley of the Dead Kings.

Daphne knew she must change the topic of conversation because Jack was in one of his beastly didactic moods. But the only thing she could think to remark upon was the nasty weather. "A pity we couldn't have come two months earlier. I daresay the weather would have been far more pleasant in the spring."

Despite that a young Negro boy fanned over their table with long plumes, Mr. Arbuthnot nodded as he wiped prodigious amounts of perspiration from his brow with his table napkin. "It distresses me to have to tell you that Alexandria is much cooler than Cairo—or Upper Egypt—because of its sea breezes." His frown pulled down his already heavily jowled face. "I cannot deny that it is sometimes an almost unbearable heat."

"It's not that uncomfortable," Mr. Maxwell said, "if one can manage to stay out of the sun."

Rosemary turned to the Orientologist. "But, Mr. Maxwell, did you not join caravans across the desert in the summer?"

He nodded solemnly. "I did, and I will own, it does get beastly uncomfortable. It is helpful, though, if one dresses as the Arabs dress."

"Did you kohl your eyes to protect them like the Bedouins do?" Rosemary asked.

"I did."

"I suppose it's a very good thing you're not as fair as Rosemary and I, for I daresay so many days under the boiling sun could have blistered away your skin."

Rosemary was even fairer than Daphne. In fact, the two sisters could not be more dissimilar—and not just because Daphne was tall, skinny, and bespectacled, and Rosemary was petite and curvy. Everything about them was different. Daphne deplored fashion; Rosemary adored pretty dresses and everything that went with them. Daphne was possessed of excessively curly, very dark blonde hair, and Rosemary's hair was pale blonde, gently curled, and always in the latest fashion.

Daphne was well aware of her own shortcomings. The only two men to ever admire anything about her appearance were her father and her husband, while everyone found Rosemary quite pretty.

The lone trait the sisters had in common was a high degree of intelligence.

Mr. Maxwell smiled. "I was told that without my spectacles I could pass for a native—though my skin was much darker then, because of the sun exposure."

"And the beard you then wore," Rosemary said, grimacing. "I dislike beards."

Daphne could not resist a tease. "What if Captain Cooper has grown a beard?"

Her sister sighed. "If any man could wear one well, it would be my captain."

Daphne cringed at the thought of that odious flirt being Rosemary's.

"I cannot think the wearing of a turban very cool," Jack said.

Mr. Arbuthnot shook his head. "Nor can I."

"I shouldn't at all mind wearing the native dress," Daphne said. "In fact, in this heat I would have no objections to wearing dancing girls' costumes."

Mr. Arbuthnot nearly spit out his food. Mr. Maxwell went stiff and stared into his lap. Jack's eyes slitted and his lips tightened. "My wife will most certainly not dress as a dancing girl!"

"Really, my lady," Mr. Arbuthnot said, his voice tentative. "It wouldn't at all be the thing. I shouldn't like to bring up so indelicate a topic in the presence of a maiden, but dancing girls are noted for showering other favors upon the gentlemen who admire them."

Rosemary blushed. Mr. Maxwell, nodding slightly, continued staring into his lap.

Mr. Arbuthnot, having cleaned his plate, reached to the center of the table and with his bare hands scooped out a heaping handful of olives.

Then he steered the talk away from bare-skinned strumpets. "I suggest you be early to bed tonight because we leave at dawn."

"How long is the journey to Cairo?"

Mr. Arbuthnot shrugged. "It depends upon the winds. Five days, average."

"Will we go near Fort Rached?" Rosemary inquired. "I'm not precisely sure where Captain Cooper is at this time, but he could very well be at Fort Rached. How delightful it would be to see him!"

"We will not be stopping at Fort Rached," Mr. Arbuthnot said.

Rosemary frowned.

If the self-centered, insensitive Captain

Conceited possessed half the attributes Rosemary heaped upon him, she would never have met him (and Daphne would not have had to suffer his praises), for the man would be a heavenly Deity.

When the meal was over, Jack came to stand at his wife's chair. "Time for bed, love." Her husband's voice had softened considerably.

She knew very well how to read this man she'd married, and that voice meant he had romantic notions. She went all buttery inside. How exciting it would be to make love under Egyptian moonlight.

* * *

The first thing she did when they went upstairs to their rather austere bedchamber was shed the sweaty clothing. "Pray, love," she said as she backed into Jack. "Unlace my stays. I have to divest myself of them! I feel as if they've melted into my flesh."

Dear Jack could never unlace her stays without cupping his hands over each of her exceedingly modest breasts. Her breath coming more quickly, she said in a husky voice, "Douse the candle."

Her husband, who had already removed his heavy coat and waistcoat, obliged.

Taking her husband's hand, she padded barefoot to the open window screened with lattice. The two of them stood there, surveying the exotic city beneath the moon's glow, Daphne's back nestled into Jack, and his arms encircled her. "I cannot believe we're here in the Orient, my darling. Is it not magical?"

Behind the gates that closed each night, the city had grown so much quieter. She heard the meow of the cats foraging for food, the lone clop of a donkey, men's muted laughter far in the distance. Minarets scattered about the city soared into the softly moonlit sky.

He nibbled at her neck. "It is rather."

To make the scene complete perfection, the melodious tones of the Arabic Call to Prayer began to ring from every minaret in Alexandria.

"The Isha," Jack said. "The day's final Call to Prayer."

The two of them stood there spellbound until the city went silent again, then they went to their white bed and lifted away the mosquito netting. Jack drew her into his arms. "I mean to collect favors from this most intoxicating aspiring dancing girl."

$\mathcal{C}$hapter 2

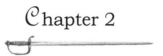

"We must praise Allah for the shade," Daphne said as she sat beneath a white cloth canopy on the deck of their *felucca* the following afternoon as they sailed slowly along the yellowed waters of the Nile. When they'd left Alexandria early that morning, there had been a tolerable wind, but it was as absent now as that city's silhouette with its graceful minarets reaching toward the heavens. Now their boat barely moved. It would not have moved at all were it not for the bronzed Egyptian crew members powering their oars into the placid water.

Trailing their *felucca* was an identical one carrying the Regent's House Guards, one of them always standing at watch with orders not to let Captain Dryden's party from their sight.

"Ah, but my lady, you must enjoy this whilst you can," said Mr. Arbuthnot as he blotted his drenched forehead with a massive handkerchief. "It's always cooler on water than it is in the desert."

Jack bit back a retort. The man was possessed of a propensity to remark on the bloody obvious. Did he think none of them had ever read a blasted book about the Arabian desert? Arbuthnot was well-meaning and attempted to be helpful, but his incessant elucidations were growing tedious.

Jack, uncomfortably hot, looked up from the notes he'd made on the most commonly uttered

Arabic phrases. On the banks of this fertile Nile Delta, sinewy brown men tended the fields. As their boat drew closer, Jack's eyes rounded. Good Lord, were those men completely naked?

Before he could react to the sight, Daphne shrieked. "Close your eyes, Rosemary!"

Rosemary, who had proclaimed this part of the journey boring, looked up from her book to face her sister. "Why must I close my eyes?"

"Because there are naked men not forty feet away. Two, three, four . . ." Daphne squinted toward the river bank. "Five of them!" In spite of her own warning, Daphne was incapable of peeling her eyes from the sight.

Rosemary quickly squeezed her eyes shut. "Oh, dear."

Would that his wife would do the same. Daphne acted as if she'd never before seen a naked man. But then, what English woman would ever have seen five naked men in broad daylight?

"I daresay one becomes accustomed to the nude male body if one spends much time in Egypt," Maxwell said as calmly as if he were commenting on the weather. Jack was not sure which shocked him the most—the naked Egyptians or meek Mr. Maxwell's compliant acceptance of the nudity. In his wildest imagination, Jack could not imagine the modest scholar ever condoning disrobing in public. That the man even peered at such was surprising.

"Will somebody tell me when I can open my eyes?" Rosemary asked.

"Yes, dear. Keep them closed for the present." Daphne was still eyeing the lithe tillers of the soil. Every exposed piece of their dark flesh. "I will let you know."

Jack scooted closer to Maxwell and dropped his voice. "Will there be nudity in the Cairo bazaar?" He knew his investigation would have to originate there, and he knew Daphne would not allow him to go to the bazaar without her.

Maxwell spoke in a low voice the ladies in front of them could not hear. "No, but I once witnessed a copulation there in the Kahn el Khaliti. It was performed without the slightest effort to be discreet."

Jack grimaced. "I bloody well wish I hadn't allowed the ladies to come."

Maxwell flicked a glance at Lord Sidworth's youngest daughter—something he was too shy to do were the girl facing him. "It would be easier going without them."

Rosemary should not be permitted to go to the bazaar, but Jack would have the devil of a time keeping her from it.

It wouldn't do for a maiden to witness . . . a copulation. In spite of the prurience of the act Maxwell had witnessed, Jack nearly burst out laughing. Copulation? Only a socially inept scholar would use such a word. The soldiers Jack had served with spouted a stream of far more colorful words for the deed.

"I presume Khan el Khaliti is the Arabic name for the bazaar?"

The scholar nodded. "It's easy to get lost there. It's a labyrinth of crooked, narrow streets where one can find anything."

Jack swatted at the flies that continuously pestered them. "Would one be able to procure antiquities at such a place?"

"One can procure almost anything at Cairo's Khan el Khaliti. Cairo's a termination for the great caravans coming from as far away as China. You'll find any manner of food, tobacco, spices, along with fine silks, other fabrics, Chinese pottery, jewelry—and Egyptian antiquities."

"I don't suppose you'd know where in that labyrinth I could find the most reputable antiquities dealer?"

Maxwell nodded solemnly. "I've only been to Cairo once and didn't spend much time in the bazaar or in Egypt. I'm afraid I've no good connections here, but I daresay Arbuthnot must know everybody."

"How long have you been in Cairo, Arbuthnot?" Jack asked.

The attaché turned away from the ladies and faced Jack and Maxwell. "It will be seven years in September."

"Then you must know everyone," Jack said. It couldn't hurt to feed the man's vanity. In the short time Jack had spent with the jolly Englishman he had come to realize Arbuthnot had a great fondness for casually mentioning any connection he might have to English peers, Persian potentates, or desert sheikhs.

"I'm sure I don't know everyone, but it is my duty to know men of importance from all the nations which have sent their officials to Egypt. One must represent King and country to the best of one's ability."

Keep feeding the man's vanity. "How fortunate we are that due to the Regent's mechanizations, we've been able to associate with you," Jack said. "You are just the man to steer us in the right direction." Jack swatted a mosquito, killing it on his forearm, leaving a drop of blood behind. "Where would one go in the . . . Khan el Khaliti if one wished to purchase a very valuable Egyptian artifact?"

"No question about it. One would seek Ahmed Hassein, but I must warn you the man is most disreputable."

They had now passed the naked farm toilers, and Daphne transferred her attention to her husband's queries. "You may look up now, Rosemary. We've passed the offensive sight." Jack wondered why his wife had not closed her own eyes if she found the sight so offensive.

Both women turned to face Jack and Maxwell. Arbuthnot was on a bench between the two others. "What do you mean by disreputable?" Daphne asked. "Do you mean he sells fakes?"

Arbuthnot shook his head. "His goods, for the most part, are authentic. They ought to be at the prices he demands."

"Then how is the man disreputable?" she asked.

Arbuthnot's brows lowered, as did his voice. His gaze went to the native crew. "Ahmed Hassein will do anything to get his hands on things of value."

Daphne swallowed. "Even murder?"

Arbuthnot shrugged. "Hassein is very wealthy. I doubt he does the dirty deed himself, but it's believed that he's responsible for a great many deaths."

"Can you direct me to him?" Jack asked.

"Us. What my husband meant to say is can you direct us to the man."

Jack glared at Daphne.

"The bazaar is easy to get lost in, but anyone there should be able to tell you how to find Hassein's shop."

"Oh, but I must go, too," Rosemary said.

Maxwell eyed her. "I would be honored, Lady Rosemary, to escort you throughout the Khan el Khaliti." He eyed Jack. "I would take her only to the most respected shops."

Daphne spun to her sister. "Yes, dearest, you must allow Mr. Maxwell to give you a proper tour of the bazaar whilst Jack and I undertake our dull inquiries. Remember, the duchess is longing for some vibrant silk from the Orient."

"It's very kind of you to offer, Mr. Maxwell," Rosemary said. "I'm aware that shopping is of little interest to most males."

"I assure you, Lady Rosemary, it will be my pleasure. There is something to interest everyone at the Khan el Khaliti."

"I wonder if the soldiers from Fort Rached ever come into the bazaar." Rosemary faced her sister. "I can think of nothing that could be more exciting than being surprised by the sight of my dear Captain Cooper."

Her brows elevated, Daphne whirled at her sister. "I'm surprised to hear you say that for I would have thought the discovery of a pharaoh's tomb would be much more gratifying."

"I beg that you ladies don't get your hopes up over such an occurrence," Mr. Arbuthnot said. "It's been many years since a new unmolested tomb has been discovered."

Jack's brows lowered. "And may I remind you ladies that we are not here in the role of archeologists? I can't even promise that you'll get to see a pyramid."

"I daresay," the attaché said, "it will be very little effort for your entire party to see the pyramids at Gizeh. They can be seen from Cairo—if it's not too smoky--and it's not a long journey to view them—not like it would be to go to the Valley of the Kings."

"Could we ride camels to Gizeh?" Rosemary asked excitedly, peering at her brother-in-law.

"We'll see." Jack's voice lacked conviction.

Daphne raised her arm and hurled her hand to slap Jack on the face. "I got him!" she squealed.

His wife had never before displayed a violent bent. Did she care so much about riding a bloody camel?

She held out her palm where the shriveled remains of a mosquito reposed. "No blood. I daresay that means I got him before he had a chance to take a bite out of my husband. I can't think why they haven't pestered me, only poor Jack."

"And me too," Rosemary said, her eyes narrowing. "I declare, these horrid insects must find me enormously tasty."

"It may be difficult for you to believe—not being plagued by mosquitoes in England," Arbuthnot said, "but they're ten times worse once the sun goes down."

Arbuthnot took such perverse pleasure in announcing distressing news, Jack would not be surprised to see him jump with glee at the sight of a menacing crocodile swimming these waters.

"Similar to blood-sucking bats that come out only at night," Rosemary said.

Maxwell nodded. "Yes, rather. And I must warn you that mosquitoes are attracted by two things other than human flesh—candlelight or water, such as the Nile or even puddles."

"Oh, dear," Daphne said. "Does that mean no candles at night during our voyage?"

Both Maxwell and Arbuthnot nodded.

"Unless you care to be a feast for the mosquitoes," Arbuthnot added.

No mere frowns for his wife. When Daphne was upset, she pouted. And when Daphne pouted, her entire face collapsed. Even her body seemed to tighten with displeasure. "What shall we do for amusement after dark if we can't play cards, can't read a book?" She looked at Maxwell. "I so enjoyed our nightly games of whist during our sea voyage."

"As did I, my lady."

Jack could think of one nocturnal activity he and Daphne enjoyed excessively, but he could never voice such a thought in front of others.

"We could play Who Am I?" Rosemary suggested. "I adore guessing games."

Daphne nodded her agreement. "And my sister's very good at them."

"I daresay it will be difficult to stump a learned man like Maxwell," Jack said.

"It would be an honor to play with so learned a man." Arbuthnot took out his hefty handkerchief and wiped his brow dry. "I shouldn't like to brag, but I'm accounted to be a tolerable player at Who Am I?"

"Then we do have something to look forward to tonight," Daphne said. "We must hope we can think of enough famous persons to last the five of us for four nights."

"That could prove most challenging," Maxwell murmured.

Jack eyed the self-professed tolerable player. "In the meantime, Mr. Arbuthnot, I should like to ask if you know other men in Egypt who are interested in the more valuable antiquities."

"There's Lord Beddington."

"The one who was ambassador to the Ottoman

Empire?" Jack asked.

Arbuthnot nodded. "He developed his interest in ancient artifacts whilst serving in Constantinople, but he's become enamored of all things Oriental. He's been in Egypt now for the past two years."

"He's said to be amassing some of the country's greatest treasures," Maxwell added.

"He's in Cairo?" Jack asked.

"Not at present. He's gone up to Thebes. He has a villa near Cairo, near the Pasha's. The two have great respect for one another."

"I daresay Lord Beddington can acquire whatever his heart desires," Daphne added. "He's obscenely wealthy."

Arbuthnot gazed admiringly at Daphne. "You know his lordship?"

"If I ever met him, I would have been too young to remember. He went off to Constantinople when I was very young. My father laments that he's never returned to England. They were school chums, you see."

"When he returns to Cairo," Arbuthnot said, "I'm certain he'll be happy to see the daughters of his old friend. An Englishman living abroad longs for news of home."

Jack hoped they would have successfully completed their mission by the time the former ambassador returned to Cairo.

"Do you know what types of antiquities his lordship collects?" Maxwell asked Arbuthnot.

"Mammoth ones. He's planning to donate some to the British Museum, and much of the statuary has been sent to his gardens in Somerset."

Daphne's brows lowered. "Do you know if he has interest in smaller things like sarcophaguses or adornments, such as funerary masks?"

As far as Jack knew, Arbuthnot did not know what kind of item the Regent had agreed to purchase from Prince Singh. He and Daphne were the only ones in their party who knew, and he wanted to keep it that way. His loving gaze raked over his wife. He never had to instruct her when they were in one of their investigations. She thought like a man. She was the only woman he knew whose mind was as analytical as his.

"Who doesn't seek to get their hands on those?" Arbuthnot said with a shrug.

The man probably had a point there. Jack supposed acquiring an artifact that had come from a pyramid was no different than bringing back old Italian masters and statuary from the Grand Tour. "Is there any other major antiquities dealer in Cairo at present?"

"Not one I'm aware of," Arbuthnot said. "No, wait! The Sheikh al Mustafa is visiting Egypt as the Pasha's guest, and I believe he's rather interested in acquiring authentic antiquities."

He would only be of interest to Jack were he here when Prince Singh was in Cairo. "Was he here last year?" Jack asked.

Arbuthnot screwed his face in thought. "I couldn't say. He's been coming to Cairo for many years."

"If he's a sheikh," Rosemary said, "he must be a Bedouin, and I shouldn't think they would have much interest in acquiring objects."

"Not all sheikhs are Bedouins," Maxwell said. "Sheikh al Mustafa is one of the most revered Arabian princes of the desert. He has a palace in Baghdad. You see," he explained to Rosemary, "there are tribal sheikhs, and then there are the royal sheikhs of the al Hasmal dynasty."

"Is he a murderer like Ahmed Hassein?" Daphne asked.

Jack frowned at his outspoken wife. "Daphne! You can't go around publicly accusing people of murder."

"Well, I wouldn't do it to their faces."

Rosemary effected a superior countenance as she looked down her pert nose at her elder sister. "Did Mama not tell us that one should never say behind one's back what one wouldn't say to one's face?"

Daphne put hands to hips and glared at her sister. "Murderers, my dear sister, nullify all Mama's rules of etiquette."

Jack cleared his throat. "Back to the Sheikh al Mustafa . . . Could you get me in to see him?"

"The Consul would be the one to do that, and I don't need to tell you how eager he is to assist you—and help our dear Regent."

"I am told the Sheikh does not speak English," Maxwell said. "You will need an interpreter, and I shall be honored to assist you in such a commission—provided you secure a meeting with him."

"If he's still in Cairo, you can be assured of meeting the man," Arbuthnot said.

                              * * *

Daphne's prophecy they would run out of famous people to guess in Who am I? during the remainder of their voyage proved to be true. That first night they drifted down the Nile beneath a moonless sky they went through every king and queen of England, France, and Spain during the last three hundred years. They exhausted the list of Greek philosophers and Roman poets. (She was exceedingly proud that she had been the only one to guess Marcus Aurelius—even though Mr. Maxwell was in the same guessing pool.) Every Chancellor of the Exchequer had been tapped. She only hoped poor Mr. Arbuthnot wasn't too humiliated that all four of his companions displayed significantly superior guessing skill to his own tolerable skills.

In spite of depriving themselves of any kind of light, the travelers were still gnawed on by swarms of mosquitoes. It was as if the pests had been drawn by magnets.

Daphne preferred not to think on the depravities and discomfort. She was far too grateful to have the opportunity to see the Orient. She'd seen caravans of black cloaked men on camels. She'd heard the Call to Prayer ring from graceful minarets. She'd sailed along the same river as Cleopatra. And then there had been the five naked men. Yes, she thought that final night aboard the *felucca* as she lay beside her sleeping husband, mosquito netting over them, this was going to be quite an adventure.

Chapter 3

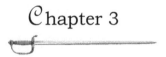

When Jack saw a significant clustering of tall palm trees, he knew they were coming to the port at Bulak. Moments later, his guess was confirmed by Maxwell. "The mosque at Bulak dates to the ninth century. You can see the top of it right there." He pointed its direction.

"And if you'll look there," Arbuthnot added, pointing to a substantial, three-story structure built of light-colored stone. It, too, was ringed by more tall palms and surrounded by a patch of velvety grass and a garden. "You'll see the Pasha's villa." Arbuthnot's voice could not have displayed more pride had the building been his very own residence.

"So that's Cairo?" Daphne asked.

Arbuthnot shook his head. "Oh, no. We're about a mile northwest of Cairo. Definitely walking distance. Only commoners and some Consuls, as well as a handful of French merchants, reside in the old walled city of Cairo."

"I believe, my darling," Jack said, "we are to take lodgings in the European quarter which is located outside of the city."

"One must be within the gates of the European quarter, too, by dark," Maxwell said. "I had a beastly time being admitted to my lodgings there when I arrived half an hour after the gates closed."

Daphne turned up her nose. "It all sounds

rather primitive."

Maxwell uncharacteristically chuckled. "You, my lady, have just perfectly described Arabs."

"I live in the European quarter myself," Arbuthnot said.

As their vessel drew up alongside its mooring, and their dragoman busied himself bringing up all their valises, Arbuthnot turned to Jack. "If it's all the same to you, we can just send your dragoman ahead with a pair of donkeys laden with your bags, and I can take you straight away to the Consul."

Jack nodded. "That would be most agreeable."

After they docked at the busy quay, Jack waited until the other members of their party, save his wife, had disembarked. He wanted a private word with her. "I wish for just you and me to meet with Briggs."

"Exactly what I was thinking. In fact, I had planned to request that Mr. Maxwell give Rosemary a tour of Cairo. She's awfully keen to see a mosque. Mr. Maxwell told her that she could drape a shawl over her hair and be permitted inside the Ibn Tulun Mosque." Daphne shuddered. "I hate to think of a shawl on a hot day like this."

Daphne slipped her slender arm through her husband's, and they left the boat.

It was good for a change to have someone else directing them where to go. For many years of clandestine activities in foreign locales, Jack had been forced to rely on his own cunning for even the most elementary things—like where one could draw water from a well. Now he could be a tourist. Almost.

He watched with fascination the long-robed, bearded men in turbans toiling alongside bare-chested Negroes, all of them loading or unloading boats laden with fruits and vegetables and sacks of grain. Magnificent camels lined the wharf, some with Bedouins straddling the mighty beasts. Curiously, some had one hump, others two. He noted, too, that the Bedouin men's headdress was different. Their head covering was held by a circular braided crown. Exactly like he'd seen in biblical illustrations.

Amidst all the men mingling at the quay, one stood out. A European. Jack tensed. Gareth Williams. Jack had once sworn that if ever again he crossed paths with the coward, he'd beat him to within an inch of his life. Even before the heavy fighting at Badajoz that sent Williams fleeing to Morocco, the vile piece of dung had been suspected in a multitude of thefts from his fellow soldiers.

When Jack's gaze locked with Williams' intense blue eyes, the other man spun away and disappeared into the crowd. Jack had seen enough to observe that the years spent in the desert climate had not been kind to the deserter. Williams couldn't be much more than thirty, like Jack, but he looked considerably older. His face had become leathered and nearly as dark as an Egyptian's, but his hair was considerably fairer. He was thinner, too (which Jack could certainly understand after eating the unappetizing native meals for the past five days).

Unaccountably, Jack wondered if Williams had been watching the docks for Jack's party to land. One thing was certain—the man was up to no good. His allegiance could be traded like a pair of used boots.

As Jack disembarked from the *felucca*, Habeeb

drew him aside. Jack had spoken to the dragoman only two or three times since he'd met their ship at Alexandria, but he was surprised at the young man's competence in English.

"I must warn you, sir, about the ladies."

Jack's first thought was to protect Daphne and her sister. "What's wrong?"

"I speak of the . . . I believe your word is whores. You do good to avoid them. Always best to go with dancing girls. Much cleaner. Less sickness."

Even when he'd been a bachelor, Jack had avoided that sort of woman. He patted well-meaning Habeeb on the shoulder. The slender dragoman was more than a head shorter than Jack. "I thank you for the warning." *Even if I don't need it.* The dragoman continued packing their bags onto the braying donkeys, which were contributing to the discordant noise that surrounded them.

Perhaps he should convey that information to the soldiers. He moved to Harry Petworth, the man Jack had pegged as their leader simply because he was the only one among the raw youths who had ever served with Jack. He spoke in low tones to Petworth, and then rejoined his wife and the others.

"Had Mr. Briggs known the exact time of our arrival," Arbuthnot said when he rejoined them, "he would have sent his own coach to collect us."

"I don't believe I've seen a European coach in Egypt," Daphne said.

"They are rare." Arbuthnot bestowed a smile upon Daphne. "If you'd prefer, I can still procure a pair of horses for the ladies—to shorten the time in the sun."

"My wife may be slender," Jack said, "but she's uncommonly tenacious. And she will never concede defeat against anything, even the desert's almost unbearable heat."

"I daresay I've just been complimented," Daphne said drolly.

Maxwell cleared his throat. "I say, the same can be said for Lady Rosemary." He flicked a shy smile at her.

"Thank you, Mr. Maxwell," Rosemary replied.

Following their group were two columns of the Regent's House Guards. Jack felt bloody foppish that he had to be guarded by men whose combat experience was vastly inferior to his own. But the Regent had insisted, and one did not disagree with one's monarch. He felt sure the Regent had assigned the soldiers to their party merely to placate Lord Sidworth, but Jack was still embarrassed about it.

"Mr. Arbuthnot, will the House Guards lodge with us?" Daphne asked.

He shook his head. "I'm afraid there aren't enough available rooms in the European quarter. We've taken the liberty of procuring tents—European-style—for them, and there's room to pitch them on your hotel's grounds. Two of their rank will be posted at the front of your lodgings and two at the back at all times. The Regent's orders were specific."

"The dear man means to lessen my dear Papa's worries about us," Daphne said.

The Regent had asked that Jack not wear his regimentals during this investigation. Dressed as a civilian, he'd had little to do with men of his own kind, and he felt beastly about that too. It was some consolation that he had other, more important things on his mind.

In a little over ten minutes they reached the massive Ezbeekiya Square which, Arbuthnot told them was just outside the old city walls. This square was many times larger than the largest of London's squares. A small city could be built atop its brick foundation. "It's a great gathering place but has never been built upon because the Nile floods it every August," Arbuthnot said.

Within minutes, they'd passed through the old timber gates to the city and were walking along lanes far too narrow to be called streets. Houses on either side were constructed of wood as well as stucco, and white-painted lattice covered the windows. These allowed them privacy even though their windows were open.

Jack found himself thinking how easy it would be to burn all this down, especially given the local addiction to smoking the hookah pipes—a practice Maxwell had explained to him. "Even women smoke them," he had told Jack.

Every few hundred feet old men gathered to smoke and to drink very dark coffee from cups not much larger than a thimble.

"I declare," Daphne said, "one could get lost here."

"Yes," Maxwell said. "It's not laid out on a grid and can be very confusing."

"But once you learn where the Consulate is, it becomes easier. The Consulate," Maxwell explained, "is completely different from these buildings we've seen thus far."

Arbuthnot nodded. "Indeed it is. They say it was constructed from stones pilfered from pyramids."

"That's a sacrilege!" Daphne exclaimed. "How

could anyone have set out to destroy that which has stood for three thousand years? I shall give Mr. Briggs a piece of my mind. Why, dismantling a pyramid is even worse than an Egyptian coming to England and dismantling our Tower of London!"

"Oh," Arbuthnot defended, "it wasn't the English who stripped away stone from the pyramids. The Egyptians themselves did it many years past."

Daphne's mouth formed a straight line. "It's disgusting."

"What is even more distressing," Maxwell added, "is this country's failure to protect their antiquities. If they don't act soon, there won't be anything left from the days of the great pharaohs."

"What do you propose?" Daphne asked.

"For starters," Maxwell said, "their own museum. Do you realize how much of their history is going to the British Museum?"

"Then it's a very good thing the pyramids won't fit there!" Daphne said.

Squinting against the afternoon sun and frowning, Rosemary joined the conversation. "The Egyptians need to take control of their treasures."

"They have implemented the requirement that foreigners—or anyone, really—obtain a permit—a firmin—before excavating or removing anything," Arbuthnot said. "The pity of it is power curries favor, and those willing to bribe get more favorable firmins while others are repeatedly denied."

They followed Arbuthnot around a corner, and Jack knew without a doubt they had come to the British Consulate. The proud building constructed of solid stucco stood out like a jewel in a bed of coal amongst the haphazardly constructed wooden dwellings surrounding it.

As was Arbuthnot's custom, he pointed it out with a proprietary air. "Ah, we've come to the Consulate. Wait until you see the interior! You'll welcome a little piece of England in the Orient."

"I particularly came here to get away from the dreary English ways," Rosemary said.

Maxwell gazed admiringly at her.

"Then it's a very good thing you'll not be visiting the Consul." Jack turned to Maxwell. "I am in hopes that you'll be able to conduct Lady Rosemary on a tour of Cairo."

"It will be most agreeable to me to do so."

"I expect you'll conduct a fascinating tour because you're so clever," Rosemary told the scholar.

That the Consulate was not guarded by English soldiers was quickly rectified when four of the Regent's House Guards, beastly hot in their woolen uniforms and towering beaver hats, took up their posts at its entrance when the Drydens and Arbuthnot entered the dwelling. Rosemary and Maxwell—with half the guards—went off to explore the city and were to meet them in front of the Consulate in an hour.

* * *

Mr. Briggs had them shown directly into his office, a large chamber furnished completely in the English style. Although there were many windows and it was a sunny day, little light illuminated the chamber, owing to the dark narrow streets outside of it and the rickety buildings that obstructed the sun from his windows.

Jack had told her that the Consul had a military background, and everything about his surroundings spoke to his attention to precision. Books lined up tidily, chairs all faced the Consul's desk, and instead of a portrait of King George, a large map of Egypt covered the interior wall, with markings for each of the places where the Consulate had served. Most efficient.

Mr. Arbuthnot effected the introductions—according to protocol presenting first Daphne, as the highest ranking person present, to the Consul. "She's the daughter of Lord Sidworth."

Mr. Arbuthnot possessed a decidedly inflated (and unwarranted) admiration for all things aristocratic, Daphne thought.

Once the introductions were complete, Jack turned to the toadeater. "We are most appreciative for all you've done for us, Arbuthnot, but I beg you allow me to speak to Mr. Briggs in private."

The man attempted to conceal his disappointment by slapping on a smile and telling them he'd show them to their lodgings as soon as they were finished with Mr. Briggs. "I have many duties to attend to now that I'm back in Cairo, but I'll be in my office just down the corridor should you need me."

Jack and Daphne sat in a pair of identical mahogany chairs facing the Consul. Daphne had heard that Mr. Briggs had grown tired of the Orient and longed to return to England. With his dull gray eyes and gray hair with withered skin, he looked tired.

"I hope the lengthy journey wasn't too strenuous for you," he said. "The Regent—in his correspondence to me—indicated his concern for Lady Daphne."

"If you please, Mr. Briggs," she said, "I prefer to be referred to as Mrs. Dryden."

His eyes widened. "How very singular." Then he addressed Jack. "Not that being the wife of

Captain Jack Dryden wouldn't be something of which to be exceedingly proud. I've been hearing of your intelligence and bravery for years, Captain."

"How kind of you," Jack said. "But enough of us. You know the nature of our mission here?"

The Consul nodded. "I know that Prince Edward Duleep Singh had been engaged to procure for the Regent an extremely valuable funerary mask that had been taken from a pharaoh's tomb. It was constructed of solid gold, I believe. And I know that no one's seen Prince Singh in many months. I daresay it's now been nearly a year."

"Do you know Prince Singh?" Jack asked.

Mr. Briggs hesitated a moment before he answered. "I can't say that I actually know him, but Prince Singh is an extremely wealthy man who is received everywhere. He's frequently a guest of the Pasha, and I had occasion to be introduced to him at one or two functions."

"By guest of the Pasha," Daphne asked, "do you mean that when he's in Cairo, he's a houseguest of the Pasha?"'

Briggs shook his head. "No, Prince Singh has his own villa near the Pasha's. It's considerably smaller than the Pasha's palace."

"Do you know if he keeps servants there even when he's not in Cairo?" Jack asked.

"I can't say for certain, but it is customary to do so, and you must know native labor comes very cheap."

Yes, Daphne did know. Mr. Arbuthnot told them he'd procured their dragoman for a mere three guineas a month.

"Could Mr. Arbuthnot show us to Prince

Singh's villa?" Jack asked.

Daphne shook her head. "Remember, darling, Mr. Arbuthnot said he does not know Prince Singh."

Briggs' brows drew together. "I am surprised to hear that, given that Arbuthnot makes it a practice to get to know anyone who's wealthy and powerful, though it's irrelevant whether he knows Prince Singh. He's sure to know which house belongs to Prince Singh."

That he'd said belongs rather than belonged indicated that he held out hope the prince was still alive. Daphne wished it were so, but she was pragmatic enough to know it was unlikely. "Do you think it could be possible that Prince Singh found someone who paid him more than the Regent, and that he's gone back to India?" Daphne asked.

"I suppose it's possible."

"And another thing," Jack said. "You are acquainted with Lord Beddington, are you not?"

A smile lifted Mr. Briggs' saggy face. "It is indeed my honor."

"I should very much like to meet him," Jack said. He sounded so commanderly. Daphne could easily understand why her husband was so well-respected among the soldiers who served with him and under him. (And she refused to contemplate how the ladies made absolute cakes of themselves over her handsome husband.)

"I would be happy to facilitate a meeting between you and Lord Beddington. At present, he is not in Cairo."

Jack pressed on. "And the Pasha?"

Mr. Briggs bowed his head solemnly. "As far as I know, he is in Cairo, and I will be happy to assist with that introduction, too."

"There's one more," Daphne said. "Do you know if Sheikh al Mustafa is in Cairo?"

This query proved fruitless. "I wouldn't know."

"But I daresay the Pasha would," Jack said.

"I should think he would," Mr. Briggs answered.

"I am counting on you speaking to the Pasha on our behalf," Jack said. "I beg that you ask him to orchestrate a meeting with us and the Sheikh."

* * *

Rosemary's excitement over Cairo was so great she reminded Daphne of Papa's jubilant pups greeting them after an absence. Had Rosemary been a hound, she'd be leaping upon them right now, tail wagging profusely.

"It was positively the most interesting thing I've ever done in my life," she declared. "And I never for a moment felt afraid. How could I when each of our steps was shadowed by a handsome soldier from His Majesty's House Guards?"

"And, of course," Daphne added, sensitive to Mr. Maxwell's devotion to her sister, "Mr. Maxwell was also there to protect you."

"Oh, yes. He was such a fount of knowledge. It was as if I had an entire reference book at my disposal every step of the way."

"I wouldn't have thought there would be much to interest a young lady such as yourself," Mr. Arbuthnot said.

"There you are wrong, my dear sir," Rosemary said. "Everything I saw was filled with exotic beauty, and I've grown enamored of the smell that emanates from the hookah pipes. And the Ibu Tulum Mosque! We actually were there for the late afternoon Call to Prayer and bowed down on our knees facing Mecca. Of course I prayed to our heavenly Father rather than Allah, but I suspect it's all rather the same. I shall never forget it. Now I am most eager to see the bazaar, but Mr. Maxwell says that's to be saved for another day."

They followed Mr. Arbuthnot to the European quarter and passed through green gates to a tangle of narrow streets that looked like something from the old part of London. Or Paris. Only the buildings weren't as tall. Unlike the dwellings in Cairo's walled city, these were not constructed of wood but were solid stucco.

One of the first buildings they came to was their lodging. "I hope you don't object to having a French landlord," Mr. Arbuthnot said. "Few Englishmen have settled in Cairo."

"I daresay it's because that fiend Napoleon tried to claim it first," Jack said. "As much as the soldier in me hates to credit the navy, we owe a very great deal to Lord Nelson."

Her husband had no love for the French.

"I think, dearest," she said, "that after we defeated the French at Abukir, it was very magnanimous of the British government not to lay claim to the lands Napoleon had earlier seized."

"It seemed rather unBritish to me," Jack mumbled, "But it was, indeed, magnanimous."

Mr. Arbuthnot nodded his agreement as he came to a halt. "I'm sure you'll find your dragoman has already delivered all your things here. Allow me to speak to the soldiers about their accommodations."

* * *

After dinner Jack and Daphne went to their room. He did not know if he approved of how very European the chamber was. He rather fancied spending his nights in a lavish tent such as those belonging to sheikhs of the desert. A place where one sat on plump cushions smoking hookahs and eating grapes. He must have a sultan fetish.

Their chambers were, thankfully, clean. The room's only furnishings were an iron bed enclosed by gauzy mosquito netting, two tables and one wooden chair. One of the tables was for writing, the other beside the bed. The floors were wooden, and the windows--open on this broiling summer night—were covered with more of the gauzy netting. Over the windows were filigreed shutters of hand-carved wood.

Their bags stood in one corner, courtesy of the competent Habeeb.

At the thought of Habeeb, she whirled at her husband. "Pray, my love, what in the devil was it that Habeeb had to speak to you about when we got off the boat?"

"The *felucca*, my love. Not a boat."

"You're changing the subject, love. Why did our dragoman need to speak to you?"

Jack drew a breath, but did not answer her.

She had lived with him (and madly loved him) long enough to know that stance of his. Her dear husband never liked to speak of things not fit for a lady's ears. He was such an adorable prude. "He wasn't trying to entice you to a brothel, was he?"

Jack turned to her, a half smile pinching his lean cheek as he drew her into his arms. "How did my own temptress know?"

"Your own temptress knows her husband. Whenever you hesitate to speak of something, it's usually something one does not discuss in mixed company." Her arms came fully around him, and her head nestled into his powerful chest. "Pray, where is the brothel?"

Jack dropped soft kisses into the curly mass of her unruly hair. "Actually, he wasn't trying to entice us but to warn us. He warned against common. . . Well, you know. He said they weren't clean. Diseases and all that. He suggested that if a man were in such a need, it would be better to go to a dancing girl."

"And surely you told him you had no use for women of that sort."

"Of course, my love," he said with a wink as his head lowered to hers for a kiss as passionate as an Oriental night.

$\mathcal{C}$hapter 4

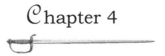

The Call to Prayer ringing out from minarets throughout the ancient city awakened Jack the following morning. Their mosquito netting had been pulled away, and Daphne was no longer beside him. He propped himself up on one elbow and looked around. His wife was standing in her night shift in front of the open window. His eyes narrowed. "Oblige me by telling me why you stand in front of the window half dressed."

She turned around. Her face looked as if she'd just seen a celestial being. "Oh, my darling, isn't it wondrous that we're actually in the Orient? You must come look. Today we can see the pyramids at Gizeh off in the distance."

He slung two bare legs over the bed's edge and started to throw on his clothing. "I'd as lief we didn't have to constantly be followed by a platoon of soldiers. Makes me feel like a milksop."

"Ten soldiers does not a platoon make. Did you not tell me a platoon is three sections of eight soldiers?"

He grumbled beneath his breath. "Don't take me so bloody literally, woman." He came to stand beside her, the gentle touch of his hand at her waist compensating for the gruffness of his voice. The first thing he viewed was a pair of tents in the grassy garden beside their hotel. The lodgings for the soldiers.

Since it was early in the day, the skies were

clear enough from Cairo's smoke that the Great Pyramid and two smaller ones could be seen off in the hazy distance.

"It's exciting to be in the Orient. I didn't think I'd ever see the pyramids." She looked up at him with a hopeful expression. "Can we not go to see the pyramids today? While we're awaiting further introductions."

"Have you forgotten Ahmed Hussein?"

"The murderer in the bazaar?"

"We don't know that he's a murderer, but, yes, that's the man we need to see today."

"Seeing the bazaar would be almost as good as seeing the pyramids. But not quite."

"The bazaar interests you? I've never known you—unlike most other women—to enjoy shopping."

"I will own, I have no interest in damasks and silks and jewels, but I should love to smell all the spices mixed with the pungent hookah smoke. I should like wandering down the dark maze of streets and alleys that haven't changed in centuries. I wish to admire the rich colors of the Oriental carpets and watch the old men sipping their muddy-looking coffee and the women with veiled heads."

The very things he'd like to see.

"I pray we can get off before the excruciatingly helpful Mr. Arbuthnot comes for us," he said.

Without breaking her view, she backed into him, and his arms came fully around her, his mouth pressed to her ear for soft kisses. "I was thinking the same thing about Mr. Arbuthnot. His helpfulness can be most annoying," she said. "I feel dreadfully guilty admitting it because poor Mr. *Arbuth-knows-it-all* means well."

"All the same, I think we'll enjoy the bazaar better if we have just Habeeb and Maxwell along to interpret."

"A splendid idea. But what about Rosemary? You know how passionately she wants to go to the bazaar."

"Once we've found Hussein, Maxwell can proceed with your sister. Habeeb can serve as our interpreter, should the need arise."

She shook her head. "That won't do. What do we really know about Habeeb?"

He sighed. "You're right. I don't know how I could have slipped so completely. For all sensitive inquiries we'll need Maxwell. I'd stake my life on his trustworthiness, and the man is discreet."

"I think I'd worry if Rosemary had only Habeeb to see her through the bazaar. The fellow's no bigger than she!"

"I was surprised at how small he is. Did you notice how small the Bedouins are? I would be surprised if any of them exceed five-six."

She nodded. "They weren't at all what I expected a desert prince to look like. But I expect it's rather difficult to grow tall when one is forced to live off sand."

"The Bedouins don't eat sand."

"I know that. But what manner of food grows in the midst of a desert?"

"I do see your point, and I don't mean to disparage the men because of their small stature. A man's courage cannot be judged by his size."

"True. In Mr. Maxwell's book, he wrote about the Bedouins' uncommon capacity to tolerate pain. And that is a true indication of bravery."

Jack wouldn't tell her how many times he'd seen large men cave in like children under torture.

Then she would want to know if he'd ever been tortured. He couldn't lie to her, nor could he allow her to know the hardships he'd had to endure in enemy camps.

He thanked God every day for giving him the ability to withstand torture while maintaining his dignity—and his secrets.

"How right you are."

He turned her around to face him. "Now I should like to assist milady in dressing."

"First, love, I'm in dire need of back scratching. Those wretched mosquitoes from the boat feasted on every part of me."

"Because you're so delectable." He scratched the mounds of bites on her back, careful to avoid using his nails. It wouldn't do to break the skin.

There was one other thing Jack hadn't told her. He'd not mentioned seeing Gareth Williams at Bulak. He had no reason to think Williams being here had anything to do with him. Still, it was impossible for Jack to shake the conviction that if something sinister were occurring, Gareth Williams could be involved. This conviction was not dissimilar to that which always signaled the evil-doings of Jack's arch nemesis, the duc d'Arblier.

* * *

They did manage to slip away before Mr. Arbuthnot had a chance to call for them. Unfortunately, there was nothing they could do to disengage themselves from the train of soldiers who followed them everywhere.

They started early in the day, hoping to spare themselves from the oppressive afternoon heat. As they walked along the streets of packed dirt, sometimes Daphne and Rosemary would link arms, chatting and leading the way through the labyrinth of narrow streets. But most of the time, they paired up as couples. Jack and Daphne, Rosemary and Mr. Maxwell. Whenever Daphne was in a foreign land, she rather clung to her handsome husband. It wasn't that she was a frightened ninny as much as that she never felt closer to him than when they were exploring new vistas together.

Mr. Maxwell was quiet and shy, but when he spoke, he was fascinating. He didn't point out the bloody obvious as Mr. Arbuthnot did, nor did he sound didactic. He was possessed of a gift of remarking candidly upon the most interesting topics.

"One can find the finest jewels outside of Constantinople here in Kahn el-Khaliti," Mr. Maxwell said. "Jewel traders have been coming here for centuries."

As they drew up to the outskirts of the bazaar and she saw majestically colored Persian carpets waving like flags, Daphne's excitement began to mount.

Since Europeans, especially delicate blonde women like Rosemary, were uncommon, their party drew considerable attention. The merchants were pushing and shoving one another to gain position to foist their goods on the rich Franks, as all Europeans were known. A pity, Daphne thought, she could not understand a word of the rapid Arabic that assailed them from every quarter.

One Egyptian pulled at Jack's sleeve, imploring him to admire the oddest thing. In spite of the two foot long object being rather pointed, it looked organic. "Pray, Habeeb, what is that thing?" Jack asked.

"It is a rhinoceros horn," the dragoman responded.

Mr. Maxwell cleared his throat. "It's said to have aphrodisiac properties."

"I daresay that explains how something that ugly could be considered of value," Jack said.

Next they came to the perfume bazaar. Even before they reached it, heavy floral scents drew them in its direction. The ladies had to stop. An Egyptian in a striped robe held a clear flask beneath the pretty blonde's nose. "I declare," Rosemary said, "these are as fine as any French perfumes."

"I agree," Daphne said. "We must have some." She turned to Habeeb. "You shall have to sufficiently deprecate the perfume to get us a good price." That was the single piece of advice she'd learned about bazaar shopping. Goods, she'd been told, could typically be had for a quarter of the starting price.

For the next several moments, Habeeb and two different perfume sellers went back and forth before Habeeb finally looked up at Daphne, a cocky expression on his face. "I get you very good price. Only five paras for one of each fragrance."

Jack paid for the perfume, and they continued on. Stall after stall featured grain, flax, salt, staples of life that presently held no interest for her.

Mr. Maxwell kept apologizing for not being more familiar with the bazaar, but Daphne was sure even locals must get lost within the tangle of narrow streets crammed with Arabs, Indians, veiled women, brown children, goats, and donkeys. Always, the pungent aroma of the hookah pipes was present, but the scent of rich coffees, exotic sandalwood, freshly caught fish, and many other foods she could not possibly put a name to permeated the dark alleys.

It was even more exciting than she'd thought it would be. Except that she was rather a freak. Of all their party, it was she who drew gawks from everyone they passed. Because of her spectacles and her height and her thick mop of unmanageable golden hair. "I have decided to purchase veils and burkas or whatever these Egyptian women wear."

Her husband looked down at her. "You can't mean you wish to dress as the natives?"

"I am strongly considering it. I know that as a European, I will continue to draw curious glances, but you must admit my hair resembles nothing so much as a deranged sheep who's been too close to the sun. If I were to wear veils, it would at least be covered."

"I do wish you wouldn't criticize your hair," Jack said. "I love it."

"That, my dearest love, is because you love me. The natives don't."

This row they were walking along was comprised of small pens for a variety of cackling poultry. She was vaguely aware of satisfaction that chickens looked much the same the world over. As much as she appreciated foreign customs, she rather drew the line at strange animals that might launch at one.

She stopped, swatted at the incessant flies, and turned to Habeeb. "It is the desire of my husband and me to each have one native costume. Can you procure them for us?" She had not apprised her husband of her scheme, but knowing his history of clandestine inquiries, she knew he might have need of such a costume. She knew, too, he would not publicly repudiate her request. Though in private she would be braced to face his mild rebuke.

The dragoman nodded.

"And," Daphne added, "take care that both my husband's and my height are considerably taller than most Arabs."

"Yes, *Sitti el-Kebin.*"

Jack had told her the title Habeeb had given her roughly translated to *great lady.*

"I daresay one would be more comfortable in native dress today," Mr. Maxwell said.

A moment later, he came to a stop where several stalls intersected. He turned left. "If my memory serves correctly," Mr. Maxwell said, we're moving in the direction of the more permanent structures where so-called antiquities are offered."

"What do you mean by so-called?" Jack asked.

"The shopkeepers will tell you they're authentic papyrus, authentic scarabs, amulets, but more often than not, they're fakes."

Rosemary spun toward him. "Pray, Mr. Maxwell, can you tell the difference?"

"It is no special accomplishment, especially for one who has spent his entire life examining old scrolls."

"Then you can read ancient Egyptian?" Rosemary asked, her eyes flashing with admiration.

He shook his head. "No living man can read them at present, but I've been working with a Frenchman to decipher a stone discovered in the Egyptian delta a decade ago. We think it will unlock the keys to ancient Egyptian picture writings."

"How thrilling," Rosemary said.

"I did not think anyone but me would find such a tedious task thrilling," he said. As always, the scholar spoke without inflection. His voice, like himself, was unassuming. Were he on an English street and not in Cairo, his modest person would never demand a second glance.

Not like her Jack. She was thankful he was not wearing his regimentals. He was far too handsome in them. Not that he wasn't exceedingly handsome as he looked today, all brawny height and dark good looks, dressed in brown woolens and camel-coloured boots made of fine leather.

When they reached the soaring brick buildings that signaled the gold market, she knew they were getting closer to the antiques. Even though Daphne was not interested in jewels, she could not help but be dazzled by the stunning gold collars, bracelets, and rings of every description, including some filigreed like she'd never before seen. Ornate gold jewelry was being thrust at them by aggressive merchants speaking in rapid Arabic, and Rosemary found it difficult not to stop. "I must return here after you've conducted your important business."

Minutes later they found the "street" where antiquities were offered. The merchants here pegged them as British and were the first to have somewhat of a command of English. "Papyrus from many thousands years past very cheap," one said.

The very next shop offered sarcophaguses. "Hareem must take fine sarcophagus back to England."

Daphne eyed Jack. "Hareem?"

"Lady."

As he'd been directed, Habeeb made inquiries as to where they could find Ahmed Hassein. The most important antiquities dealer's shop was located at the end of this very street. It would be easy to find, they were told, because of the gilded pillars at its door—and a pair of very tall guards.

At the end of the lane, two very large men stood at the dazzling entrance as if they were sentries— which, in fact, they actually were. They did not dress in the Egyptian manner but looked similar to the Turkish soldiers who still had a presence in this farthest outpost of the Ottoman Empire. Instead of turbans, each of these men wore a tasseled fez. They were armed with muskets.

Like the Regent's fine House Guards, these guards did not so much as blink as the five of them walked into the shop. The soldiers who always followed them remained outside of the shop, eyes drilled on the five of them. Ahmed Hussein's business establishment was as different from its neighbors as Habeeb was to scholarly Mr. Maxwell. It was as if bright daylight filled the first large chamber. She looked up and found that the roof of Ahmed Hussein's shop was a glass dome.

Because of the abundant light, his sparkling, bejeweled goods could be clearly seen. There was but one sarcophagus here, and she would wager (if Jack allowed her to do such) that it was authentic. There really was no substitute for real gold, and she was certain it was adorned with that most valuable metal.

A man taller than ordinary Egyptians parted silken curtains and entered the room in which they had gathered. He wore the turban she'd come to expect of Egyptians, and his spotless robes looked as if this was the first time he'd ever worn them. (Daphne could never voice her observation that the average Egyptian did not look at all clean. In fact, the stench of humanity flowing through the narrow streets of the bazaar had not been pleasant.)

She eyed the Egyptian. He looked to be in his early forties and was possessed of an aristocratic face with high cheek bones and aquiline nose.

"We seek Ahmed Hussein," Jack said to him.

The man—obviously not acquainted with English—shrugged.

Jack tried French.

The man smiled, nodded, and in French replied that he was Ahmed Hussein.

"My wife and I seek a private word with you," Jack said in French.

He shrugged again. "My French is not good."

Jack's gaze locked with Mr. Maxwell's and he spoke in English. "I should like you to serve as interpreter with the Egyptian." Jack then looked at his sister-in-law. "If you and Habeeb can amuse yourselves in this room until our meeting has concluded, I shall give Mr. Maxwell leave to take you throughout the entire bazaar when we finish. I'm certain you'll be able to find the silks you're looking for, and you'll be able to revisit the gold bazaar."

She nodded solemnly.

Mr. Maxwell stepped forward and spoke to Ahmed Hussein in Arabic. The antiquities dealer nodded, then offered a sweeping hand gesture for the three visitors to move to the room beyond the silken curtains.

That room was lit only by two massive candlesticks of silver. (She was sure they must be authentic antiques.) He indicated a scattering of colorful floor cushions for them to sit upon. The three of them obliged. Beside Ahmed Hussein was a tall hookah pipe contraption. He began to smoke it after he took his seat. He then passed it to Jack.

Jack nodded, closed his lips around it, drew in the pungent tobacco, then passed it to Daphne, mumbling, "You will be expected to sample this."

This was awfully thrilling for her. In England she'd be branded a doxy if she did such a thing. It did seem odd that in a country in which women were suppressed, subservient, and not even accorded fidelity by their husbands, they should be permitted to partake of this clearly masculine pursuit. She happily closed her lips around the pipe.

"Now you're to breath in the tobacco," Jack instructed.

She did so.

It did not have an agreeable effect upon her. She launched into a coughing fit, and she truly feared she might cast up her accounts right upon their host's lovely Oriental carpet. She had not been so humiliated since her wretchedly retching wedding night. How vexing! And she had truly liked the smell of the hookah thing. Clearly her head and her stomach experienced a serious breach.

She attempted to act as if the pipe smoking had not so adversely affected her. She casually passed the pipe to Mr. Maxwell—if one were capable of doing anything casually when one was hacking her head off and praying to the Almighty to spare her the humiliation of defiling their host's carpet. Knowing his reputation, the carpet was likely hundreds of years old. She was so completely distressed, she was not able to attend to what was being addressed at present.

She was forming a crisis plan. If her stomach did, indeed, threaten to spew, she must spew into the skirt of her dress. She began to fan the thin muslin around her. Then she decided that wouldn't do at all. Better the man's carpet than the dress she would be forced to wear all the way back to their hotel.

Now how to appear interested in the speaker without turning? Such an action could upset the precarious balance that leveled the contents of her stomach. Even if she could manage to feign interest in the speaker, the man was sure to know she couldn't possibly understand anything he said since she had no knowledge of Arabic.

Finally, she gathered enough composure to watch as Jack told Mr. Maxwell what he wanted to ask Ahmed Hassein. "Ask the gentleman if he knew Prince Edward Duleep Singh. And if he answers in the affirmative, ask if he's seen him in the past year."

In spite of her mortification and misery (because she still felt as if a noxious substance had polluted her body—which, in fact, had occurred), she was exceedingly impressed at how fluidly Mr. Maxwell spoke Arabic. Her untrained ear could not detect any difference in the speech between the two men speaking the Arabic tongue.

After the Arabic exchange, Mr. Maxwell turned to Jack. "He says he has known the Prince for years as they are friendly competitors, but he hasn't seen the Prince since last summer."

"Ask him if he's ever heard of the Amun-re funerary mask," she directed.

The other two men went back and forth in

Arabic, and then Mr. Maxwell addressed Jack. (She would have to inform Mr. Maxwell she was Jack's full partner in everything and expected to be included in every conversation pertaining to their joint investigation.) "He said he did indeed see it a year ago. He wanted it badly, but the Indian Prince paid far more than it was worth."

"Ask him if it's come on the market again since Prince Singh obtained it," she said in a strident voice the belied her queasy insides.

She watched as Mr. Maxwell spoke. And Hassein shook his head.

"If you will, Mr. Maxwell," she said, "ask him if he knows if Prince Singh's servants remain at his villa here."

The two men spoke back and forth for a moment. Then Mr. Maxwell turned to her. "It has always been the Prince's custom to keep a staff to run the house here whilst the Prince travels between here and his native country, but Hassein cannot attest to the practice being continued."

Daphne nodded and turned to her husband. "Can you think of anything else?"

Jack shook his head. "I beg that you thank him for speaking with us."

* * *

While Mr. Maxwell was escorting Rosemary down every single crooked street of the massive bazaar—with armed soldiers assuring their safety—Jack and Daphne, along with their faithful watchdogs and Habeeb, strolled to the area near Bulak where they'd seen the Pasha's palace.

By now the sun was high in the sky, and there was no way to avoid its scorching heat. She felt beastly sorry for Jack, whose thick, heavy, woolen clothing was unfit for the desert. To compound their discomfort, they attracted swarms of flies as if they'd been coated with honey.

Because of what Mr. Briggs had told them, they knew Prince Singh's villa was near. It was only a matter of having Habeeb make an inquiry to learn which house belonged to the Prince.

Once Habeeb made his inquiries, he led them to a villa that seemed quite small when compared to the Pasha's, but it was still an impressive residence. Tall palm trees fanned around the stucco house, much of which was built around a garden. How incongruous it seemed to find such verdure here in the midst of the pale dirt and sand mixture that Cairo was built upon.

Jack rang the bell, and a servant scurried to the main entrance. "Do you speak English?" Jack asked.

Immediately, the thin young attendant shook his head and whirled away, leaving the door open as he scurried down the corridor. A moment later he returned with an older man. This distinguished-looking Indian wore a turban but curiously dressed in the European style with trousers. After seeing so many men whose faces were obscured by untamed beards, Daphne was rather pleased to see a brown-skinned man whose face was clean shaven. "Mohammed tells me we have English-speaking visitors." He bowed. "Won't you please come in?"

The soldiers had already stationed themselves at the perimeter of the villa. Jack and Daphne entered, then he turned back to Habeeb. "You may be seated while my lady and I speak privately with this man."

The interior of this home was furnished in the style of a raja's palace. Not that she'd ever been to one, but she'd seen illustrations of them. There were only a few Oriental rugs here, likely to better display the mosaic-tiled floors that were works of art in their own right. It was a shame to cover them with rugs, but a few Persian carpets were scattered on the floor.

The wood of most of the furnishings was cut in a filigreetype of pattern. There were no floor cushions. She was most happy to see chairs. After their exceedingly hot and uncomfortable walk, she was grateful to sit in a shaded room. It was much cooler in here than outside, but it was still beastly hot.

"I am the Prince's . . . your English equivalent would be butler, I suppose. You know the Prince is not here?"

They both nodded solemnly. "That's why we've come," Jack said, his voice grave. "The Prince Regent of Britain is concerned over the Prince's disappearance."

The Indian man, who had remained standing, spoke more somberly. "As am I."

"Are you aware of the item your master had procured for our Regent?"

"The Amun-re mask?"

"Yes," Jack said. "It appears you were a valued servant who gained the confidence of your master."

"I have been with the Prince nearly all our lives." He shook his head, a sorrowful expression on his face. "I fear he's dead."

"We were told that the Prince was always cautious, that he always was surrounded by guards."

The other man nodded. "It's his custom to use his guards whenever he carries large sums of money—or one of his valuable antiquities."

"Had the Prince actually taken possession of the mask?" Jack asked.

"Yes."

"He kept it well guarded?" Daphne asked.

"All of his residences have impenetrable chambers where his most valuable items are held until they are delivered to their buyers. He and I are the only ones with a key." His shoulders slumped. "The mask is no longer there."

"Did you see your master take it away?" Jack asked.

"No."

"Is anything else missing?" Daphne asked.

"Only a rug. It was not one of great value."

"Can you tell us everything you remember about the last time you saw the Prince?" Jack asked.

He drew a long breath. "I was sent away, supposedly to meet a friend of his from India who was to be docking that night." He shrugged. "No one ever came. I know now it was a scheme concocted to keep me away while he met the man responsible for his . . . disappearance."

"How do you know he met the person at his house?"

"Because he would never leave at night without the armed men sworn to protect him."

"Did any of the other servants see this mysterious stranger?" she asked.

He shook his head solemnly. "They were all given the night off."

"I don't mean to disparage your master, but it sounds as if he was up to no good," Daphne said.

The servant shrugged. "His behavior had been uncharacteristic all week."

"Was . . ." Daphne quickly corrected herself. "Is Prince Singh married?"

"Yes. The Princess lives in India."

"Then I don't suppose she'd be any help," Daphne mumbled.

"When did you learn the mask was missing?" Jack asked.

"It was several days. The first night he wasn't here I thought he'd just gone to . . ." He stopped. "The city."

Daphne wondered if the man was covering up the fact that Prince Singh might have had a mistress with whom he regularly cohabitated.

"After the second day," he continued, "I knew something was wrong. That is when I went into the locked chamber and discovered the mask gone."

"Could it be possible that it became imperative for the Prince to take a trip? Were any of his clothes gone"

The other man shook his head. "He would never go off without his guards—and nothing was gone. Except for the mask and that single rug. How I wish the Prince had never developed his obsession for dealing in antiquities!"

Daphne's green-eyed gaze met his dark one. "Can you give us the direction of Prince Singh's mistress?"

Jack's head jerked toward her. "Daphne!"

Her dear husband was such a Puritan!

The Indian man nodded. "She is in the old city. Her name is Amal. I do not know precisely where she resides, but I am told she is accounted to be the loveliest woman in all of Cairo."

Jack stood. "That should help."

Daphne came and settled a gentle hand at the

servant's sleeve. "We will do everything we can to find your master."

* * *

They had no trouble finding the lodgings of the loveliest women in Cairo. Unfortunately, no one answered the bell. Daphne tried the door, and it opened. She padded into the first chamber.

And screamed.

$\mathcal{C}$hapter 5

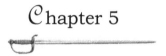

Even in death, Singh's mistress had been beautiful. Her lifeless body sprawled on the cold tile floors, the colourful silk of her robes draping elegantly around her slender body. Long, black lashes swept against a flawless face, and thick, dark wisps of hair had tumbled from her veil, which still managed to crown her lovely head.

Someone had strangled the life from her.

Jack had quickly swept Daphne from the scene. This was one time he was thankful that their every step in Cairo was dogged by soldiers. British soldiers, thank God. He handed his hysterical wife off to them, and he and four of them went back into the courtesan's disheveled house. While the soldiers looked in every room of the three-story house for the murderer, Jack examined the body. He'd had enough dealings with death to know that this woman had not been dead long.

They must have barely missed witnessing the murder. From the overturned furnishings, it appeared the poor woman had fought tenaciously for her life. He looked beneath her fingernails for a clue. A piece of fabric, something.

But he found nothing.

As he went to get up, he saw it. A single hair on the falls of her robe.

And it was not black.

His first instinct was that it was the

murderer's, but then he realized if the woman was a common courtesan, she could be with many men. He lifted the brownish-blond hair. Definitely a European's. His thoughts flashed to Gareth Williams. It was the colour of that vile man's hair. Coincidence? Perhaps. But the only trust Williams had ever engendered was mistrust.

Jack stood and examined the room for further clues. Where in the devil were the woman's servants? By the looks of her rich silk clothing and her fine stucco house, she was well-enough off to afford many servants. Perhaps, if she had an assignation with a lover, she had dismissed them. There was also the prospect the servants had heard the struggle with the killer and fled, especially if they were defenseless females.

The soldiers who had been combing the house found nothing. "Half of you need to stay here until the authorities come," Jack told them. "I'll leave my dragoman here to interpret. If any of the dead woman's servants return, he's to question them. I'll want to know anything they may have seen or heard. Now I'll pop over to the Consulate to have them report the murder. Then I'm taking my wife back to the hotel."

At the Consulate, they sought Arbuthnot and told him about the murder. His mouth dropped open. "How beastly." His voice softened as he turned to speak to Daphne. "My poor lady. I'm so distressed that you had to witness something so ghastly."

"We hoped you'd know who to report this to," Jack said.

Arbuthnot nodded. "You must take dear Lady Daphne back to the hotel. I'll run along and tell the Turkish officials."

"So that explains the presence of all the Turkish soldiers swaggering through the town with their muskets so prominently displayed," Jack said. "They serve to keep law and order."

"Right-o."

While Jack and Daphne were returning to their hotel, both of them were somber. It had been a ghastly day. The heat had been almost intolerable. The damned flies that buzzed around their faces were the most annoying pests he'd ever encountered. And, worst of all, a beautiful courtesan was murdered.

Their cool bedchamber beckoned. More than ever, now he understood the afternoon respites practiced in lands of intense sun. Siesta, they called it in Spain. He wondered what the Arabic word for it was. He'd have to ask Maxwell.

As soon as they reached the seclusion of their own bedchamber, he closed the shutters over their window opening, then proceeded to divest himself of his sweaty clothing.

Daphne was doing the same. "Do you know, my dearest, if I dressed as the native women do— except I refuse to cover my face—I believe I wouldn't have to wear these odious stays. Feel them. See how wet they've become." She moved to Jack.

He grinned, holding up a hand for her to yield. "I will take your word for it. As soon as I'm out of my own drenched clothing, I'll help you remove the damned things."

His mind was so engaged with the murder of the lovely Amal that for the first time since he'd married Daphne, he unlaced her stays without cupping his hands over her breasts.

Even though their bedchamber was hot, he'd

estimate it was twenty degrees cooler than it was outside in the sun. He collapsed on their bed. Before Daphne lay down, she gathered the mosquito netting around the bed, then slipped in. It thankfully also kept out the damned flies. It was too hot even for the spooning position she normally adopted. There was a sizeable—and uncustomary—gap between their two stretched-out bodies.

It was some time before they spoke. He knew, like him, she'd be analyzing the murder of the lovely Egyptian woman.

"Do you think Ahmed Hassein had her killed?" Daphne finally asked.

"Why would you think that?"

"Mr. Arbuthnot as good as said that the man was a murderer. Or the orderer of a murder."

"What would he have to gain by her death?"

"Perhaps she's also been giving her favors to Ahmed Hassein. Perhaps he used her to get what he wanted from Prince Singh. And now that we're making inquiries, he must silence her."

"Your supposition has merit. It's clear that her life was not put into jeopardy until we showed up in Cairo. Singh's butler also knew we were going to try to find Amal. Perhaps he's the murderer. Or, as my wife says, the murder orderer."

She shook her head emphatically. "I believe Singh's servant is genuinely distressed over his master's disappearance. I cannot believe he had anything to do with the beautiful courtesan's death."

"I'm inclined to agree with you. For one reason—he wouldn't have to have told us of Amal's existence."

"Which brings us back to Ahmed Hassein."

"Not necessarily. The Consul knew about our mission. Perhaps he communicated with someone who wished to silence the mistress."

"Or even Mr. *Arbuth-knows-it-all*, though I can believe no malice of him," she said.

"I'd describe him as annoyingly toadeating but not malicious."

"The poor woman must have known the identity of the person meeting with Prince Singh that last night," Daphne speculated.

"She may even have been there—and it unfortunately cost her life."

"Did you find any clues as to the murderer's identity?"

"What makes you think I looked?"

"I know thee well."

"Actually, I did. I found a hair on her that was not black."

"Very promising.   Though, if she were a courtesan- - -"

"She could be with many men."

"I do hate that our presence in Cairo may already be responsible for someone's death."

"As do I," he said gravely. "It makes me even more determined to find the culprit and bring him to justice."

Their speech stopped. The Call to Prayer was being sung out at minarets throughout the city. All other noise in the bustling metropolis stopped. Whilst he was in their country, Jack felt semi-bound to honor their customs by ceasing dialogue and listening. Because of his brief studies with Maxwell, he understood some of it.

Afterward, Daphne drew a deep breath. "I can't help wondering about that hair. May I see it?"

Jack fetched it for her then climbed back upon

the bed and refastened the mosquito netting.

"There aren't that many Englishmen in Cairo. It certainly doesn't match either Mr. Briggs' or Mr. Arbuthnot's," she said.

"Arbuthnot has no hair. Or at least nothing as long as this."

"True. There is still a heavier French presence in the city. This hair must belong to a Frenchman."

He had withheld information from her long enough. He sighed. "I didn't tell you that when we docked I recognized a man. A deserter from Badajoz. A thoroughly disreputable man named Gareth Williams, who was also suspected in many thefts."

"Did he see you?"

"Yes. He quickly turned away and got lost from my view in the quay-side crowd."

"And you think this hair would match his?"

He nodded.

"If he's a British deserter, it's not likely he'd have anything to do with the small English community here."

"It wouldn't surprise me if he's befriended the damned French."

"He dressed in the European style?"

"Yes."

"We shall have to ask Mr. *Arbuth-knows-it-all* if he knows the man."

"I doubt he'd be using his real name."

"Is he Welsh?"

"I believe so."

"Then we'll ask Mr. Arbuthnot if he's come into contact with a Welshman living in Cairo."

* * *

Later that evening, Arbuthnot came to their

hotel, joining them in the dining room. "I do hope most sincerely that Lady Daphne has recovered from the beastly scene she witnessed today."

"I am much better, thank you. We have a question for you, Mr. Arbuthnot. Have you become acquainted with a Welshman living in Cairo?"

His bushy brows lowered. "I can't think of one."

"I do hope you've brought us promising news," Jack said to him.

"Yes, very. Mr. Briggs has been successful in scheduling you a meeting with the Sheikh al Mustafa. The Pasha arranged it as a favor to Mr. Briggs."

"When will the meeting take place?"

"I will call for you tomorrow morning at nine and take you to the Sheikh's villa."

* * *

Jack's face was grim when he turned to Daphne the following morning. "Habeeb has never returned from the house of the murdered woman."

"I was afraid of that."

"You thought he was going to desert us?"

"No, Silly. I thought the servants would be reluctant to return to the murder house. Especially if they can identify the murderer. Their lives may also be in jeopardy."

"I hadn't thought of that. I would go back into the city to speak to Habeeb, but Arbuthnot should be here any moment to collect us."

She was standing beside the window. "As we speak, he's walking up to the hotel. Let's go down."

"First," Jack said, "I've decided we need to completely explain to Maxwell. I can do that in a low voice while you distract Arbuthnot."

"How can I distract *Arbuth-knows-it-all?*"

"Ask him to explain something to you."

A moment later, Arbuthnot greeted them. "I would have brought the Consul's carriage, but since we are required to be accompanied by your soldiers at all times, that wouldn't work," Arbuthnot said. "It's only a thirty-minute walk."

They began to walk to Shubra, the area where the Pasha's palace and other villas were located. Maxwell began to query Arbuthnot about an excursion to Gizeh, which held great interest for Daphne. Jack's mind was elsewhere. He wished like the devil he hadn't allowed Rosemary to come to Egypt with them. She could not be on hand for their sensitive talks, nor could he grant her request to travel to Gizeh to see the pyramids. He couldn't spare Maxwell, whom he needed to interpret, and he would not consider allowing her to travel without himself or the Arabic scholar.

He took some consolation that she had exceedingly enjoyed shopping in the bazaar the previous day, and he had feigned interest when she proceeded to unfurl lengths of brightly coloured silks and sparkling gold ornaments for his perusal as she gushed on about how very cheap everything was.

If he and Daphne could successfully conclude this mission, he would see to it that they all got to see the pyramids at Gizeh. Right now, though, there was a murderer to apprehend.

He hated, too, informing his wife's sister about the murder, but she needed to know the dangers that could lurk in this exotic city.

"Maxwell, I beg a word with you," Jack said.

Maxwell dropped back a few steps and began to walk beside Jack.

"Mr. Arbuthnot," Daphne said, "I was hoping you could tell me about Pasha Mohamed Ali. Have you had the honor of actually meeting him?"

Arbuthnot readily launched into a description of the Pasha and a long catalogue of all the times the Pasha had acknowledged him.

During this time Jack explained to Maxwell why they had come to Egypt and the possible suspects in Prince Singh's disappearance and concluded by telling him of the murder of Singh's mistress. "So, you see, old fellow, this is dangerous, and I'll understand if you wish to return to England."

"I wouldn't think of it."

There was one other matter plaguing Jack. How was he going to extricate himself and Daphne from Arbuthnot when they arrived at the Sheikh's villa? Jack wasn't sure why he even needed the man's escort since the Sheikh al Mustafa's villa was the closest one to the Pasha's. Wouldn't that description have been enough for them to find it?

As it happened, when they strolled up to the Sheikh's sumptuous villa that was encircled with artistic clusters of tall date palms, Jack casually turned to their escort. "Thank you very much, my good man. Lady Daphne and I will be in good hands now with Mr. Maxwell to interpret for us, and we should have no problem finding our way back to our hotel."

As Arbuthnot walked away, the Sheikh's servant opened the large timbered door, came into the fountained courtyard, and bowed to welcome them, greeting them in Arabic.

Maxwell responded. Jack had instructed him to convey the information that the English ruler who sent them insisted on the soldiers' presence but explained the soldiers were to stay outside of the property. Jack felt like a bloody milksop, but he knew their presence protected the ladies from harm.

He felt badly that Rosemary had been forced to stay back at the hotel—with a pair of soldiers to watch the entrances and exits for her protection.

Before they entered the house, Jack turned to Petworth, the only one of the House Guards with whom Jack was previously acquainted. He gave the soldier a sympathetic expression. "Awfully sorry, old fellow, that you must stay in this heat."

The redhead, who was likely in his thirties and very fit, smiled. "It's good we've come early. I hope to spare my men from the day's harshest heat."

"As do I, my friend."

"But, sir, you and I have served in Spain. We should be accustomed to heat."

Jack shook his head. "It was hot in Spain, but not this bloody hot."

Petworth grinned, nodding.

The Sheikh's barefoot servant led them along a corridor built in much the Moorish style, with a square arcade giving on to still another courtyard at the center of the house, this one of grass.

Like Prince Singh's floors, these were intricately tiled in another Moorish pattern. Their group came to a large room strewn with colourful pillows upon which they were to sit. Before they did so, a man rose to greet them in Arabic. He was about the same height as Daphne, slender, and likely in his thirties. A full black beard covered much of his face, and he wore black robes and head covering. "I am Sheikh al Mustafa." His black eyes bore into Daphne's, a sinister look on his face. He likely had no use for women, especially women who did not cover their hair.

Though it had been gracious of him to consent to their visit, nothing about his countenance was particularly welcoming.

Maxwell spoke to him, and then the man in black robes beckoned for the three of them to sit down.

Once they were all seated, he said, in French, "My French is very good. Can we communicate in that language?"

Jack and Daphne both nodded. "I am Captain Jack Dryden. This is my wife, Lady Daphne, and we are accompanied by Mr. Stanton Maxwell, who, as you know, speaks Arabic."

A faint smile was directed at Maxwell. Then the Sheikh faced Jack, an expression of contempt on his face. "You have come on behalf of the English ruler, no?"

"That is correct," Jack replied in French.

As they spoke, two scantily clad young Negro boys carrying plumes three times their height came to stand on either side of the Sheikh and proceeded to fan him and his guests. This addition made it feel almost cool in the shady room with its cool glazed tile floors.

"I saw the soldiers you brought." The Sheikh's mouth was a grim line.

"I can explain," Daphne said, continuing in French. "Our ruler promised my father that he would see that I was well guarded in this foreign land."

"The soldiers' only function here is to protect English citizens from potential harm," Jack said.

"I do not understand why you wish to see me. I have never had any connection to the British, especially not with your king."

"Actually, our king is too sick to serve. In his stead is his oldest son, the Prince Regent. He's the one who sent us," Daphne explained.

"He sent you to Egypt to see me?" the Sheik looked incredulous.

Jack shook his head. "No. He wanted us, first, to find Prince Edward Duleep Singh, and secondly, he wished to recover a valuable gold funerary mask."

The Sheikh nodded. "Then you seek this meeting with me because I knew Prince Singh?"

Knew? Not know? "We understand that you're interested in acquiring antiquities," Jack said.

"That is true."

Jack eyed the Sheikh. "Did you ever acquire any through Prince Singh?"

"On many occasions."

"Did you know about the Amun-re mask?"

"No. Prince Singh knows that I am not interested in small antiquities. What I currently seek is a sarcophagus from a pharaoh. That is as small as I'm interested in."

This time he used the word knows. Jack wondered if the verb tense was significant since he and Daphne also vacillated between using present and past when referring to the missing Indian. And if the Sheikh was acquainted with Singh, he would know the man had mysteriously disappeared.

"Do you recall the last time you saw Prince Singh?" Daphne asked.

He shrugged. "It could be as long as two years ago. I wasn't in Egypt last year, and I'm almost certain I haven't seen Singh this year."

"How long have you currently been in Cairo?" Daphne asked.

"I came after my pilgrimage to Mecca."

"That pilgrimage would have been in December," Maxwell told them in English.

If the man spoke the truth, then he would certainly be eliminated from suspicion in their inquiry. But how did one go about proving that he indeed had not come to Egypt last year?

"You have heard that Prince Singh has disappeared?"

He nodded. "My friend the Pasha told me some time ago."

"The Pasha was acquainted with Prince Singh?"

"The Pasha is a great ruler. He welcomes important men to his country whether they practice our faith or not. He wants what is best for Egypt."

It looked as if they were going to have to speak with the Pasha. Another commission with which to charge Briggs.

* * *

As he and Daphne strolled back to their hotel, Jack said, "How in the devil can we verify if the Sheikh was telling us the truth about not being here last year?"

She frowned. "If he's telling the truth, then we can eliminate him from suspicion."

Jack eyed Maxwell. "Sorry, old boy, for dragging you along. I had assumed we'd need you to translate."

"My only purpose is to be of use to you in this inquiry."

"You could have stayed in the relative cool of the hotel."

"I wish I had one of those little Negro lads fanning over my bed," Daphne said wistfully. "Only I suppose I'd have to have a little girl since it would not be proper for a boy to see me in my night shift. But then, it wouldn't do for a little girl to see you in your . . . oh, dear."

Jack flashed his wife a grin. "We'll just have to suffer without our personal fanner."

"Tell me, Mr. Maxwell, when you traveled through the Levant, did these wicked flies follow you everywhere?" She batted them away from her face as she spoke.

"Yes. I believe they're worse than the intense heat." Maxwell waved away a circle of flies from his face, but a stubborn one sat on his eyelid without budging. He flicked it off.

Jack admired him for not cursing since such restraint had thus far eluded Jack.

"I've got it!" Daphne exclaimed.

"Got what?" Jack asked.

"How we'll prove the veracity of the Sheik's claim he did not come here last year."

"And how, my love, do you propose to do that?"

"I won't. Habeeb will."

"I see," Jack said, nodding. "Our dragoman can query the Sheikh's servants."

A peacock could not have looked more proud than Daphne did when she nodded, a smile stretching across her face.

"I don't suppose the fellow can just walk up and ask perfect strangers such a question," Maxwell pointed out.

Daphne's smile faded. "There is that."

Maxwell addressed them. "Since you're not going to need him to interpret, perhaps you can do without his services for a couple of days and have him claim he wants employment in the Sheikh's household. Or stables."

"The difficulty is that Habeeb never returned

last night. We ordered him to question the dead woman's servants."

Habeeb always stationed himself on a bench in front of their hotel when the Drydens had no duties for him.

As they were approaching the hotel, Jack said, "He's still not returned."

$\mathcal{C}$hapter 6

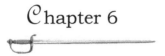

So many things flashing through her mind conspired to deprive Daphne of sleep. Always, she came back to the vision of the lovely dead Egyptian courtesan, Amal. Daphne feared for Rosemary. She would not have brought her sister along had she actually thought they would be dealing with a disgustingly vile, loathsome reprobate who would crush the life from a helpless woman.

It was bad enough Daphne had seen the beautiful woman's lifeless body just minutes after life had been strangled from her. Even worse were Daphne's regrets that they'd arrived a few minutes too late. The woman might still have been alive. If they had never come to Cairo, Prince Singh's lovely mistress probably would still be alive. Daphne had no doubt their coming here stirred up the vipers responsible for Prince Singh's disappearance. The woman's death had to be linked to the other.

Someone obviously wanted to keep Amal from talking to her and Jack.

Was it possible that whatever Amal knew, her servants also knew? All that Jack and Daphne sought was the identity of that last person seen with Prince Singh. It was more imperative than ever that they speak with Amal's servants.

Daphne hoped she was right about Habeeb. In her gut, she knew he was loyal to her and Jack.

The reason he'd been gone for more than four and twenty hours had to be that he was still trying to locate Amal's servants.

As soon as dawn eased into their dark bedchamber, she swept from their bed and rushed to the window to look for Habeeb. A smile broke across her face when she saw his turban-topped head. He sat on the bench in front of their hotel.

She hurried to get dressed, her movements awakening Jack. "What the bloody hell are you doing up so early?"

"I've got much to do today, and it's best to get an early start to avoid the day's worst heat." She sat down on the room's only chair to put on her stockings. "Habeeb's here."

"That's welcome news." With a big sigh, he threw off the mosquito netting, climbed from the bed, and began to dress. "Explain to me, madam, these things you've got to do today."

"I'm enlisting the aid of Habeeb. He can be of tremendous help to us."

"Questioning the servants of Sheikh al Mustafa?"

"That will be later. It's more imperative that I learn if he was able to speak to any of Amal's servants."

"Yes, I've been thinking about that also."

She turned a smiling face at him. "Now when would that thinking of yours have occurred since you went to sleep within a minute of dousing our candle, and you just this minute awakened?"

He jammed a foot into his boot, then looked up at her, grinning. "You're jealous. I have the ability to sleep, and you obviously were awake most of the night, the wheels in that mighty brain of yours spinning continuously."

"Thou knowest me well."

As soon as they were finished dressing, they went to Habeeb. He rose and greeted them when they approached.

Daphne could tell from his broad smile that he'd met with success and had to practice restraint to keep from launching her grateful self into the young dragoman's arms for a congratulatory hug. "Did the dead woman's servants ever return?"

He nodded. "She had two women servants. One was gone to the fish market when the murderer came. The other one answered the door to a European man who demanded to see her mistress. He spoke Arabic. She showed him into the . . . I believe the English would call it a drawing room, and she left. A moment later she was aware of a struggle between that man and her mistress. Thinking he must be some madman, she fled out the back door."

"She had never before seen the man?" Jack asked.

"Never."

"Please, Habeeb, take me to her and help me speak with her," Daphne said.

He shrugged. "I do not know where to find her."

Jack's brows lowered. "She's not staying at her mistress's house?"

Daphne glared at her husband. "No woman— especially a woman who could identify the murderer—would want to sleep in that house after so horrible a crime."

"You do have a point there," Jack conceded.

"Both servants were very, very sad and cried much. They waited until the day after the murder to come and get their things. One of them brought her father for protection."

"How will we ever find them?" Daphne spoke to herself.

"A quarter of a million people are crammed into this city," Jack said.

"You want me to try to find them?" Habeeb asked. "I know the city well. I know which areas of the city they might have gone to."

"Yes, please," Daphne said. "And Habeeb?"

His big brown eyes regarded her.

"I should like you later this afternoon to undertake another commission for us. Of course, if you locate the dead woman's servants you must let us know immediately."

"Yes, Sitti el Kebin."

"Before the sun goes down I should like you to go to the Sheikh al Mustafa's, which is near the Pasha's palace. Never let them know you are dragoman to the foreign couple. Don't go to the front entrance. Go to the back and make inquiries as if you would like to become a servant in their household."

"What kind of inquiries?"

"Somehow I shall need you to ask if the Sheikh was gone from Cairo this past year. It is important that I know when he was gone."

"It's also important," Jack said in a stern voice, "that no one knows we are responsible for asking you to find out that information."

"You are my masters. I answer to no one else."

It was then she noticed there was a sack on the ground.

Habeeb bent down and handed it to her. "I have those costumes, Sitti el Kebin, that you asked me to procure. I flatter myself that they are long enough for you and the Captain."

"I am very grateful. I must reimburse you the expense. How much did they cost?"

"Only four paras."

Jack gave him the money.

* * *

Owing to their early rising, they were the sole occupants of the breakfast room. The Egyptian servants who had previously set up the food on a rough-hewed sideboard had also put a fresh cloth on the table. She and Jack helped themselves to strong Turkish coffee, watermelon, toast, and freshly churned butter.

"I feel so bloody impotent," Jack said when they sat down. "This is our fourth day in Cairo, and we've learned nothing that we didn't know when we left London."

She grimaced as she swallowed the sludgy coffee. "We have learned that Prince Singh had a mistress."

"Whose death we are most likely responsible for."

"There is that. There is also the fact that we can possibly eliminate one suspect—if the Sheikh's absence can be verified."

"So that leaves us with the shady antiquities dealer, Ahmed Hassein."

"Let us not discount Lord Beddington, though it's unlikely a man as wealthy as he would ever resort to murder to obtain what he wants."

"I'd like to question the man, but I understand the voyage up the Nile to Thebes can take almost four weeks, one way."

She shook her head. "Certainly not worth two months of our time for so slim a prospect."

"My thoughts exactly."

"I will own we have nothing to go by. We must

find your Gareth Williams."

"I feel almost certain he's the one who killed the woman."

"But what we really need to know is who is it he takes orders from."

"Exactly. I fear the Welshman won't be easy to find, even though a British man is scarce in this city."

She nodded. "You'd think even if he were going by another name, Arbuthnot would know of a Welshman living here. Isn't that part of his position—knowing all the British subjects?"

"Unless the British subject doesn't want his countrymen to know he's here. Treason is punishable by death."

"There is that." She then brightened. "I know what!"

He stopped buttering his toast and shot her a mischievous glance. "What does my lady know?"

"Your fellow officer—the one who served with you and the Welshman in the Peninsula . . ."

"Harry Petworth?"

Jack leapt up, then bent down to kiss her cheek. "Another excellent suggestion." He raced from the room, out the front door.

Mr. Maxwell strolled into the eating room. She had been waiting for the opportunity to speak privately to him.

"Please, come sit by me," she said.

He obliged.

She lowered her voice. "I wished to pass along a vital warning to you."

His brows drew together. "About the suspects?"

"Oh, no. Something altogether different." She drew a breath. "Since you are a man and since you may seek a female for a certain activity, as men are want to do, I must encourage you to only go to the dancing girls."

"But, my lady, such an activity as dancing has no appeal to me for I never learned to dance.

At that moment, Rosemary entered the chamber, and Daphne knew such conversation must cease.

"Why are you discussing dancing girls?" Rosemary asked.

Mr. Maxwell's brows scrunched together. "I believe your sister was under the misapprehension that I was desirous of dancing."

Rosemary's eyes widened. "You don't like dancing?"

He shrugged. "It is a skill I've never acquired."

Rosemary shot a hostile glance at Daphne. "I don't know why you would try to force him to dance. It's not as if he doesn't have enough to occupy him."

Jack returned with the soldier.

"Have I ever formally presented you to my wife, Petworth?"

"No, sir."

Jack turned to Daphne. "Lady Daphne, may I present to you Harry Petworth of His Majesty's House Guards?"

"Delighted."

Petworth bowed. "It is my pleasure to protect the wife of the infamous Captain Dryden—as well as to serve our Regent."

Jack then introduced him to Rosemary, then to Mr. Maxwell.

"Please," Jack said, "help yourself to some breakfast and come sit with us. We have a new assignment for you."

The soldier piled his plate, poured the coffee,

and came to sit beside Jack.

"When we were in the Peninsula, did you know Gareth Williams?" Jack asked him.

The other man's eyes narrowed. "That dirty, no good . . ." He glanced at Daphne. "'Tis only my lady's presence that keeps me from launching into a string of curse words. I ain't never served with a more despicable man than Gareth Williams."

"He's in Cairo," Jack said.

Petworth whirled at Jack. "You've spoken with the coward?"

Jack shook his head. "No. I saw him the day we disembarked at Bulak."

"He knows you saw him?"

"Yes. He spun away and disappeared into the crowd of Arabs, and I haven't seen him since."

The normally pleasant-faced Petworth sneered. "I'd like to get my hands on him."

"There's still another vile act we believe he's guilty of," Daphne said.

Jack's voice was grave. "I have some reason to suspect he's the one who killed the Egyptian woman yesterday."

Petworth winced. "Then I hope to God I do get my hands on him. How could a man do something so despicable? She was . . . even in death, the prettiest thing I ever saw. What depravity could make a man commit so heinous a crime?"

"Most crimes of that sort are committed for two reasons: rage or financial gain," Daphne said. "We believe he did it for the latter."

Petworth set down his cup of coffee and swung his glance from Daphne to Jack. "What can I do to bring the blackguard to justice?"

"We need you to find him," Jack said. "He apparently hasn't had any connection with the

English authorities here, and it's very likely he's using another name."

Petworth's eyes slitted. "He's probably gone over to the French. Dirty traitor."

"I'm not certain he could speak their language," Jack said.

"But we believe he's learned to speak in Arabic," Daphne said. "At least the murderer who called at the dead woman's house was a European man who spoke Arabic," Daphne said.

"He had fled to Morocco—where he would have been obliged to learn Arabic in order to survive," Jack said.

"What about the dead woman's servants?" Petworth asked. "Have they returned? When we left the scene at nightfall, they still hadn't come back. I suppose your faithful dragoman waited until they finally showed?"

"Yes, Habeeb's been most competent," Daphne said. "Unfortunately, the female servants merely gathered their things and disappeared again."

Petworth nodded. "I can understand them not wanting to sleep there."

As trustworthy as she knew Petworth was, there was a limit as to how much information she was willing to share with him. The less people who knew about the hair, the better.

"Delicious stuff," Petworth said as he finished his watermelon. "I take it you'll want me to wear civilian clothes whilst I look for the slayer of women?"

"Yes. Did you bring other clothing?"

He shook his head.

"You're very near my size. I'll get you some of mine," Jack said.

"Jack even has a native costume, if you'd care

to dress in it."

"With my red hair?" He burst out laughing. "Besides, I draw the line at dressing in those robes. Looks too much like a woman."

It occurred to Daphne that Harry Petworth's red hair was even more of a freakish display here in Cairo than her own unruly golden mop.

"You may think a Bedouin's dress not masculine, but the Bedouins are noted for their courage," she said.

"That they may be, but you'll not catch Harry Petworth dressing like no lady."

"Even though it's easy to recognize Europeans, it will still be difficult to find that swine Williams since there are a quarter of a million people in Cairo," Jack said.

Petworth whistled.

"You'll need to take your dragoman with you to serve as interpreter. Hopefully, you will be able to find people who will know the direction of the British man," Jack said.

Petworth pushed aside his emptied plate and cup and got to his feet. "I'll find the cheating, stealing, murdering coward. You can count on it."

* * *

While they were awaiting word from Mr. Briggs on a possible meeting with the Pasha, Jack and Daphne, along with Rosemary and Mr. Maxwell, strolled toward the old city gates where a great caravan was entering Cairo.

Daphne was especially impressed about these people's packing skills. Each of the camels—even larger in real life than she'd expected—hauled huge bundles that held tents, cooking utensils, food stores, as well as the goods they were bringing to market.

"Mr. Maxwell," Daphne said, "You are just the person who can explain why these camels have just one hump."

"The dromedary that's native to the Arabian peninsula and neighboring lands, like Saharan Africa, will always have just one hump," Mr. Maxwell explained. "The dromedaries of India, on the other hand, will have two humps."

Rosemary turned admiring eyes upon him. "I didn't know that. How clever you are!"

Daphne would wager Rosemary's worshipped Captain Conceited wasn't half as clever as Mr. Maxwell.

The poor man's lips clamped shut. Rosemary's praise embarrassed him to the point he was incapable of saying anything.

"Do you know, Mr. Maxwell," Daphne said by way of changing the subject to something more comfortable for the bespectacled man, "Jack and I have obtained Arabic costumes."

He smiled at them. "Capital! I've brought mine as well. Now we need only get one for Lady Rosemary for our own caravan."

Rosemary frowned. "I do wish, Daf, you'd have told me you were getting a costume. You know I would adore that sort of thing."

"Oh, would you? You're so particular about your dress. I had no notion you'd like to dress as a native. We'll have Habeeb get something made for you. Your height is comparable to most of the native women we've seen here."

"Where is Habeeb?" she asked.

"He's undertaking a commission for us," Jack said.

"Once Rosemary has her costume, we must make a caravan." Daphne's smiling face looked up into her husband's. "I should like to travel to Gizeh to spend one night in a tent and pretend that we are desert nomads. Would that not be fun, dearest?"

Her husband frowned. "We didn't come here to have fun."

"Don't be such a curmudgeon. One night in the desert. Two days. What would it hurt?"

"In case you've forgotten there's a murderer out there."

"I daresay he's not in Gizeh," Daphne said.

"Oh, please, Captain," Rosemary implored, "I beg that you will consider it."

It took him a moment to respond. "I'll consider it."

While they stood there, fascinated over the lengthy caravan of Bedouins, Arbuthnot approached them. "I have more good news. Mr. Briggs will take you to meet the Pasha this afternoon."

$\mathcal{C}$hapter 7

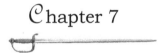

"You know, dearest, now that Rosemary has found out about Amal's murder," Daphne said, "I think we should take her into our confidence."

"I've been thinking along those same lines myself. It's not as if Maxwell doesn't already know everything. And I think it's for her own protection that she be given a complete accounting of our mission."

"I'll go speak with her. Then when Mr. Briggs collects us in his carriage, she can come. She would love to see the inside of a Pasha's palace."

"I don't think all of us will fit in the carriage. I wanted to bring Maxwell, too."

"If Rosemary and I sit on the same bench as the slender Mr. Maxwell, I think we'll all fit fairly comfortably."

Less than an hour later, Daphne had apprised Rosemary of their investigation, and they were all traveling to the palace in the Consul's coach. Even with its windows open, the heat was stifling, but the shade was welcome.

The flies were not.

"The Pasha was a most able Albanian soldier," Mr. Briggs told them. "His native tongue is Turkish, but he can communicate in French."

"Do you speak Turkish, Mr. Maxwell?" Daphne asked.

"Enough to get by tolerably," he answered.

"I have been wanting to ask," Mr. Briggs said,

eyeing the scholar, "are you the Stanton Maxwell who wrote *Travels Through the Levant*?"

"Yes."

"Mr. Maxwell's terribly clever," Rosemary said. "He speaks in at least ten tongues."

"I enjoyed your *Travels* very much," Mr. Briggs said, eyeing the author. "Are you by chance related to Osborn Maxwell of Cambridge?"

"That would be my father."

"Now that's a clever man for you. He is one of the only Englishmen I've read who understand Arabs."

"You must direct me to your father's writings," Rosemary said to Mr. Maxwell. "You know how profoundly interested I am in anything to do with the Orient."

"I may have something with me I could share," he said, his head turning to the slender lady beside him.

The coach stopped in front of an entrance to the Pasha's palace. They disembarked. Steps leading to the massive doorway cut between broad sweeps of rich green grass adorned with clusters of towering palms.

This close, the palace was even larger that it had appeared from a distance. She tried to determine how it compared in size to the Regent's Carlton House and decided that even though this stucco palace was choppier with varying heights and jutting appendages, the two royal residences were comparable in size.

As they followed one of the Pasha's servants down an interior arcaded corridor, Mr. Maxwell commented, "You will see the Pasha and his staff dress more colorfully, less austere than other Muslims. The Turks are not as fiercely religious as are many Muslims. It has been my observation that the closer one lives to Mecca, the more religious one is."

"Astonishingly astute statement," Mr. Briggs said. "It makes perfect sense to me."

The servant's dress was vastly different from what Daphne had become accustomed to in Cairo. The servant they followed wore a belted dress that stopped around the knees, and on his feet he wore fuchsia-colored satin slippers with toes that curled up. His head was bound with an ivory turban, and his face was mostly covered with a bushy black beard.

They came to a large and relatively cool chamber. The tiles which paved the floors here were glazed terracotta. The walls were pale stucco more than a foot thick. The ceiling soared at least twenty feet—possibly more.

Dominating the opulent chamber was what appeared to be a giant bed. This was no ordinary bed. Its large, square tester was covered in silk in an intricate pattern of gold and green with borders of crimson. From it, thick gold silk tassels wagged, and more of the rich gold braid and tassels adorned the pillows piled around the Pasha. Each pillow was of a different colour. There was magenta, emerald, royal blue, purple, orange, red, and much gold.

The Pasha himself sat on the bed, regarding them. He was a middle-aged man possessed of a beard that had a few years previously must have been all black but which was now primarily gray. On his head was an aquamarine silken turban, and his orange robes were also of silk. Like his servant, he wore the shoes with the turned-up toes.

Mr. Briggs had said the Pasha had been a formidable soldier. She could not for the life of her picture the man going into battle dressed like that. Then, in an odd juxtaposition of thoughts, she thought of Jack dressed in such a manner, and she almost burst out laughing.

She was immediately remorseful. Daphne had always prided herself on her ability to empathize with those of different cultures, never to mock them.

The Pasha Mohammed Ali regarded them through his black eyes, a smile curling at his lip as Mr. Briggs effected the introductions in French.

He bade them to sit upon the silken cushions scattered about the floor before him.

Once they were all settled, the Pasha's servant began to pass around the hookah pipe, starting with his master.

"Uh, oh," Daphne thought.

When the pipe came to her, Jack held up a hand. "I am sure your Excellency will understand that the ladies in our country are not permitted to smoke."

The Pasha nodded. How grateful Daphne was that she'd told her husband how dreadfully sick the pipe had made her. How grateful she was to Jack for extracting her from the awkward situation.

Jack began to address the Pasha in French. "As Mr. Briggs may have told you, we have come from England to your land on behalf of our ruler, the Prince Regent. He was a friend of Prince Edward Duleep Singh. Did you know Prince Singh?"

The Pasha nodded. "For many years I have known him."

"Had you ever heard of the Amun-re funerary

mask that Prince Singh procured?"

He nodded. "Some time before Prince Singh procured it, I heard that a Frenchman had murdered the Egyptians in whose possession it had been. I believe Prince Singh purchased it from the vile Frenchman. I had wanted to bring the Frank to justice, but it was not to be. He returned to France a very wealthy man."

"Did Prince Singh ever tell you what he planned to do with the Amun-re mask?"

"I was acquainted with the prince, but I do not think I was in his confidence."

Daphne drew a breath. It probably wasn't her place to speak—knowing that the place of women in the Arabic world was in no way equal to that of men and that were she Arab, she wouldn't even be allowed to be here—but she was unable to stay quiet when Jack simply didn't ask the intuitive questions she did. "Your Excellency, had you ever heard of anyone else who wished to obtain the mask? Anyone who ever spoke to you of it after it came into Prince Singh's possession?"

He thought for a moment before answering. "I have many sources throughout the country. I hear many things. Some may be reliable; some, not. I heard an Englishman got it after Prince Singh disappeared, but I do not know if that is true. I heard that it later sold in Constantinople for a very great price and that the seller was an Englishman."

Her first thought was of Gareth Williams. Now that she had the Pasha's attention and had not drawn his wrath, she pressed on. "What have you heard about the disappearance of Prince Singh?"

He shrugged. "The Prince had been missing for some time before I was told of it. Apparently, his servants became alarmed when two days passed with him not returning to his villa." Unconsciously, the Pasha's head turned in the direction of Prince Singh's nearby villa. "They say none of his clothes were missing. Only the Amun-re mask."

It surprised her that he would have been told that the Amun-re mask was discovered missing after the Prince disappeared because Prince Singh's servant did not appear to be one who would casually disclose information about the contents of his master's locked chamber.

"Does your Excellency have any idea who could be responsible for Prince Singh's disappearance?" Jack asked.

"It must be an Englishman."

Did he really believe that, or could he be protecting his friend, Ahmed Hassein? Or perhaps even the Sheikh al-Mustafa? "Does your Excellency know Ahmed Hassein?"

His head dipped into assent. "He also has a villa near here and is often my guest."

"It surprises me," Jack said, "that Hassein did not want to obtain the Amun-re mask, given his taste for very expensive antiquities."

"I was surprised when I learned that he allowed Prince Singh to take possession of something which was so much the kind of thing he specializes in," the Pasha said.

Daphne could well understand why Hassein wouldn't hand over many thousands of guineas when he could wait and steal it from Prince Singh. She felt strongly that Hassein, not some mysterious Englishman, was the culprit.

Unless the Englishman was really a Welshman.

"Have you considered how one would go about

locating the missing Indian prince?" Jack asked.

A pained expression passed over the Pasha's chubby face. "I fear he is dead. You know it is the Arab custom to bury their dead in the desert sands. Our deserts are littered with sun-whitened bones."

Daphne certainly hoped she never had to view rotting human carcasses if she ever did get to go out into the desert.

The Pasha changed the topic by inquiring about their opinion of Egypt and told them they must travel to Thebes to see many more antiquities from ancient Egyptians.

Daphne wondered if he were subtly alluding to Lord Beddington, who was known to have traveled to Thebes. Was he trying to cast suspicion on that Englishman?

"But, your Excellency, it would take us two months to make such a trip, and we don't have that kind of time," Jack said.

"Then you must at least see Gizeh."

* * *

It was dinner time before Mr. Briggs' coach dropped them off at their hotel. Jack was pleased to see that Habeeb awaited them just outside.

"You've found the dead woman's servants?" he asked.

Habeeb hung his head. "I have not yet found them, but I will not stop looking until I do. Especially the woman who saw the murderer."

"Good," Daphne said.

Jack could tell by the pleased expression upon his face, Habeeb had something good to impart.

"I did go to the house of the Sheikh al-Mustafa and was able to learn that he—and most of his servants—took the long journey to Mecca at the end of your last year."

"Your dragoman is pointing out that our calendar differs from the Muslim lunar calendar," Maxwell helpfully pointed out. "That would put the Sheikh gone from Cairo autumn through winter."

Jack looked up at the scholar. "How long would it take to travel from Cairo to Mecca and back?"

Maxwell shrugged. "There are a variety of conditions to consider, but I would say it could take up to nine months."

"Then that exonerates the Sheikh from suspicion, I'd say," Daphne said.

Jack redirected his attention at Habeeb. "Will you look again tomorrow for the women?"

"I will look tonight, too. I will search and search the city until I find them. This I vow to you." He bowed and turned away toward the old town.

Once they were in their bedchamber, Daphne said, "It has been our first productive day." She went to stand before the open window to watch the sun setting over Gizah's pyramids.

He came to stand beside her. "Your definition of productive and mine are decidedly different."

She looked up at him, smiling. "First, we've eliminated the Sheikh. That's progress."

"I'll give you that."

"And we've learned that there's a possibility an Englishman may have been responsible for Prince Singh's abduction and possible murder."

"Or a Welshman."

"That, too, is possible. But I wondered if the Pasha were trying to tell us we should investigate Lord Beddington."

Jack stiffened, his thoughts spinning back to the Pasha's comments. "I have allowed my hatred of Williams to close my mind to other suspects. You're right. The Pasha may have been telling us something about Beddington. Perhaps we need to learn more about him. When was he last in Cairo? Did he know of the Amun-re mask? Has he a history of ruthless activity?"

"Excellent questions, my brilliant husband!"

"Daphne?"

"What, dearest?"

"What have I told you about using the word brilliant in connection with me?"

"You forbade me to. That and handsome. And brave. And all those things you are, but I didn't say it in front of anyone. It's you and I. Don't be so hard on me."

He put his arms around her. "All right, love." And he nuzzled soft lips into her neck.

* * *

The next morning they had asked that Mr. Arbuthnot join them for breakfast. "So, Arbuthnot," Jack began. "What kind of man is Lord Beddington?"

"His lordship is everything one would want to represent Britain at a powerful post like that of ambassador to the Ottoman Empire. He's exceptionally well dressed and, as you know, exceedingly rich. He has a facility for languages and learned how to communicate in Turkish. He has a high respect for other cultures and an ability to adapt to them." Arbuthnot set down the wine glass he'd been twirling in his hands. "He was gracious enough once to invite me to accompany the Consul when he dined at his lordship's villa. While it's not large like the Pasha's, I think I would not be speaking an untruth if I were to say it is undoubtedly the finest residence in all of Egypt."

The middle-aged attaché put much store in outward appearances and all the trappings of wealth. Jack was no dandy, but he knew enough to know that the attaché's clothing was of the highest quality. Excellent tailoring, costly wools, finest leather boots. He wondered if Arbuthnot ever considered dressing as the natives. He'd been told that Lord Beddington often did.

"I believe you told us earlier that his lordship came to Egypt two years ago?" Daphne regarded him with a quizzing brow.

He nodded. "That is so. With his extraordinarily deep pockets, he was able to have his villa constructed in only three months. It was summer, and the days' sunshine longer. He immersed himself in the local culture, studied the language, and took many excursions to Gizeh. After he had thoroughly explored Gizeh, he said he was ready for Thebes and the Valley of the Kings."

"Do you recall when he left Cairo?"

"I do. Mr. Briggs hosted a combination Christmas/farewell party for our highest-ranking fellow countryman."

"This past Christmas?" Daphne asked.

The portly man nodded.

Damn, Jack thought, the former Ottoman ambassador was in Cairo when Singh went missing.

Daphne passed along a bowl of olives, then a plate of fresh-caught fish. "Do you live at a hotel, also, Mr. Arbuthnot?"

"No. I have been fortunate enough to purchase my own house in the European quarter. I'm not getting any younger, and it seemed a good time to begin acquiring property. For many years I lived at this hotel. I miss the variety of cooking. I now have a native cook who knows nothing but Egyptian cooking."

"Then we're very glad to have you come eat with us."

He unconsciously lapsed into the Arabic style of eating with his hands, scooping up the olives in his bare palm. "It's uncommonly good to have the opportunity to speak to others from good old England, especially refined personages such as Lord Sidworth's daughters." He nodded toward Rosemary, then reached down and twisted off the fish head with his bare hands. "Daresay we don't need that ugly thing."

It was a deep disappointment for Jack to learn that Lord Beddington had been in Cairo during the time of Prince Singh's disappearance. As unlikely as it was the English peer and former diplomat would stoop so low as to murder and steal, the man could not be eliminated. Especially after the Pasha's allusion to Thebes.

How in the devil could they determine the man's guilt or innocence when he was nearly a four-week journey away?

There was also the fact he could not have ordered the courtesan's death from so great a distance.

This was their fifth day in Cairo, and he was still no closer to solving the disappearance of Prince Singh. Barring the absent Lord Beddington, he and Daf had run out of people to interview. A full day stretched before them, and he couldn't think of a single thing they could do that would advance their inquiry.

Much still depended on the ability of Habeeb to locate the missing woman and on Petworth to locate that villainous Gareth Williams.

"I should like your assistance, Arbuthnot, in planning an expedition for our party to travel to Gizeh," Jack said. "My wife fancies sleeping in a tent."

"I will be happy to assist in any way I can, but your dragoman is much more competent than I am in such matters."

Daphne's face collapsed. "Our poor dragoman has been called away today. One of his wives summoned him because of some family distress. Do you have a dragoman you could lend us?"

"What of the soldiers' dragoman?" Arbuthnot asked.

Jack's voice was grave. "I've sent one of our soldiers and their dragoman on a line of inquiry for me and don't expect them to return today."

Arbuthnot nodded authoritatively. "I shall send around one of my servants shortly. When will you be departing?"

"As soon as possible."

"If you start this early in the day," Arbuthnot said, "by day's end you should have gathered together everything you'll need for an expedition of some little duration. You could leave in the morning."

The hotel door opened, and Petworth strolled in. "If you can wait until Mr. Arbuthnot is finished, I can speak with you," Jack said to him.

"Oh, I'm finished." Arbuthnot stood. "I'll send my servant to assist." He left the chamber.

Rosemary smiled at Jack. "Oh, Captain, you've made me the happiest creature imaginable."

"Me too, my dearest." Daphne leapt to her feet and kissed his cheek. "We must procure a native costume for my sister. How fun it will be if we all dress in the native fashion for our expedition."

"Fun and necessary," Maxwell said. "Since I have some experience with desert expeditions, I'll begin drawing up a list of needed supplies and food stuffs."

"Then I'll put you completely in charge," Jack said.

After Rosemary and Maxwell departed, Jack turned to Petworth. "Pray, won't you get a plate and have some breakfast?"

"I've already eaten."

He came to sit beside Jack.

"I hope you've good news for me," Jack said.

Petworth nodded solemnly. "I still don't know where the man lives. We spoke to many people who claim to have seen him in the old city. One person said he was told the English foreigner lived with an Arab woman, but no one seems to know where. We were directed to one place where he and a native woman had, indeed, lived, but they left some months ago. They had not been there long and were said to have kept to themselves."

"I get the impression that Williams is in the habit of moving frequently," Daphne said. "I daresay he's wanting to avoid the hangman."

Jack told Petworth about the upcoming expedition to Gizeh. "But I'm afraid, old boy, I'm going to need you to stay in Cairo and intensify your search. It's imperative that we find Williams."

"I'm not complaining. I'll take the shady streets of Cairo any day over the desert with intense sun beating down."

After he left, Jack turned to Daphne. "How did you know Habeeb has many wives?"

"Oh, I didn't, Silly. You know how I just make up things off the top of my head when we're involved in one of our inquiries."

"That makes me exceedingly nervous. Arbuthnot engaged the man for us. He might know personal things about Habeeb."

"I believe he'd have said something if he did."

A moment later, Arbuthnot's servant timidly stood in their doorway and introduced himself.

"Capital!" Daphne exclaimed. "The first thing I'll need you to do is procure a native costume for my sister. I'll run and fetch her so you can see her size."

Jack sat there in the dining room, steeped in gloom. He hated that his inquiry was stymied at present, but he had to own he was as eager for their little expedition as the others were.

$\mathcal{C}$hapter 8

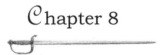

With Mr. Maxwell's efficiency, the handful of servants procured by Arbuthnot's dragoman was able not only to get everything needed for the expedition in just one day but also to pack it all. Four dromedaries were obtained as well as horses for the soldiers and the extra workers.

The four English, each dressed in native costume, mounted the dromedaries laden with bundles that held some of their tents and food supplies.

Just as they were about to leave at dawn, Arbuthnot came galloping up on a horse and spoke to them with a winded voice. "Mr. Briggs has asked that I accompany you on your trip to Gizeh." He was dressed in English riding clothes. "Surely I can share Maxwell's tent?" He eyed the scholar.

"I shall enjoy the company," Mr. Maxwell said.

A deep disappointment spiraled through Daphne. For once, she was speechless. She had wanted this to be just their little party with no outsiders except the hired hands and soldiers. She could well imagine the insufferable man stating the bloody obvious like, "A pyramid, as you may know, has a broad base and comes to a point at the top."

Even Jack withheld a warm welcome. His inscrutable gaze flashed to her.

It was an awkward moment before Mr.

Arbuthnot drew his horse alongside Jack's camel.

"Mr. Maxwell, with much help from your servant, organized this entire expedition in just one day. He's terribly resourceful," Daphne said to Mr. *Arbuth-knows-it-all.*

"I'm looking forward to the experience," Mr. Arbuthnot said. "While I have been to Gizeh several times, owing to its close proximity to Cairo, I've never actually traveled through the desert caravan style as we are today. Most of my travels throughout Egypt have been confined to being conveyed along the Nile and my trips to Gizeh on horseback."

Daphne sighed. "Such a pity Thebes is so very far down the Nile."

"Yes," Jack said. "It would have been nice while we were in Egypt to see Upper Egypt."

"My darling," Daphne said facetiously, "while I may not be as proficient as you at reading maps, I can tell you you've been to Upper Egypt. In Alexandria."

All the men started to laugh. Daphne could not imagine what she had said that was so comical.

"My darling wife, this is one instance where the map is deceiving. Yes, if you look at a map of Egypt, Alexandria is at the northern tip. However, that area is known as Lower Egypt. Thebes is in Upper Egypt."

Her mouth dropped open. "How can that be?"

"I suppose it has something to do with the flow of the Nile," Mr. Maxwell speculated.

"Forgive me for laughing at you, Lady Daphne," Mr. Arbuthnot said. "I'd never heard Alexandria referred to as Upper Egypt before—though I will own, it was awfully clever of you."

Perhaps Mr. Arbuthnot wasn't so unwelcome,

after all.

By the time Cairo and its hundreds of chimneys smoking with the day's bread baking were behind them, she was happy to inhale the clean desert air beneath the awakening sun. She was only now becoming accustomed to riding a camel. At first it had been rather terrifying because it was so steep a fall to the ground. And the silly thing made outrageous noises that had initially frightened her.

Before they'd ridden half an hour, the full sun was bearing down on them. She was awfully thankful she had dressed as an Arab woman. Most of all, she was thrilled to be able to leave off her stays. Why women had to be laced into the wretched breast smashers was totally beyond her comprehension. As was most fashion.

"How do you like wearing native dress?" she asked her sister.

"It's thrilling."

"Even if I say it myself I do believe my husband would have made an exceedingly handsome Arab. I tried this morning to persuade him not to shave. A couple of days beard growth, and he could pass for a native."

"Daphne . . ." Jack was using his scolding voice.

He did so dislike it when she boasted on him. "Sorry, dearest, I didn't mean to embarrass you by boasting out loud about your handsomeness."

She could almost hear him gritting his teeth.

Rosemary flicked a glance at Mr. Maxwell. "I believe Mr. Maxwell did forgo this morning's shave."

"I am flattered that my lady noticed. Whenever I dress as a native, I prefer growing a beard."

"I promise to withhold my judgment until it's grown a bit more," Rosemary said playfully.

"I cannot think when I've ever had so much fun," Daphne said. "I don't even mind the heat."

"You will find," Mr. Arbuthnot began in his didactic voice, "that even though we are close to Cairo, the desert heat is much more intense. For one thing, Cairo is near the river, and there are often breezes on the water. So, as hot as it was in Cairo, compared to what you will experience today, it's almost cold. For another thing, the sun reflecting off all this sand with its heavy glass content acts rather like a heat igniter, much like when one holds a piece of glass over a piece of paper in intense sun. Flames have been known to erupt."

"I hope none of us erupts into a fire ball," Daphne said with a little laugh. "One can see a shimmering heat radiating off the sand. It's quite lovely to view from up here on the dromedary."

Mr. Maxwell's dromedary came to a complete stop. "I should like to direct your attention to those two stones that are placed about five feet apart."

They all stopped. The stones were smaller than a woman's head.

"Oh, allow me to guess!" Rosemary said.

"Please, my lady," Mr. Maxwell answered.

"The stones mark the shallow grave of a desert nomad."

Mr. Maxwell nodded. "Very good."

"I don't suppose they use coffins?" Daphne inquired.

"No," Mr. Maxwell said. "Muslim belief dictates that they be buried on the day they die. The head of the deceased must point to Mecca."

"One would think the hyenas would get to the body," Jack said.

"If they are known to be in an area," Mr. Maxwell said, "then stones are placed all over the location of the grave."

"No markers ever?" Daphne asked.

Rosemary and the scholar both shook their head. "It's very likely the grave will never again be visited by loved ones," Mr. Maxwell said. "It's quite odd, though, to find a single grave this close to a large city." He encouraged his dromedary to move forward.

"Yes, I quite see," Daphne said. "One on the verge of death wouldn't be riding a camel in the desert unless there was no civilization around for hundreds of miles."

Maxwell nodded.

"How long, Arbuthnot, to get to the pyramids?" Jack asked.

"We ought to be there in an hour. I will be happy to serve as your guide."

"Actually, Maxwell has already offered," Jack said. "He's been here before, and he's studied the Seventh Wonder of the Ancient World extensively."

"Then I shall look forward to hearing what he has to say." Mr. *Arbuth-knows-it-all's* voice could not conceal his disappointment.

"Will we be able to see riches in the tombs?" Daphne asked.

"All the graves were robbed long ago," Rosemary answered. "A pity. Still, I couldn't be more thrilled. I've brought my sketch book and plan to fill it with drawings from Gizeh."

Mr. Maxwell regarded the young lady admiringly. "I did not know you were an artist, my lady."

She shrugged. "I try."

"I wish you'd been along on my other travels, then. How I longed to be able to capture in an image the things I saw—especially Petra. I curse that I have no abilities in that direction."

"I will be happy to share some of my drawings with you, sir. I shall be very jealous that you actually got to visit Petra."

"You are not thinking of entering the Great Pyramid, are you, Lady Rosemary?" Mr. Maxwell asked.

"Nothing could keep me from it."

The scholar was silent for a moment. Daphne knew his silence was in reaction to her sister's desire to go inside the pyramids. After some little while, he cleared his throat. "I will have to advise you against it."

Rosemary whirled at him. "Why, pray tell?"

"I've not heard of a woman entering a pyramid. You see, even in winter, one must strip off most of one's clothing in order to crawl around within the stifling hot shafts."

"I have heard of this," she admitted, "therefore I also have procured for myself and for my sister the type of costume that the dragomen wear. It's not unlike our Scottish kilts."

Daphne was shocked. "You mean we will allow our bare calves to be seen by the gentlemen?"

"I've been thinking about that," Rosemary answered. "Before you and I emerge from our tents in the young men's clothing, we will ask that all the Egyptians and all our soldiers turn their heads whilst we move to the entrance of the Great Pyramid."

"What about Mr. Maxwell?" Daphne asked.

Rosemary turned to face him. The poor fellow's

face had flushed, and Daphne was certain it wasn't from the sun. "You are of such noble character and so knowledgeable about those from other cultures, I know you won't presume to judge my conduct, nor would a gentleman like you ever try to take liberties," Rosemary said.

He coughed. It was a moment before he could articulate his thoughts. Daphne would wager that Rosemary was the first unattached, pretty female with whom the man had ever conversed. Finally he spoke. "My lady can trust me with her life as well as her virtue, and I vow that I would never presume to be judgmental against you."

"Then it's settled," Rosemary said. "My sister and I will explore the Great Pyramid."

"You know there are some shafts in which you'll have to crawl through dirt?" Mr. Maxwell said to her.

"Yes, I've read about that."

"There may be bats," he continued.

"I have read that if you will discharge a pistol, it will scare the wretched creatures away."

"That's true."

"Do you have a pistol, Mr. Maxwell?" Rosemary asked.

"Always when I travel in the Orient."

"Then I anoint you my protector."

Daphne found herself wishing that Mr. Maxwell were more handsome. If he were, Rosemary may have been able to transfer to him the affections she held for the odious, egotistical, heart-ensnaring, sinfully handsome Captain Cooper. Dear Mr. Maxwell was so much more worthy.

As it was, Rosemary seemed unaware of Mr. Maxwell as a man. Or a prospective suitor.

When one was the daughter of an earl, it rather

scared off suitors who weren't of the aristocratic class. Were Mr. Maxwell handsome and were he to fall blindingly in love with Rosemary, he would never act upon it because of their unequal stations.

Jack had been in that position once. Now even Papa, who favored Daphne over all his daughters, never questioned that Jack was good enough for his most beloved child. If anything, Papa had learned to love Jack as if he were his own son.

"I suppose all the men will be climbing to the top of the Great Pyramid," Mr. Arbuthnot said.

"It is perhaps the most memorable experience of my life," Mr. Maxwell said. "I do don breeches for better accessibility in climbing the stones of the Great Pyramid."

"Good thing I brought mine, then," Jack said.

"What about the women?" Daphne asked. "Can we not climb?"

"It would be most difficult," Mr. Maxwell said. "First, one needs to have unrestricted use of one's legs, and there's also the fact that it takes great strength to climb. Each stone to be mounted is at least waist high. I do not believe a woman's arm strength up to the task."

Jack's camel drew up beside Daphne's. "Don't get any ideas, love. You know you're not the least bit strong."

"But, my dearest husband, I shall have you to assist me."

"There is that," he said, frowning. He then lowered his voice and spoke so that only his wife could hear him. "I shouldn't like for other men to be peering at my wife's drawers."

Daphne's cheeks turned hot. "Instead of commissioning a native costume, it appears I should have asked for men's trousers."

"How I wish I had trousers," Rosemary said. "I should love to climb to the top of the pyramid above all things."

Mr. Maxwell turned toward Rosemary. "I can understand your great disappointment, but truly, my lady, you could never be physically strong enough to hoist yourself up nearly five hundred feet of those massive stones."

"I suppose I shall have to satisfy myself by going into the interior of the pyramid—and with drawing you as you climb atop the pyramid."

"I hope you're not afraid of small dark places," Mr. Maxwell said.

Rosemary shrugged. "I don't think I am, but I've not been put to the test."

"Mr. Maxwell?" Daphne asked.

"Yes?"

"Are there rats inside the pyramid?"

"I've not seen them there. There's no food stuff for them there any longer."

"I should die of fright were I to be crawling through the Great Pyramid with rats," Rosemary said.

"Mr. Maxwell?" Daphne asked again.

"Yes?"

"Are there snakes?"

He hesitated a moment before answering, his tenuous gaze on the young lady beside him. "The desert is filled with snakes. It is possible that sometimes they could be inside the pyramids."

"I wish you hadn't brought that up, Daf!" Rosemary chided. "Now I shan't be able to crawl inside of the pyramid. I am mortified by the idea of snakes."

"It's not my fault snakes are crawling around

the pyramids," Daphne protested.

Mr. Maxwell cleared his throat. "I didn't actually say they were crawling around the pyramids, Lady Daphne."

"But you said it was possible," Daphne defended.

"Not everyone wishes to go inside the pyramids," Mr. Arbuthnot said. "And there are also many people who go happily barreling into the pyramid only to emerge moments later, feeling as if they're suffocating."

Mr. Arbuthnot was a gleeful font of negativity.

"The heat and stuffiness can be almost unbearable," Mr. Maxwell admitted.

Mr. Arbuthnot nodded. "And some people realize they are not able to tolerate small spaces. A sort of apoplexy seizes them under such conditions."

They had all been so busy conversing they hadn't realized they were coming upon the Sphinx. Daphne was the first to gaze upon it. "Allah be praised! Look at the Sphinx!"

There before them, several hundred feet away, the famed Sphinx's lion's body rose from the shimmering sands that were much the same bland, almost colourless shade. From this distance it did not appear to be any taller than her dromedary. But within a few moments, they came close to it.

The granite head of a man atop the giant Sphinx soared far above her camel. From bottom to top, the Sphinx was as tall as her parents' London house. Four stories. They drew up their horses and camels and began to climb down. Daphne was obliged to wait until a servant brought her steps upon which to climb down.

"Please," Rosemary said, "Can we not pitch our tents here? I'm dying to get at my sketch books so I can draw the Sphinx."

Daphne looked at Jack.

"Very well. Maxwell, will you direct the servants to begin unpacking the camels?"

While the Egyptian crew of eight began unpacking and assembling tents, Jack strolled to the Sphinx. "When would you say this was built, Maxwell?"

"Over four thousand years ago."

Jack whistled, his gaze swinging to the Great Pyramid, which was no very great distance away. "Was the pyramid constructed at the same time?"

"Yes, the Great Pyramid was built for the pharaoh Khufu, and it's said the man's head on the lion—what we know as a Sphinx—is the head of Khufu."

Jack's gaze shifted to the Great Pyramid. "What an incredible engineering marvel."

"It's even more impressive," Mr. Maxwell said, "when one considers that it was constructed before the invention of the wheel."

"Do you mean those giant blocks of rock were conveyed solely by men's strength?" asked an incredulous Daphne.

"Remarkable, is it not?" Maxwell began to mount the Sphinx. "By the time Lady Rosemary finds her sketchbook, I hope to be atop the Sphinx."

"My sister will have to draw your picture." It took much self-control to keep Daphne from scurrying up the Sphinx after him. It looked like such a fun thing to do. But she remembered her husband's admonishment not to display her drawers to these men.

Jack quickly followed Mr. Maxwell.

Daphne turned to Mr. Arbuthnot. "Are you not going to climb the Sphinx, sir?"

"Since I have many times previously, today I shall be mindful of preserving my riding costume. It's more difficult to replace English clothing when one lives in the Orient."

Daphne was well aware of how much stock the attaché put on the quality of his clothing. Such a pity that he was on the corpulent side and almost bald. It mattered not what the man wore. Still, she realized his deep-seated appreciation for fine things.

For the next several moments, she watched the soldiers re-assembling their tents and the Egyptians pitching three low-slung tents on the order of those used by the Bedouins. One of those would do for Rosemary, another for the two bachelors, and the third for Daphne and Jack. She'd been told the Egyptian servants were not going to sleep in tents, that they dug themselves into the sand to sleep.

The very thought of snakes made that option horrifying. But, then, those Oriental-style tents would not keep out snakes as the English soldiers' tents would. She would have to beg that the soldiers swap with her and Jack. While she was by nature more of a tomboy, when it came to creepy, crawly things, Daphne was sheer female. Of the vapors variety.

Rosemary, too, had watched the workers, and as soon as she saw her small valise, she snatched it and secured her sketch book. She plopped right down in the billowing sands and began to draw the Sphinx with her brother-in-law and Mr. Maxwell appearing as miniscule appendages to the massive stone figure.

"Do have a care, my darling," Daphne called up as Jack neared the top. "I shouldn't like for you to fall."

"How did I ever climb the Pyrenees without you to keep me safe, my love?" Jack gave her a mocking look.

"I assure you, sir," she responded, "I shan't have a moment's peace until you are restored to me on level footing." Daphne came to sit beside Rosemary, even though the sand felt like hot tin. She looked over her sister's shoulder at her sketch just as Rosemary finished getting the entire Sphinx.

The men had reached the top, then started down.

"No," Rosemary said, lifting a halting hand. "Please stay until I've captured you."

"I should treasure my own copy of this, Lady Rosemary," Mr. Maxwell said, sitting atop the Sphinx's head and grinning at the artist, the sun reflecting off his spectacles.

"You shall have it, sir."

After they climbed down, Daphne asked. "Do we rest in our tents for the hottest part of the day and go in the pyramids later?"

"I don't believe there's that much change in the interior temperatures of the pyramids between noon and dusk," Mr. Maxwell said. "It's entirely up to you."

She looked at Jack. "What do you think?"

"Everyone's dying to go. Let's go."

All Daphne could think of was the serpents.

Their group made a curious discovery while walking to the pyramids. Opposite of the Great Pyramid from where they had pitched their tents was a much larger camp. And these tents were of the same style used by British soldiers.

"Let us go introduce ourselves," Mr. Arbuthnot said.

As they came closer, he exclaimed. "Lord Beddington's returned from Thebes! He's the only European who travels rather like a king."

That might have been an understatement. Daphne counted no less than four-and-twenty tents. "I know most of his lordship's family prefers living in England. Does he travel with a large group of friends?"

The attaché shook his head. "Those tents are all for his servants. And assistants. He has two secretaries, a French Orientologist, a French chef, and a Turkish Man Friday. I'm so pleased I shall be able to introduce you to him."

They walked into the camp and Arbuthnot approached the first European he saw, querying Lord Beddington's whereabouts.

"Allow me to announce you," his aide said. "He's just come from one of the mestabas and is changing into clean robes. He'll be delighted to see fellow countrymen."

Daphne pictured the dirt-coloured, flat-topped rectangular structures. The first mestabas she'd seen were near the Sphinx, but she'd been so fascinated over the Sphinx she'd paid little heed to the rows and rows of these windowless structures. There were so many, it had been impossible to count them.

"You might wish to tell him that Ladies Daphne and Rosemary Chalmers, daughters of the Earl of Sidworth, are among our group," Mr. Arbuthnot said. "I believe he's old friends with their father." Mr. Arbuthnot could not have looked more self-satisfied had the Earl of Sidworth been his father.

The aide returned a moment later. "His lordship wishes you to come to his tent."

Five of them? His tent must be considerably larger than theirs. She soon saw that it was. It immediately brought to mind things she had read about Napoleon's massive tent in which he carried an assortment of portable furniture. Only Lord Beddington's two-chamber tent—one was for sleeping, the other for entertaining—was more influenced by the Orient than the French. Silken pillows were scattered on the floor, and on one of these, the Englishman sat.

The bearded man rose to greet the ladies. He dressed neither in the Turkish style nor in the Egyptian style, but wore the robes of desert sheikhs, his headdress held in place by a circlet of rope. He looked first at Daphne. "You must be Lady Daphne. I have always remembered your beautiful bountiful curls—that and your father's complete captivation over one very small, very charming girl. Since I only had sons, I was mystified."

"Your memory is astonishing, considering that it's been almost twenty years since you were in England," she said.

When he eyed Rosemary, Daphne facilitated the introduction. "Your lordship, this is my youngest sister, Lady Rosemary."

He gallantly kissed her hand. "Another Chalmers beauty. I do believe you favor your lovely mother."

Daphne completed the introductions, then he asked them to sit on the silken pillows.

"I am surprised to find you here, my lord," Mr. Arbuthnot said. "I thought you'd thoroughly explored Gizeh last autumn."

"I thought so too. Until I went to Thebes. Mailet and I wanted to compare stone work of the various periods. We've been here all week and shall return to Cairo tomorrow."

"As will we," Jack said.

"Do you mean you've also brought tents?" Lord Beddington asked.

Jack frowned. "Yes, the ladies fancied a night in the desert."

Lord Beddington effected a disappointed look. "A pity I cannot ask you to dine with us tonight. We're very low on food. That's another reason we return to Cairo tomorrow. That and the fact I long for my cool villa after living the life of a desert nomad."

"I would ask you to dine with us," Mr. Arbuthnot said, "except that our fare will be very plain Egyptian food, and I know as much as your lordship has assimilated into the Oriental culture, you indulge in your French chef."

Lord Beddington smiled.

"We would be honored if you'd come to our camp after dinner for a glass of port," Mr. Arbuthnot said. "The Consul has kindly supplied our little group with some of his own stores that he brought from Madeira."

"I shall." Lord Beddington looked at Jack. "So you have come to see Gizeh? Will you be going into the Great Pyramid?"

"Yes," Jack said. "In fact, we were on our way when we noticed your camp."

"Should your lordship like to join the party?" Mr. Arbuthnot asked.

He shook his head. "I was in there yesterday. Had the devil of a time breathing."

"Have you ever encountered snakes in the pyramids?" Daphne asked.

The former ambassador chuckled. "I have not, but your fear of reptiles reminds me why I prefer to leave my wife in England."

"Would that I could have," Jack mumbled.

"What brings you to Egypt, Captain?"

"We're all very interested in Orientology."

Lord Beddington eyed Mr. Maxwell. "It's fortunate you've got so noted an Orientologist to be your guide. Are you not the Stanton Maxwell who wrote *Travels Through the Levant*?"

"Indeed I am. I heard you mention Mailet. I have read all his works and look forward to meeting him."

"As will I," Rosemary said. "I have also read his works."

"He's still down in a mestaba this afternoon, but I shall bring him to your camp tonight when we join you for port." He sighed. "When I was a younger man, I used to be able to work at archeology all day, but no longer. I have adopted the practice of taking an afternoon nap."

Daphne took that as a dismissal. She stood. "We need to go explore the Great Pyramid, my lord. We're only here for one day and need to see all we can see."

"Tonight, then," he replied.

$\mathcal{C}$hapter 9

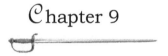

As they had happily ridden across the desert, Jack had temporarily forgotten that a murderer had likely been dogging their every step. He'd felt carefree. Was it the unrestrictive native dress? He hadn't even minded the sun so fiercely bearing down on them as his camel plodded through the deep desert sand.

But now that they were about to file into the depths of a dark pyramid, he was seized with misgivings about having come. Especially with the ladies. His gut told him something wasn't right. In these many years of clandestine activities involving life-threatening situations, his gut had never once misdirected him.

The five Europeans stood beside the massive pyramid, looking up. They had put aside their flowing robes for clothing that would not inhibit their ability to crawl. The men wore their trousers but had left off the hot outer jackets. The ladies' dress was no different than their young Egyptian servants, who wore short, belted dresses the same length as a Scottish kilt. The soldiers, as well as the native servants, had been ordered to look away so as not see the ladies' exposed calves.

"It's the tallest structure in the world," *Arbuth-knows-it-all* said.

"Completely amazing that it was built more than four thousand years ago," Rosemary murmured, her gaze peeled to the upward progression of massive stones.

"Are those limestone?" Daphne asked.

"Yes," Maxwell answered. "The original facing was smooth and highly polished but has been stripped away for other buildings over the centuries."

Just before they were about to enter the pyramid, Jack drew Maxwell aside and spoke in a low voice. "I want you to keep Lady Rosemary close to you at all times."

"I was rather thinking the same thing."

"You've got your pistol?"

Maxwell nodded. "Have you one also?"

"Yes. What about a knife? Do you have one?"

"Always –"

"When you're in the Orient."

Maxwell chuckled.

"Tell me, is it really safe in there?" Jack asked, fingering his own sheathed knife. "The ceilings won't come tumbling down or anything, will they?"

"I've not heard of any fatalities."

Jack eyed Arbuthnot, who was ten feet away. "Are you going to allow those nice clothes to get dirtied in the Great Pyramid?"

The attaché shook his head. "As I've been in many times before, I shall pass this time. In fact this will be a very good time for me to catch up on some of my correspondence in the shade of our tent." He bowed. "I wish you all a fascinating journey." He started for the tent he would share with Maxwell.

That left the two couples.

"Where's the entrance?" Rosemary asked.

"In the ninth century, the Arab Caliph Abdullah al-Mumun and his battering rams excavated the tunnel which is the present ground-level entrance," Maxwell said. "It is believed that in antiquity, the hidden entrance was much higher— up the equivalent of three or four stories of an English house."

He led them around the base of the giant pyramid until they found the irregularly shaped opening. The actual arched opening was inset a few feet inside of the huge surface stones that were settled in a haphazard fashion. Maxwell then gave each person a lighted waxed candle.

"At first we'll be able to walk." He peered at Rosemary. "In this case I think it will not be ladies first. I shall go first and scare away any offending creatures." He stepped into the tunnel, drawing his pistol, and fired off a shot.

The sound was almost deafening.

It was followed by mad flapping of wings and a flurried mass of black streaking by. Bats. Nasty, vile creatures.

Soon the four of them were inside and were climbing upward. It wasn't a wide enough passage to walk two abreast.

"Mr. Maxwell?" Daphne asked.

"Yes?"

"Has anyone ever become lost in here?"

"Not to my knowledge."

Jack fancied himself a brave man. He'd faced cannon fire. Musket balls. Killers with knives. Hissing vipers. And the duc d'Arblier. But this damned dark tunnel beneath a four-thousand-year-old structure had him sweating profusely. And not just from the abominable heat. His pulse was behaving in a strange fashion, too. He'd be damned glad when they got out of this dark, suffocating shaft. And even happier when they got out of the bloody pyramid.

He had the damnedest feeling that he could barely breathe. And he'd never been so hot. He shut his eyes against the rivulets streaming down his face.

"Now we've come to a wall where the narrow surface resembles a ladder. We will need to climb it," Maxwell said.

No easy task when one was holding a candle.

"Are you all right?" Jack asked Daphne, his voice tender.

"I don't think I can honestly answer that. This isn't what I'd imagined it would be like. I thought we'd just waltz in down a broad, lantern-lighted corridor and come to the pharaoh's burial chamber, see it, and come walking back out."

Maxwell chuckled. "You ladies don't have to continue if it's too frightening for you."

"I stay," Rosemary said, firmly. "As long as you vow to slay any serpents, Mr. Maxwell."

"I give you my word."

"You're not afraid of them?" Rosemary asked.

"I don't suppose I am."

"You're awfully brave," she said.

Jack had to tip his hat to the man. Maxwell might be small of stature, and his vision so defective that—like Daf—he had to wear spectacles, but Maxwell was an extraordinarily brave man. During their sea voyage, Jack had read his *Travels* and marveled that a young man only just having left university would travel to the Orient completely alone and attempt the grueling trek across hundreds of miles of desolate desert without a single person from his own homeland.

What courage!

The higher they climbed, the hotter Jack became. How could the women possibly keep up with them under these stifling conditions? "Still all right, love?" he asked.

"Allow me to say I'm still here," she said with a little laugh. "I'm still trying to determine if I'm all right."

"What about you, Lady Rosemary?" Maxwell asked.

She sighed. "I'm doing tolerably. Will it be much longer?"

"Not long."

"Are you sure there's air up there for us to breath?" Jack asked. The higher their elevation, the more he felt the need to gasp for air. Air that didn't seem to be there.

"As I said, Captain, I've not heard of any fatalities."

"I do hope we're almost there," Daphne said, "for right now on the pleasure scale, I'd have to rank this right up there with my honeymoon."

Silence.

"Just so that you all will know," Daphne clarified, "my honeymoon was not what one would think."

"Allow me to elaborate," Jack explained. "My wife spent our wedding trip on a man-o-war violently retching out the contents of her stomach. For several days."

"If you're feeling like that," Rosemary said without the least shred of concern, "then I am most happy that you're at the bottom of this ladder contraption."

"I didn't actually say I was feeling like spewing. I said this ranks with spewing on a pleasure scale."

"We've reached the end of this phase," Maxwell said, not a morsel of relief in his voice. "Now is when we have to crawl on our bellies through a very narrow shaft."

Jack frowned. "And I suppose it, too, is dark."

"My dear brother," Rosemary said, "everything inside a pyramid is dark."

"Now you're sounding like Ralph *Arbuth-knows-it-all*," Jack quipped.

The others chuckled.

"Speaking of Mr. Arbuthnot," Maxwell said, "I don't mean to be uncharitable, but I'm a bit skeptical about his success in making it through this narrow shaft."

"Because of his size, you mean?" Jack asked just as he slithered his considerable bulk along the narrow passage. While Jack was not portly like Arbuthnot, he was a large man whose above-average height was balanced with above-average bands of muscle.

And he could barely maneuver through the dirty tunnel. It was bloody difficult to raise oneself upon one's elbows in order to propel oneself forward when there wasn't enough room to raise upward a few inches. He found himself shimmying from side to side in order to advance forward. At least the ladies were thin enough to more easily maneuver.

"I declare, I would truly die if there were a snake in here," Rosemary said.

"I'll protect you, my lady," Maxwell vowed.

"This may surpass my wedding trip in unpleasantness," Daphne said, her voice thinning from the lack of air in the crowded tunnel.

"We'll soon be able to stand," Maxwell said. "We're coming to the upper saloon. I think we'll breathe better there too."

The upper saloon was much more tolerable,

Jack decided as he drew up to his considerable height, then turned back to help Daphne get up.

In this upper saloon, a giant could have stood.

"Next up," Maxwell said, "the pharaoh's chamber."

Maxwell stopped. "I'm perplexed. Usually there's a lantern burning in the pharaoh's chamber, but I don't see anything. It should be around here."

A moment later, Maxwell said, "Here's the door."

"Praise be to Allah," Daphne said.

They heard the sound of Maxwell stepping into the room. He could then be heard addressing Rosemary. "Here, take my hand."

What they heard next was horrifying.

A crash of stones falling to a floor. Rosemary screaming.

Jack's pulse splattered and pumped as he scurried toward the chamber, toward Rosemary. "Stay here, Daphne."

$\mathcal{C}$hapter 10

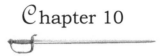

Jack somehow flung himself into the debris in the funerary chamber. Powdery particles from fallen stones clouded his vision and momentarily choked him. "Rosemary, are you all right?" he called frantically.

In the split second before she responded, he saw that she was in an opposite corner, standing, Maxwell in front of her, his knife unsheathed.

"I . . . I think so," she managed in a shaky voice. She had also managed to hold on to her candle.

"What in the devil happened?" From behind him, he heard the soft fall of his wife's feet and whirled to face her. "Did I not tell you to stay back there?"

He could now see Daphne plainly. What a sight she was! Her white belted costume was covered with so much dirt that its original hue was unrecognizable. Everything—from her spectacles to her knees—was covered with dirt. Her hand holding the candle was shaking violently. She squinted madly at him. "I've told you before, if you're going to die, I'm going with you."

He yanked her away from the site of the accident. "Have a care. Right where you were standing is where that heap of stones came tumbling down." He turned back to Maxwell. "I thought you said this place was safe."

"I've never heard of the stones becoming

dislodged. And it's not as if either Lady Rosemary or I could be so heavy that our weight coming down would cause the stones to fall."

"Go over there with your sister," Jack commanded his wife. Then he took his own candle to examine the entry corner where Rosemary or Maxwell could well have been killed. He held his candle high into the inky depths of the ceiling's corner.

His blood curdled at what he saw. "Someone has set a trap here."

Maxwell rushed forward to survey the upper corner. "By God, someone constructed a bloody lever to send the stones crashing when one of us entered this chamber!"

Jack's attention had transferred to the floor. Something there must have triggered the lever which released the volley of stones. Then he saw it. A length of string which reached from the floor all the way up to the lever near the ceiling. The pressure of one's foot would send the stones crashing down upon them.

He stood there in silent contemplation for some moments. Who had known they were coming here today? Briggs and Arbuthnot, naturally, had knowledge of it, and since there was no reason for secrecy, either of them could have told others. There were the eight new Egyptian servants. Everyone associated with their hotel knew.

Someone who knew their plans had come here—or sent a hired cutthroat—earlier to either kill them or scare them away from this inquiry. It wasn't even as if they'd learned anything of value. Yet someone was nervous. Were they getting close? Damned if Jack could figure out how.

"Did any of you see anyone who was not with

our party?" he asked.

The three others answered in the negative.

Jack came to stand in the center of the chamber and drew a breath. "I'm going to ask that all of you keep this to yourselves. If the culprit is watching us for a reaction, he won't get it. Let him think his plan failed. If he doesn't think we'll be suspicious, he might let down his guard."

"I applaud such a plan, dearest. When we do return to the others, each of us needs to be particularly vigilant, meticulously observant. Watch all the servants. Trust no one."

"That's a risk one takes when hiring workers as we did yesterday. We don't really know anything about them," Maxwell said. "I have to think at least one of them could be in league with the person responsible for Prince Singh's disappearance."

"You're likely right," Jack said. "If any of you want to return to Cairo—or even England—now, I will completely understand."

"I'm staying," Rosemary said firmly.

"And I've vowed to protect Lady Rosemary," Maxwell answered.

"Then it looks as if I will get to sleep in the tent with a tall, dark, Arabian-looking man," Daphne said.

Jack hated to alarm them further, but he didn't like the idea of Rosemary sleeping in a tent alone. He would make sure the soldier on watch tonight paid particular attention to the young noblewoman's tent.

Rosemary stepped out from behind Maxwell's protection. The trembling in her voice had subsided. "So that single granite box is the only object left in Khufu's tomb? It's not even decorated!"

Nothing could have been plainer. In this dim light, the rectangular gray sarcophagus looked as if it had been fashioned from mortar.

"True, my lady," Maxwell said. "All the contents were likely stolen in antiquity—thousands of years ago. When the Caliph arrived here in 870 AD, this is how he found it. Even the missing chunk of stone was reported then—nearly a millennium ago."

"Would someone have switched out a more ornate sarcophagus for this plain thing?" Rosemary asked.

"I don't believe so," Maxwell replied. "I have a theory. Since Khufu's body and his entire funeral procession of several boats had to be carried a great distance down the Nile for the burial, it's possible the original highly ornamented sarcophagus might have sunk, and they were compelled to fashion a new one in a hurry for the entombment."

"What brings you to such a conclusion?" Rosemary asked.

"The fact that I've never seen a plain sarcophagus before. The condition of the stone—though I'm no expert—tells me it dates to the same time as the construction of the pyramid. Also, there's the fact that since the Great Pyramid and its surrounding satellite pyramids are grander than anything that came before or since, I have to believe the furnishings that were fashioned to go inside would also have warranted opulence."

"I think your theory's brilliant, Mr. Maxwell," Rosemary said. "Such a pity the mummy was stolen long ago. I wonder whatever became of it?"

"From the beginning of recorded history, man

has been fascinated with death. Mummies were highly prized throughout the ancient world and could—and still do—fetch a great deal of money."

"As intriguing as mummies are," Daphne said, "I'm happy the Regent had not commissioned Prince Singh to bring him back a mummy for Carlton House. I don't know how anyone could sleep in the same house as a mummy."

"I can understand why the Regent might not wish to sleep in a house with a mummy," Jack said.

"I most certainly understand," Maxwell said with a chuckle. "When I was a wee lad my father brought home a mummy to study, and I had the devil of a time going to sleep. I was so terrified, my mother insisted he remove the thing from our house."

It seemed odd to Jack to imagine this capable resident scholar as a frightened lad.

"Mummies are fascinating—in a macabre sort of way," Rosemary said. "I shouldn't wish to have one in my house. Nor would I wish to spend a night in this chamber—as vastly curious as I am to see them."

"I don't know about the rest of you, but I'm ready to get out of this place," Jack said.

To his surprise, none of the others were inclined to dwell in this oppressive place any longer. He'd hoped getting out would be quicker than getting in, but that was not the case. At least this time, they all knew what to expect.

Once they were back beneath the harsh sun, the four of them contrived to act as if they were on a jolly outing.

"The first thing one does after emerging from a pyramid," Mr. Maxwell said, "is to take a long drink of strong liquor. It's said to keep away the pleurisy which can form in the lungs after the lungs have been so starved for air." He withdrew a flask from his trousers and began to pass it around. Each of them took a swig.

"I suppose you gentlemen will be wanting to climb to the top of the pyramids?" Rosemary eyed each of the men.

"Nothing could stop me," Jack said, "but I beg a moment in my tent to tidy myself a bit before I don my own breeches."

Rosemary could hardly contain her glee. "After I clean up, I'll go fetch my sketchbook and come to draw you men acting like monkeys."

"I do hope you'll get some good likenesses of the pyramids," Daphne said.

"Oh, I will."

"Rosemary!" Daphne exclaimed.

"What?"

"Can I implore you to draw a picture of me on top of my dromedary?"

"What a good idea! Papa would love to have that."

"I don't want it for our dear father. I want it for me."

* * *

That night they enjoyed their first completely Egyptian meal in front of a fire. Two of the servants had spent two hours preparing the dinner. The fresh bread and fruits of every possible colour were eagerly eaten, but the main course—boiled onions, not so much. Daphne noticed that Mr. Arbuthnot snatched up a plump onion and began to bite into it whole. She endeavored to do the same, but did not like it. She took more bread.

Then she noticed Mr. Arbuthnot was soaking his bread in juices from the onion. She endeavored to do the same, but liked it no better than she liked the plain onion.

"Is it not remarkable," she said, "that we are not being devoured by mosquitoes?"

"Why is that, Mr. Arbuthnot?" Rosemary asked.

"It's the Nile that breeds the mosquitoes. You will find some in the desert but not like in Cairo."

"One would think the light from the fire would attract them," Jack said.

"It would most certainly—if they were here," Mr. Arbuthnot said.

"It's fortuitous that none of us carried the pests with us," Mr. Maxwell said.

"The Consul asked that I bring port for us as well as the soldiers. Good English soldiers, all."

Jack got up. "I'll help you with that."

While Jack and Mr. Arbuthnot fetched several bottles of port from the latter's saddlebags, Lord Beddington and his French archaeologist Charles Mailet strolled into their camp, and there were greetings all around.

"If you don't mind," Arbuthnot said to Jack, "I'll have you serve our little party whilst I serve the soldiers."

Except for a lone soldier who was always on watch, musket in hand and saber at his side, the soldiers sat around another campfire some thirty feet away from the British subjects they were sworn to protect. They happily welcomed the two bottles of port that Mr. Arbuthnot delivered.

After Arbuthnot returned to their campfire and took his seat, Lord Beddington, in French, introduced his scholar to everyone, and Mr. Mailet's eyes widened when he learned that he was to meet Stanton Maxwell. "You are so much younger than I'd have thought."

"You may have me mixed up with my father."

Mr. Mailet shook his head emphatically. "No, I am most familiar with his works, also, but the son has handily exceeded the father's accomplishments."

Mr. Maxwell peered into his lap. "You're very kind. But I should like to ask you about your work at Pompeii."

Rosemary got up and walked to where Mr. Mailet sat, and she plopped herself between the two scholars. "I shall absorb everything you two brilliant men say."

The three of them chatted away to the exclusion of the others.

Jack sat beside Daphne, his own port in hand, and addressed Mr. Arbuthnot, bringing up a subject that had been very much on Daphne's mind. It was really too uncanny how they tapped into each other's thoughts with such acuity. "I've been thinking about the women's aversion to snakes—as well as to all things that crawl in the sand—and I've determined that I shall ask the soldiers to swap tents with us for this one night. The women will feel more secure in a good old English tent."

As much as Daphne disliked the idea of slithering things on the floor of her tent, she disliked even more the notion of her poor sister all alone in a tent with no Jack to protect her.

"Splendid idea," Arbuthnot said.

"Thank you, Captain," Rosemary said. "I was not looking forward to sleeping in that Bedouin-style tent."

"If you're truly frightened," Daphne offered,

"You are welcome to come into our tent." Even though Daphne had dreamed of spending a romantic night in a tent with her husband, she would happily forgo the romantic night to alleviate her sister's fears.

"No, I'll be more comfortable by myself."

"Then I will re-pitch my tent next to yours, Lady Rosemary," Mr. Maxwell pledged.

Mr. Maxwell's devotion to Rosemary was so noble. A pity he wasn't a nobleman.

"And we'll be on the other side," Jack pointed out.

"I shall feel perfectly safe." She bestowed a sweet smile on her bespectacled admirer.

Lord Beddington addressed Daphne. "Did you father ever sire a son?"

"No, my lord. The poor man is father to six daughters, but he treats my husband rather like a son."

"And another of his sons-in-law," Mr. Arbuthnot pointed out with delight, "is the Duke of Lankersham. You will remember he's a cousin of the Regent."

"Is your father close to the duke?"

Even his wife wasn't close to the cold duke, Daphne thought. "They get along very well."

"Speaking of the Regent," Jack said, "he said something to my wife about looking up his old friend Prince Singh. Do you know him?"

Lord Beddington did not answer for a moment. "He's a delightful man. Perfect command of English—and he's possessed of a remarkable eye for quality antiquities. I've purchased many things from him."

He did not speak of Prince Singh in the past tense. Did that mean he thought he was still alive?

"Did he ever offer you the Amun-re mask?" Daphne asked.

"He did. At the same time I had the opportunity to buy a heavily gilded sarcophagus in almost perfect condition. Both were extremely expensive. I chose the sarcophagus. And I've not regretted it. It's the jewel of my interiors collection."

"His lordship's exterior collection is an amazing assortment of statuary from antiquity for his English gardens," Mr. Arbuthnot pointed out.

"One of these days I'll get home to see it. I've had an Etruscan garden, a Turkish garden, and an Egyptian garden fashioned around the statuary I've obtained in my travels throughout the Orient."

She needed to steer the conversation back to Prince Singh. "Did Prince Singh help you with any of those purchases?"

He nodded. "With one for my Egyptian garden."

"Do you know we've not been able to locate Prince Singh. His servants say he disappeared last fall."

His brows lowered. "He's still not returned?"

Daphne sadly shook her head.

"Then you knew he was missing before you went to Thebes?"

"I had forgotten all about it until you mentioned it a moment ago, but yes, I had heard that he was missing. Surely someone knows where he's gone."

Daphne shook her head. "I was hoping you might have seen him in Thebes."

"My secretaries and I were the only foreigners in Thebes."

The port was a mellow, fitting ending to so exotic a day. Daphne snuggled closer to her husband and allowed her lashes to slowly drop. Her thoughts kept going back to the fallen rocks that could have killed her sister.

Though she found Lord Beddington perfectly amiable, she had to consider him a suspect. Could he have had spies in Cairo who knew they'd be coming here today? Could one of his servants be responsible for rigging the potential death trap in the Great Pyramid?

How she longed to discuss the trap with the others, but they'd made a pact to tell no one else. Not even kindly (though arrogant) Mr. *Arbuth-knows-it-all.*

A howling sound caused all of them to jump.

"That was a jackal," the attaché informed them.

"Are they dangerous?" Daphne asked.

"They could become aggressive when confronted by a single individual, but they normally stay away from humans."

"I hate that we have to return to Cairo tomorrow," Rosemary said. "There's so much more to explore here in Gizeh. I should love to have the opportunity to examine some of the mestabas."

"What are those mestabas used for?" Daphne asked.

"They, too, are burial chambers for lesser personages of high rank. How many do you think there are?" Rosemary asked Mr. Maxwell.

He shrugged. "Several hundred."

"Surely we can look in one before we must leave in the morning," Rosemary said.

"I don't see why we can't manage that," Mr. Maxwell said.

"I'd always assumed they'd be small," Rosemary said.

"Because they look so small when compared with the nearby pyramids," Mr. Maxwell said.

Rosemary nodded. "I was surprised that they rise to at least thirty feet."

"It does seem rather tall, given that the burial chambers are subterranean," the scholar said. "Entering them is not as easy as one might think. Like the pyramids, these were constructed with hidden doors, and even when one finds the doors, they don't lead to the burial chamber."

"That sounds odd," Daphne said.

"It's because the actual doors were so that priests and family members could bring offerings for the dead person's soul," Mr. Mailet said. "The room they came to led to nowhere."

"So, let me get this right," Daphne said, perplexed. "There will actually be two entrances: one for the offerings and another for the burial chamber?"

"Not really, my lady," Mr. Maxwell answered. "The burial chamber was initially accessed from the center of the mestaba, then sealed off."

Daphne turned up her nose. "It all sounds frightfully terrifying."

"I suppose it would be if one were buried alive," Mr. Maxwell said with a little chuckle.

"Now I will not be satisfied until I can see one for myself," Daphne said.

"Then we shall have to oblige the lady in the morning," Mr. Arbuthnot said.

Lord Beddington finished his port, rose and said his farewells. "If I don't see you in the morning, I will make it a point to have you come to the villa for an English meal. Soon."

"That would be very agreeable," Jack said, rising and shaking the man's hand.

After he and his companion were gone, Mr. Arbuthnot said, "Now, Captain, you must tell me how your inquiries go."

"I have nothing to tell."

"Surely you don't think the murder of that courtesan could be related to your quest," Mr. Arbuthnot said.

"I strongly suspect that it is," Jack said.

She was proud of her husband's terse responses. He never liked discussing his inquiries with anyone other than his life's partner. And now Rosemary and Maxwell.

"Oh, dear," the attaché said. "A pity you've brought the ladies with you—if, indeed, you're dealing with the kind of person who would murder a lady—not that that woman could precisely be labeled a lady."

"Her life was of value," Daphne snapped. "No one deserves to die in such a manner—except perhaps the duc d'Arblier, who's tried many times to murder my husband, as well as our Regent."

Mr. Arbuthnot's brows raised. "A Frenchman?"

Jack shrugged. "It does not signify." He set down his empty glass and stood. "It's time we see about switching tents."

The soldiers readily agreed to Jack's request. Then he asked who was to be on night watch.

"I am, sir."

Jack ran his eye along the young man's long, sturdy limbs. Thankfully, this soldier was the strongest looking. That, at least, inspired confidence. "I should like you to pay particular attention to this tent." Jack pointed to the tent where Rosemary would sleep. "Lady Rosemary will be alone. You're to protect her."

"You can depend upon it, sir."

* * *

When Jack awakened the following morning, dawn had not yet broken. Their tent was still in darkness, but it was a darkness diffused by the slowly rising sun. As had been his custom for so many years of clandestine activities, he was on instant alert. He whirled to Daphne, to assure himself first that nothing had happened to her. He could barely see her beloved features in the darkness but was reassured by her steady breathing.

He softened as he recalled their tender lovemaking of the night before. He had not previously understood his wife's compulsion to make love in a tent in the Egyptian desert. Until they did.

It was a night he'd never forget. Even through their pallet, they felt the cool billowing sand beneath them. It was such a comforting feeling to be lying within the shelter of their well-constructed British tent as the winds whipped along the desert planes, sprinkling their tent with sand. It would have taken no effort to imagine he and Daphne were the only two beings in this land so far away from all they had known. The only sound to be heard was a distant jackal.

Now, even though dawn had not broken, he heard servants awakening and beginning to build a fire for the morning meal. The noise awakened his wife.

She pulled up her linen to cover her bosom and smiled at him. "Good morning, my love."

He leaned to her for a petal-soft kiss. "We ought to get started before the intense heat."

He helped her dress—once again in native dress of flowing robes, and she assisted him with his boots. He had chosen to wear his own clothing. He had not enjoyed the wearing of robes.

"Your sister may need your help," he said.

"But it's still dark. She's likely still asleep."

"Because of the heat, it will behoove us to rise early. Especially if she wants to see the mestabas."

She left the tent, and a moment later he heard his wife's horrified wail.

$\mathcal{C}$hapter 11

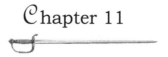

Jack bolted from their tent. "What's happened?"

"Rosemary's gone!" Daphne stood just inside her sister's tent, her hand still lifting the entry flap. "Someone's taken her!"

Shirtless and barefoot, Maxwell came rushing from his tent on the other side. "This cannot be! I never heard a word . . . I swore I would protect her," he said, his voice forlorn.

The rear of Rosemary's tent had been slashed through. Jack whirled around to chastise the soldier he'd asked to guard Rosemary.

The fellow was sitting in the sand directly in front of Rosemary's tent, his head bent, chin on chest, eyes closed, hugging his musket to him as if it were a cherished woman. He was sound asleep.

Jack mumbled an oath as he began to shake the soldier. He did not readily awaken. Then Jack smelled it. Laudanum. "The guard's been drugged with laudanum!"

"We need to determine if anyone else is missing," Maxwell said, his voice commanding.

Jack's eyes narrowed. "It wouldn't surprise me to discover that one of our recently hired servants is responsible for Rosemary's abduction." His gaze returned to Rosemary's tent. "Daf, can you see if anything of your sister's is missing?"

She nodded solemnly.

By now Arbuthnot had made his way to join the others. He was fully dressed except for his coat. "Are you saying Lady Rosemary is missing? Are you sure she's not just gone exploring? Didn't she express a strong interest last night in seeing the mestabas?"

Jack faced Arbuthnot and spoke in a growl. "Some vile person slashed through the back of her tent and apparently carried her off."

Arbuthnot's eyes narrowed, and he uttered a curse.

Maxwell looked forlorn. "And I promised her I would protect her."

Jack placed a hand on his shoulder. "Don't blame yourself. I was just as close to her tent as you were, and I slept right through her abduction."

"Dear God, I hope she's not intended for white slavery," Arbuthnot said.

Daphne poked her head out of the tent and harrumphed. "They'd be sure to bring her back. My sister is not only incompetent about cleaning floors and polishing furniture, but she's never in her life lifted a hand in pursuit of tidiness."

Jack coughed, and despite the gravity of the situation, his eyes twinkled with mirth. "It appears my wife is under a misapprehension about the nature of white slavery."

"Whatever can you mean?" Daphne asked, looking up at him quizzically.

Jack cleared his throat. "You know what a harem is?"

"Of course." Her face screwed up in thought. "Do you mean . . . some sultan might want to . . . oh, dear. It's imperative that we find her. Fast."

"I should think the best place to start is by

following their footsteps." Maxwell moved around to the back of Rosemary's tent. And let out an unintelligible oath. "There are no footsteps!" He peered up at Jack. "Desert thieves have been known to cover their path by sweeping away footprints with palm fronds"

"Arbuthnot!" Jack faced the attaché. "Go see if any horses or camels are missing."

"And I'll do a head count of the servants," Maxwell said.

Daphne moved from the tent and fell into in her husband's arms. "Everything she brought is still here. Every stitch of clothing. I sh—sh--should never have brought her."

"It's too late now for such thoughts," Jack said tenderly as he hugged her to him. All the while he was pondering how highly prized virgins were in white slavery—a line of thought he vowed never to share with Daphne. "And I don't believe she was abducted to be some sultan's bedchamber slave," he whispered. "This abduction has to be connected to our inquiries. Someone either wants to scare us off the trail—or they are questioning her to find out what we have learned about Prince Singh's disappearance."

He didn't like the trajectory of his thoughts. He could not dispel the fear that Williams had Rosemary, could not dispel the memory of the lifeless body of Singh's mistress. He was almost certain that Williams had murdered the woman.

And Jack was terrified the same fate would befall Rosemary.

Maxwell returned first, anger flashing in his eyes. "One of the Egyptians is gone!"

"And so is one horse," Arbuthnot said, panting from his brisk walk. "I took the liberty of notifying

Lord Beddington about the missing girl. He'll be
here in a moment to lend whatever assistance he
can."

Jack nodded. "While my first thought was that
she'd been carried off to a mestaba, the fact that
an Egyptian and his horse are missing indicates
she may have been conveyed back to Cairo."

"Why did none of us hear anything?" Daphne
asked.

"My guess is she too may have been drugged.
Certainly, once he was in her tent, he bound her
mouth," Jack said.

"Why in the devil did we not hear a horse?"
Maxwell asked.

"The horse must have been walked away from
the others at a slow pace," Jack said. "I've done it
many times myself when near the enemy camp."
He moved toward where the horses were tethered.
"Let's see if we can find hoof prints."

They all circled the horses, heads bent as they
scanned the smooth sand, but they found
nothing. "How can it be that the odious, vile,
contemptuous man could take time to erase his
tracks whilst carrying my unconscious sister?"
Daphne asked.

"A second accomplice could have joined him
here." Jack would not tell Daphne he feared the
second man was Gareth Williams. He wouldn't be
surprised if Williams wasn't the one who'd set the
trap for them in the pharaoh's burial chamber.

Dressed as an Egyptian, Lord Beddington
stormed up, a concerned expression on his face.
He went straight to Daphne and took her hands.
"I'm so sorry to hear that your sister is missing,
but I vow that I'll do everything in my power to see
that she's restored to you." He turned to Jack. "In

what way can I help?"

"I would be deeply in your debt, my lord, if you could direct the search of the mestabas here in Gizeh. We're leaving Arbuthnot and four soldiers. The rest of us are going to look for her in Cairo. One of our horses is missing."

"I will see that every mestaba in Gizeh is searched for my old friend's daughter."

"Captain Dryden thinks it's possible there was a second man—possibly having come from Cairo—who wiped away the tracks," Maxwell asked.

"It's merely a plausible explanation." Jack's gaze fanned the others. "None of us rests until the lady is found."

He faced Maxwell. "Before we leave, you must question the Egyptians to learn everything you can about the missing man."

By now all the soldiers had dressed fully and joined them. Jack explained about Rosemary's abduction and about their drugged colleague. One soldier dropped to his knees and attempted to rouse the useless guard.

Jack counted off five soldiers. "You're coming with me. You, too, Maxwell. And Daphne. Since it's the fastest means of traveling, we're taking horses back to Cairo." He turned to Arbuthnot. "You'll stay here and assist Lord Beddington in the search of the mestabas."

Arbuthnot's face fell, his shoulders sagged, and he slowly nodded. Clearly, he objected to his assignment. He was probably adverse to getting his fine clothing dirty.

"I'm counting on you not to return to Cairo," Jack told Arbuthnot, "until you can assure me that you and these men under your command have searched in every single mestaba for my wife's sister."

"You can't understand! There are hundreds of mestabas! It could take many days," Arbuthnot protested.

"I am aware that there are hundreds of the damn things. Look at the cheery side. You could find her in the first hour. Lord Beddington's charging his servants with examining the mestabas for Rosemary. If you do find Lady Rosemary, first, rescue her, and second, you are to hasten back to Cairo and notify us. I shall tell the Consul how valuable you've been to us." Jack spun away from the unlikeable man.

As the rest of them gathered up their things, Maxwell questioned the seven remaining Egyptians about the man who'd left their camp. They all expressed surprise that he'd gone. They said he'd lain near them the previous night in his scooped-out bed of sand and appeared to go to sleep.

Only one of them knew him previously, not well, but he did know where the man lived and conveyed that information to Maxwell, and Maxwell conveyed it to Jack.

Daphne clutched her sister's sketch book.

"May I suggest, Love, that you put that in the valise," Jack said in a gentle voice. "We must go now. Will you be up to riding on your own, or should you like to ride with me?" His wife rode as well as any man.

"We can go faster if we don't double up." She went and put the sketch book in their shared valise.

Before they left, Jack expressed his profound thanks to Lord Beddington for his assistance.

The three of them, along with five soldiers, took

off. Jack set the pace. Anyone watching them would believe they were participants in a steeplechase for large stakes. They rode like the wind.

He felt it in his bones that Williams had Rosemary and hoped to God they could find her before she met the same fate as Singh's mistress.

His thoughts went to the watch soldier. Had his port been drugged? Arbuthnot had taken the port to the soldiers. But if only one soldier had been administered the laudanum, it had not come from the bottle. Someone had slipped the powerful drug into the soldier's glass. Who?

Could one of Lord Beddington's servants have been mingling with theirs for evil purposes? None of the Europeans would have been able to discern any difference in the servants from the two camps.

One hour later, they were pulling up in front of their hotel. Since the soldiers had taken all the tents, Jack had told Petworth he could have use of his and Daphne's room the night they were gone. Jack prayed he would find Petworth there, prayed that Petworth would have located Williams' lodgings.

The first to dismount, Jack rushed into the hotel, pounded up the stairs to his and Daphne's chambers, and threw open the door. Given that it was not yet six in the morning, Petworth was still sleeping. Jack stood in the doorway. "Hate to awaken you, old boy, but we're in a spot of trouble."

Petworth leapt up, getting caught in the mosquito netting.

"Pray, put your breeches on," Jack said. "My wife is apt to come barreling in any moment."

Petworth disengaged from the mosquito netting

and, quite naked, strode to the chair where he'd carefully folded the civilian clothing he'd borrowed from Jack and began to dress. "What's happened?" he asked, brows lowered with concern.

"Lady Rosemary's been abducted, and we've got to find her. I'll not have her end up like . . ."

"Like the beautiful Egyptian woman?" Petworth said in mournful voice, eyeing Jack.

Jack nodded. "Please tell me you've located our despised former comrade."

"I believe I have, though he wasn't there last night. I waited until midnight, and he never returned. I was told the Egyptian woman he'd been living with has gone back to her village. Maybe he went after her."

"It's nothing more than a hunch, but I feel in my bones that he's mixed up with Lady Rosemary's abduction." Jack went on to explain about her tent being slashed, about the drugged soldier, and about none of the lady's things being missing.

"This is bloody, bloody awful. No wonder the no-good, thieving, murdering piece of filth never returned last night! I'd wager my year's salary that vile excuse for a man is responsible for the lady's kidnapping. I just pray to God we can find her in time." After Petworth finished dressing, he loaded his musket and—as Jack had done—strapped on his saber. The two men raced down the stairs and met Daphne and Maxwell. Outside, the other five soldiers—all mounted on their horses—waited.

"Here," Jack said to Petworth, "You take my wife's horse, and she'll ride with me." If Jack could better command his wife, he'd have deposited her at the Consulate, but he knew her well enough to know she would never stay safely out of the action. Whenever a confrontation was imminent, Daphne insisted on being present.

They followed Petworth through the gates of old Cairo and down a series of very narrow streets. In each of the lattice-fronted residences, it was apparent that many dozens of people resided there.

The city was just awakening. Brick ovens—which every house seemed to have—puffed out their dark smoke, and the aroma of fresh bread filled the air. Babies cried, and cats meowed, and sometimes the two sounds were indistinguishable.

At one narrow lane that dead-ended, Petworth drew to a stop and dismounted. His voice low, he said, "We'll leave our horses here." He stooped to draw in the dirt street with his finger. He sketched out the location of Williams' house one lane over from where they were.

"Is there a back door as well as a front?" Jack asked.

Petworth nodded, then eyed one of his fellow soldiers. "Littleton, you go to the back door, and don't let anyone pass—even if you have to kill them."

Daphne coughed. "Unless, of course, it's my sister, Lady Rosemary."

"Yes, my lady," Littleton said. "I wouldn't harm the lovely lady."

"You said Williams is on the second floor?" Jack asked.

Petworth nodded. "But all three floors are entered by the ground-floor door at the front of the building. I'll go first. We all need to make sure our muskets are ready."

Maxwell straightened up to his inconsiderable

height that was no more than five-nine. "I go first."

Jack had never heard the meek scholar assert himself so forcefully.

"I feel responsible for her. I pledged to keep her safe, and by God if I have to lay down my own life to get her back, that's what I'm going to do," Maxwell said.

"Now see here, old fellow," Jack said. "She's my sister-in-law, and I'm responsible for her coming. Besides, I've had a lot more experience in these life-and-death situations than you have, old boy."

Maxwell's eyes were steely. "You underestimate me, Captain. Do not be fooled by my spectacles and small stature. I've fought off pirates on the high seas with a cutlass, I've faced marauding nomads in the desert, and I've picked up venomous vipers with my bare hands. I. Will. Enter. First."

In that instant, Jack forgot about Maxwell's size. The man was far tougher than Jack had given him credit for. And though it went against Jack's grain, he knew he had to accede to the scholar's demand. Two things made the relinquishment of his own authority palatable. First, he had confidence that Maxwell was intelligent and quick thinking. Secondly, if Jack was not the first to enter, he would be better able to guard Daphne.

He nodded.

The soldier guarding the rear—whose walk was the farthest--took off.

Jack eyed the remaining soldiers. "I'm afraid if he—or they—see your uniforms, it could ruin our surprise. You four hold back out of view. I'll leave my wife in your care whilst we three . . . " His glance swept to Petworth and Maxwell. "We three will hope to surprise the kidnappers." His and Daphne's eyes met.

She opened her mouth. He knew she wished to protest being left behind. But then she closed her mouth and nodded.

No words needed to pass between them. She instinctively knew he could perform his duty better were he not worried about her. There was also the fact that she had no weapon. He swiped his lips across her mouth and followed Maxwell.

The three men walked like cats on soft paws. As Maxwell rounded a corner to enter Williams' street, he first stuck just his head from behind the corner house and gazed in the direction of Williams' house.

Jack knew he was looking for movement, for any signs that someone might be watching.

"I see no signs of life," Maxwell said, moving forward.

The other two men followed. Jack was unable to remove his gaze from the next-to-last residence on the short lane. He saw no smoking chimney, no shadows moving by the window, no candles burning. He hoped that Williams was catching up on missed sleep.

And what of poor Rosemary? A mixture of grief and nausea surged through his torso. He'd not been so upset since Edwards had been slain. That was long before Jack had ever met Daphne, but the sickening memory of his best friend's cruel death was as fresh as if he'd been slain last week. Jack's fists tightened and he vowed to do everything in his power to keep Rosemary from meeting the same fate as Edwards.

The ground-floor door that served several sets of lodgings was not locked. Maxwell eased it open as silently as was possible, then all three entered and carefully and quietly began to mount the stairs.

On the landing, three doors faced them. Petworth pointed to the one where Williams resided, and Maxwell padded to it, placed his ear upon the door, and listened for a moment. "I hear nothing," he whispered.

His pistol in his right hand, his left gripping the handle, he swung the door open as swiftly as a blink.

All three men charged into the room.

There was no sign of life in the dark chamber. After a moment, they were better able to see in the dark. There was not another entry into another chamber. This one room served as bedchamber, kitchen, and dining room. Since the windows were open, Jack rushed there to make sure Williams hadn't fled through the window. He looked down at the quiet street below and saw nothing except a stooped-over, gray-bearded Egyptian leading a donkey. At the corner, Jack could barely see the beaver hats of the back-up soldiers.

He turned back to scan the chamber for any sign that Rosemary had been there. The room's dominant piece of furniture was an iron bed swathed in mosquito netting. A small table on the opposite wall could seat two, and upon it, a bowl of fruit reposed. The flue to the brick oven crudely protruded into the ceiling. A hook on the wall held two men's costumes—one, Arabic robes; the other, decidedly English clothing that appeared to be several years old.

Jack had no doubts this was Williams' abode.

But where in the hell was Williams?

"I don't think Lady Rosemary's been here,"

Maxwell said, his voice grave. "Let us hope we can find her at the home of the missing Egyptian servant. Thank God one of the others knew where he lived."

$\mathcal{C}$hapter 12

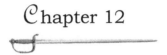

Rosemary had heard nothing. She dreamed someone was smothering her and awakened to the realization that strong hands were binding a thick cloth around her mouth. She tried to scream, but only the faintest sound came out. Her heart raced, her arms flailed. She tried to twist away, but he was much stronger than she.

It was too dark inside her tent to see who was who was trying to kill her, but from his flowing white robes, she thought it was an Egyptian. One of their servants?

God help her. He was going to try to force himself on her. She had never been so terrified, never felt so helpless. If only she could cry out. Jack or Mr. Maxwell or the soldiers would come save her from this horrible man who stank of onions.

She twisted away, but his grip strengthened. She spat at his face; he struck hers. It stung. Tears sprouted. She'd rather die than have this vile man violate her. If only she had stayed in England. She could have been safe in the bosom of her loving family right now. But now her very life was being jeopardized. For the second time in the same day.

It surprised her when he didn't immediately try to take liberties. Instead, he cinched a strong arm around her and began to drag her from the tent—not from the front but from the rear where a knife or sword had silently ripped it apart while she slept. It sickened her to realize the soldier who'd been charged with guarding her was probably sitting in front of her tent, ready to defend her, and it was impossible for her to call out to him. It would also be impossible for him to see them as her captor stole off into the night, their bare feet silent in the soft, cool sand. If only she could do something that would make a noise.

She tried kicking her captor in the hope that he would yelp, but he remained as quiet as a slithering snake. From the dark, a second man emerged. In the moonlight she could see the gleam of the sword strapped around his black robes. Then she saw that he was a European. He rushed toward them, and her heart hammered. But he went past her, and she saw he held a long frond and was sweeping the foot imprints from the sand where they'd just stepped. He was covering their tracks.

No one would be able to come save her.

As hopeless as things looked, she was determined somehow to escape from these beasts.

A few hundred yards away, two horses waited. The European said something to the other man in Arabic, and then the European mounted a black horse. The Egyptian hurled her on top of the same horse as if she were a sack of grain, and the European coiled his arm around her. She kicked madly. She elbowed the man in his ribs. He pulled her into his chest as he uttered a guttural threat in English with a bit of a Celtic accent. "Do as I tell you, and I won't have to kill a second woman this week."

The very breath in her wind pipe trapped. Her heartbeat exploded. Her blood went cold. This was the killer of Prince Singh's mistress. She stiffened.

What could he possibly want with her?

He must also be the one who rigged the falling stones in Khufu's burial chamber.

"You'll sit this horse," he ordered.

She'd been flung across it, belly first. He gave a yank, and she allowed herself to sit upright. Sidesaddle style. It only then occurred to her she was wearing nothing but a thin linen night shift. Under normal circumstances, she would be mortified for a man to see her like this. Under these circumstances, she cared not what these beasts thought of her. As long as they did not try to take liberties.

She was beginning to think her abduction was not for the purpose she had originally feared. Now she believed her interest to these men centered around Jack and Daphne's inquiries about the missing Indian prince.

It was still dark when they arrived in the old city of Cairo. They came to a narrow street where the tall, slender houses were constructed of the local brick. Long ago. Their condition was not the best. The windows all protruded, and all were shuttered in elaborate wooden works of art. Long ago. Many of the shutters were now missing chunks of wood, and many of them needed a fresh coat of paint.

How could she use this situation to escape? She couldn't call out. She did still have the use of her hands and legs. She must try to run away from them. It even crossed her mind that she could mount the horse and flee.

The Egyptian dismounted first and went to open the door to the most slender house on the narrow lane. The three-story house appeared to be just one room in width. After he opened the door, he came back and yanked her from the horse, bruising both her arms.

She lunged away and tried to sprint ahead as the British murderer was leaping from his horse. He started after her and soon was able to snatch a piece of her shift. She stumbled to a stop. Her shift ripped, but he still held it. Even though she resisted mightily, he managed to haul her into his arms and began to stride back to the skinny house—all the while suffering a barrage of kicking and pummeling from Rosemary. If only that beastly cloth weren't binding her mouth. If only she could scream. That would have summoned rescuers.

Her despair infused every cell in her body.

The European lit a candle, and she saw that unlike many houses in Cairo, this was a real house rather than a house that had been turned over to a series of one-room flats, each bulging with large families. They took her to the second floor. From the manner in which it was furnished, she thought this must belong to the Egyptian because nothing gave any indication that a European lived here. There were a few papers lying about, all the lettering in Arabic. She observed some filthy Arabic clothing. There was no sign that a woman lived here.

The British man told her to sit in the room's only chair. He began tying her to it and made no effort to be gentle. More blood-chilling fear walloped her as she thought of other vile things this man was capable of.

When he finished, he turned to the Egyptian and spoke in Arabic. The other man then promptly collapsed on one side of the bed.

It occurred to her these men had not slept all night. Quite naturally, they would be sleepy as well as tired.

"I'll question you after we get some sleep," he said. She was now certain he was Welch.

And she was certain they had abducted her to question her about Jack and Daphne's investigation. When she was unable to tell them anything useful, she had no doubt they would kill her.

Thank God they were tired. If they could just fall into a heavy sleep, perhaps she could somehow contrive a way to break free.

Her shoulders sank. So did her heart. How did someone whose mouth and hands were bound break free? She pictured the handsome Captain Cooper and fancied him showing up to rescue her from her captors as would a knight of yore.

Then she realized what an immature, unrealistic, moronic notion that was. With their footprints having been swept away, she knew no one was going to find her here in this city of a quarter of a million people.

* * *

It was still dark when Maxwell led them to another narrow street where the narrow houses on each side of the lane almost came together on the top level. As before, they took care to keep Daphne as well as the soldiers from rounding the corner in case someone was on lookout duty. "The Egyptian who knew the suspected abductor said he lives in a house on this street," Maxwell told them. "I'm not precisely sure which house, but he said we'd know it because it's the slimmest on the street. This abductor—Mohammed Asker—has all three floors."

Since Maxwell had continued to wear his Arabic garb, he would be the least conspicuous of the three to stroll down the alley-like lane for reconnaissance.

They solemnly waited for him to return. Beneath awakening skies, he strode down that street. When Maxwell reached the skinniest house, his head lifted to peer at the upper floors as he walked by. At the end of the block, he turned onto the intersecting street, presumably to walk down the block behind these houses.

When he returned, he said, "They're almost certainly there. Two freshly ridden horses are tethered in front of the house. A candle burns on the second floor, but all was quiet within. There's no back entrance, so that's good."

"The three of us go. As quietly as possible." Jack eyed the soldiers. "Wait five minutes, then come after us. I don't have to tell any of us, our mission is to rescue Lady Rosemary."

"I pray to God she's there," Maxwell said.

Jack brushed his lips across Daphne's. "Please be prudent."

She nodded solemnly. "You too."

He eyed the soldiers. "Protect my wife."

"You have our word on it, sir."

Uncharacteristically, Jack followed another man—a much smaller, more inexperienced man. He knew better than to threaten Maxwell's command. Maxwell's passion and intelligence more than compensated for his physical shortcomings.

They kept to the same side of the street as Asker Mohammed's house so they would not be seen were someone looking out a window. Jack was confident no one saw them.

At a few of the houses they passed, they heard sounds of an awakening family. But no one shared the street with them.

Maxwell went to open the door of Asker's house, then turned back. "It's locked."

Since this was not an affluent section of the city, many of its windows would be glassless, covered only by the unique wooden shutters of elaborate patterns.

Jack moved to the sole ground-floor window at the same time as Maxwell did. Their minds were on the same page. It was good to work with someone whose thinking patterns so closely mirrored his own. That was one of the reasons his and Daphne's marriage was so strong. They were mental equals.

Though the shutters were hooked together to prevent opening, the wood was so old and brittle they had no difficulty breaking off a big enough section to reach in and unfasten the latch. Maxwell managed to do this with only minimal noise. He then hoisted himself through the window and surveyed the chamber he entered. "It doesn't look like anyone's on this level," he whispered. "It's quieter for you to come through the window than risk opening a possibly squeaky door."

Once both men were inside, they passed from the front room to the only other one on the ground floor, a chamber directly behind the first and of proportions identical to the first. It, too, was empty. Maxwell then started up the narrow wooden staircase, his pistol drawn. As carefully as he moved, it was impossible to do so noiselessly. Jack was fairly certain the noise would be confined to the narrow stairwell.

The higher they climbed, the darker the stairwell became. He wouldn't have been able to see Maxwell if he'd worn dark clothing like Jack and Petworth.

When they reached the landing, they were better able to see. Maxwell padded to the first door, gently tried the handle, and eased the door open. Swiftly, he moved into the chamber.

Jack followed. There was nothing more than a cot in this small chamber. No one was here.

What if this turned out to be another fruitless search? Where else could they possibly look for his sister-in-law? Jack was beginning to feel impotent. How could he ever face Daphne or Lord Sidworth if Lady Rosemary met the same tragic fate as Amal?

After assuring themselves this chamber was unoccupied, Maxwell re-entered the corridor and crept toward the second floor's front chamber.

His pistol still drawn, Maxwell began to slowly open the door, Jack's head behind his as they looked into the room. The first thing Jack saw was Rosemary. Wearing a flimsy night shift, she was strapped to a chair, her mouth bound.

As soon as those observations registered, he realized her captors were pounding across wooden floors. Definitely more than one set of footsteps. The slight noise made by the scraping of the door must have alerted them.

Maxwell threw open the door. And came face-to-face with an Egyptian with a huge dagger. Maxwell fired at him, striking him in the gut. But the man still managed to stumble toward Maxwell, muttering venomously in Arabic as he drove his dagger toward Maxwell's chest. Maxwell spun away, but the knife still slashed his arm.

From the right, the second man lunged toward Jack, knocking Jack's pistol to the ground with his saber. Jack whipped his saber from his side and faced the man who wore black robes. It was Williams. What a pleasure it would give Jack to drive his saber through the vile man's gut. Or choke the life from him as he had most likely done to Singh's mistress. But in spite of his great animosity toward the former soldier, he knew he would do neither because it was imperative he learn from whom Williams was taking orders.

Jack had a distinct size advantage. He was almost a head taller than the deserter and considerably outweighed him. Jack also held the advantage of having studied fencing under talented masters—an opportunity that almost certainly would have eluded the lowly soldier who'd served under him.

Yet despite these disadvantages, Williams was no easy prey. He was quick, and he fought as if he were fighting for his life. He was even smart enough to avoid being cornered. He kept moving toward the open door.

An all-or-nothing lunge to run his sword through Jack sent Williams sprawling on the floor when Jack spun away. Williams slid into the corridor. Jack whirled to take victory while his opponent was down, but Williams was quicker. He sprang to his feet and raced away from Jack. "Running away, Williams? You always were a bloody coward."

Since the man held information vital to Jack's quest, Jack was not about to allow the coward to get away. He sprinted after Williams.

Williams then did an odd thing. At the top of the stairs he stood and waited for Jack. "You want a fight, Dryden, you'll get one from me."

As Jack moved closer, Williams did an even odder thing. He backed himself into the corner.

Now this was easy prey. Jack inched closer until he was in striking range. As Jack thrust, Williams put his whole body into a flying kick. The man's foot plowed into Jack's chest. The surprise move knocked Jack down, half of his body on the landing, the other half slipping downstairs. He then knew Williams' aim had been to send him bouncing down the stairs, like an egg off the wall.

While Jack was down, the wiry man ran several feet back in the corridor, which overlooked the top of the stairwell. Petworth flew from the front room, planted his feet, and aimed his pistol at Williams.

The Welshman hopped over the balustrade, and landed midway down the stairs, just missing Petworth's musket ball.

Now on his feet, Jack went after him. "This man's mine, Petworth!"

Williams scurried from the building.

Sword in hand, Jack went after him, but when he reached the street, Williams was nowhere to be seen. The horse that had been tethered there was gone.

Jack stood there dazed, not knowing if he should go to the left or to the right. Surely if Williams had gone left, he'd still be visible on the block. Unless he'd popped into one of the neighbor's houses—horse and all. He'd likely gone right since the street terminated there—just two houses away. Jack went right. But when another lane intersected this one, he looked right and he looked left, but there was no sign of Williams.

If Williams had lived in this urban labyrinth for long, he would easily know how to elude Jack.

Jack turned and went the length of the block to Daphne and the soldiers, quickly telling them what had transpired. "He doesn't know that we know where his lodgings are. Let's go there now."

Jack turned to Daphne. "Go to Rosemary. Maxwell and Petworth should have the Egyptian their prisoner by now."

* * *

When she had first seen a robed man ease the door open, fear strummed through Rosemary. Then she recognized it was Mr. Maxwell. He was the most welcome sight ever. How had they found her? Her glance alighted on Jack. Both men were exceedingly clever. She should have known they could outsmart beasts like her two captors.

Unfortunately, the captors were light sleepers. The slight scraping noise of the door partially opening must have awakened them. Each man surged from the bed, weapons in hand.

Her flicker of hope died. How could poor Mr. Maxwell compete against cut-throats like these two depraved men who'd abducted her? He was a scholar from Cambridge, for pity's sake.

She could not remove her gaze from Mr. Maxwell. He didn't seem so small of stature when going up against the Egyptian who was even smaller. He was quick of reflex, too. He managed to get off a shot before her vile abductor reached him.

Then her heart beat in a rapid staccato that pounded through her entire body. The Egyptian was attempting to drive his dagger into dear Mr. Maxwell! Her rescuer twisted away, but the other man still drove his knife into Mr. Maxwell's arm. Blood gushed. Mr. Maxwell's white robe darkened with his spilt blood.

The wound did not deter Mr. Maxwell from attempting to disarm the man he shot.

The redheaded House Guard then came to Mr. Maxwell's assistance as Jack and the European launched into a full-fledged sword fight.

"This man's mine," Mr. Maxwell snapped as he forced the dagger from the Egyptian's hand. By now the Egyptian was losing a great deal of blood and losing consciousness as he slumped to the floor.

Mr. Maxwell straddled him and barked out something in Arabic. The man did not answer him. Mr. Maxwell repeated his demand. This time the man said something that apparently satisfied Mr. Maxwell.

She was in complete awe of the Orientologist. Not even her worshipped Captain Cooper could have been so masterful.

The Egyptian went unconscious. Mr. Maxwell turned to the redhead. "Pray, Petworth, be a good man and tie up this varmint."

Mr. Maxwell got to his feet and came to her. "Are you unharmed, my lady?"

Of course, she could not respond, given that her mouth was bound.

Then the brilliant man realized how foolish was his query. "Forgive me. I should have removed these first," he said as he took the confiscated dagger and slashed through the thick fabric that had silenced her.

"I . . . I think so," she croaked. "The beast struck my face, and I suspect it's swollen, but I believe I'm doing tolerably well. Now that you've come, my dear Mr. Maxwell," Her glance fell again to the massive blood flow from his stab wound. "You must allow me to help bind your wound, sir."

He sliced through the rope that held her wrists to the chair.

She hastened to take the cloth that had covered her mouth. "We must stop your bleeding. I should kill myself if I was the cause of you receiving a mortal wound."

"There now, my lady, don't worry. I've had worse."

She was seeing Mr. Maxwell through new eyes. Worse? He could have been killed! "You must get to a surgeon."

"First, I go to Dryden. He may need help." He whirled toward the door.

She sprang from her chair and followed on his heels.

When they got to the house's street entrance, there was no sign of Jack. "Please, Mr. Maxwell, we must see to your wound. Where is my sister? She will know what to do."

"Allow me to take you to her."

It was at that moment her state of undress occurred to her. "I am mortified over my appearance. You mustn't look at me. I need clothing. Desperately."

"If it pleases you, I will close my eyes."

"Very well."

There was movement at the end of the street. She quickly saw that it was Daphne, and Daphne began to run to her. The two sisters fell into each other's arms. "Oh, my dear Rosemary, I was so afraid you'd be killed."

"I was too." The tears she'd suppressed began to flow.

As did Daphne's.

"I owe my life to dear Mr. Maxwell." Then she remembered about his wound. "Oh, Daf, he's been injured. We must see to his wound."

Daphne spun around. "Pray, Mr. Maxwell, why are you closing your eyes?"

"I didn't want him looking at me," Rosemary said in a feeble voice.

"You should be ashamed of yourself. The man practically gets killed trying to save your life and you're embarrassed for him to see your bare legs!"

Daphne was right to chastise her. Rosemary rushed to Mr. Maxwell. "See, Daf. The vile creature who abducted me tried to drive a huge dagger into Mr. Maxwell's heart. Thankfully, Mr. Maxwell was quick enough to move away, but the dagger slashed his arm."

"We'll get him to our hotel and call for a surgeon," Daphne said.

"You can open your eyes," Rosemary said to him.

She stood before him as his eyes opened. With two days' growth, his dark beard was filling out. She rather liked it. He looked more mature, more manly.

His dark eyes whisked over her. Then he shut them again.

But in that second when his eyes caressed her half naked body, she tingled all over.

Chapter 13

"Dear love, allow me to wrap my veil around you. It will quite make you decent." Daphne proceeded to cover her sister with the creamy white fabric. From the corner of her eye, Daphne noticed a man in trousers—an unusual site in Cairo, to be sure. She looked up to see the redheaded Mr. Petworth coming toward them, a dejected look on his face.

"Mr. Petworth, where's your prisoner?" Daphne asked.

"I'll need to question him in Arabic," Maxwell added.

Petworth shook his head sadly. "He's gone."

Maxwell's voice hitched. "He escaped?"

"No. He died from the wound you inflicted."

"I'm not a bit sorry," Rosemary said. "He was a horrible man. He tried with wicked determination to kill dear Mr. Maxwell, and he's the one who slashed through my tent and stole me away in the night. He also struck me. I'm not a bit sorry he's dead."

"It seems he deserved his fate," Mr. Maxwell said. But his voice lacked conviction.

"Pray, Mr. Maxwell," Petworth said, concern in his voice, "what's happened to your eyes?"

"Oh, you can open them now," Rosemary said. "I'm mostly covered." Rosemary turned to the soldier.

Mr. Petworth quickly averted his gaze from

Rosemary. His glance dropped to the scholar's bloody sleeve, and he rushed to him. "Let me see your wound! Was it his dagger?"

Mr. Maxwell nodded solemnly as he lifted his sleeve to reveal a gash so deep, it flapped open on either side.

Rosemary fainted.

Her body toppled forward—right into Mr. Maxwell's arms. "Poor Lady Rosemary." Then he picked her up. "We must return to the hotel."

Daphne hovered over her sister. She had some experience with fainting sisters and deemed this nothing out of the ordinary. "When we get there, the first thing we do is send for a surgeon. Come this way. We've three horses tethered just around the corner."

Mr. Maxwell transferred Rosemary's limp body to Mr. Petworth while he mounted. Then Mr. Petworth hoisted her up into Mr. Maxwell's arms.

"Where are the others?" Mr. Petworth asked Daphne.

She explained that Jack believed Williams—unaware they knew where he lived—would be returning to his lodgings, and they hoped to capture him there.

Just inside the walls to the European quarter, Daphne observed a curious sight. The same two men wearing fezzes who'd guarded Ahmed Hassein's shop in the bazaar stood just inside the gates. What would they be doing in the European quarter? Had Hassein sent them to spy on her and Jack?

She sighed. "Whenever we get a free soldier, we must send him back to Gizeh to apprise everyone that we've found Rosemary."

* * *

A short time before they reached their hotel, Rosemary awakened. She'd been dreaming she was being held in Captain Cooper's arms. At least she thought it was Captain Cooper. She couldn't see his face. She knew only that she felt secure. She felt cherished. She felt unbound happiness. Her arms came around him. She hadn't wanted to awaken.

It slowly became apparent that she was surrounded by the clopping of horse hooves, that the motion she was experiencing meant she was on a horse. Being carried by . . . her lover. A smile lifted the corners of Rosemary's mouth, and then her eyelids lifted. The first thing she saw was his spectacles, then the blood-drenched sleeve.

She was in Mr. Maxwell's arms! Her instant rush of affection was quickly doused by her concern for him. For emblazoned on her brain was the memory of how his mangled arm looked when he lifted away the bloody sleeve. Her spine stiffened. "Mr. Maxwell! I beg that you let me hold the reins for you. You mustn't move your injured arm." She snatched the reins from his hands.

He sighed. "Thank you, my lady. I believe I will bow to your kind offer. It seems the movement has accelerated the bleeding."

"I'm terribly worried about you."

"I was terribly worried about you. Both after the abduction and after you fainted."

"I remember now." She groaned. "Did I truly faint at the sight of your ghastly wound?"

"You did, my lady. We were all concerned."

"Save your concern for your arm, my dear Mr. Maxwell."

At the hotel, the redheaded soldier lifted her down from Mr. Maxwell's horse. While the two men and Rosemary went up the stairs, Daphne went to request one of the hotel's servants fetch a surgeon.

Rosemary could not wait to replace Daphne's veil that she'd endeavored to wrap around her. She'd had the devil of a time keeping it from unfurling to reveal her nearly naked. She longed to don one of her morning gowns. With stockings and shoes. She hurried to her chamber, tossing back a glance at her brave protector. "As soon as I'm dressed, I shall come to your chamber."

"You ought not to" Mr. Maxwell said. "I can't have you fainting again."

"I give you my word that I will not. The horrible vision of your terrible injury is embedded into my mind. I shall never be able to forget it." She wanted to say, "I shall never be able to thank you properly for endangering your life for me," but her gratitude would be expressed later. After he was on the mend.

Getting him medical attention was all that mattered now. "I won't have a second's peace until I know that you're being properly taken care of." Gone were her sweetly feminine tones. She spoke forcefully.

"There's also the matter that I will have to be undressed above the waist," he said. "It will not be proper for a maiden to see such."

She froze, glaring at him. "This maiden has bared more than half her body to you, my dear Mr. Maxwell. May I suggest that English rules of propriety be abandoned by us both under the present circumstances?"

His bespectacled eyes solemnly met hers, and he slowly nodded.

Within five minutes, Rosemary was dressed and

striding into Mr. Maxwell's bedchamber.

Daphne eyed her. "Good news. There's a French surgeon living in the European quarter, and we've sent for him."

"That is good news." Rosemary saw that Mr. Maxwell had donned his trousers and was sitting on his bed, shirtless, as Mr. Petworth and Daphne were examining his wound.

"May I come see?" Rosemary asked.

"If you promise not to faint," Mr. Maxwell said.

"The severity of it won't shock me this time." She came to stand on the other side of his bed. "Do you not believe, Mr. Petworth, that we should bind the wound to reduce the bleeding—at least until the surgeon comes?"

"I do."

"I've brought some linen we can use," Daphne said. "After the surgeon comes, he will want to stitch the arm back properly."

The very idea of driving a needle into Mr. Maxwell's flesh made Rosemary's stomach queasy, but she vowed to be strong for the most gallant man she'd ever known. Even more queasiness sloshed within her when she saw that his sheets were covered in blood.

Daphne asked Mr. Petworth to try pulling the long gash together while she attempted to wrap the linen around his arm. "We don't know how long it will be before the surgeon arrives," Rosemary's pragmatic sister said. "He could be in the middle of an amputation or something equally as vital."

Mr. Maxwell looked as if he were turning green. "I beg that you not mention amputations."

"I'm sorry, but I'm sure amputations are for . . . well, things like the shattering from a musket ball." Daphne said. "Your injuries, I am certain, can be addressed by simple stitching."

"I beg that you not mention stitching." Rosemary transferred her attention from Daphne to the patient. "Should you like me to hold your hand, Mr. Maxwell?" How had those words popped from her mouth? She hadn't meant to say them. How embarrassing!

Grimacing from the pain, he turned to her. "That would be lovely."

She placed her hand in his, and they clasped together. Despite that he was a slender man, his hand was not small. It was a great deal larger than hers, and his clasp was firm.

In her entire life, no physical action had ever affected Rosemary so profoundly. Butterflies flitted in her chest. Her breath grew short. She quite decided that hand holding was a wonderful thing.

"When I was a lad, my mother sat by my bed when I had the fever," he said, his voice gentle. "She held my hand, and I believed that it transferred her good health to me."

Rosemary tossed her head back and laughed."Pray, I hope you don't think of me as a mother."

An embarrassed expression swept across his face, and he stammered, "I . . . I didn't mean to imply- -"

"I was just teasing." She remembered that his mother had been his champion in ridding their house of a mummy. It was obvious he and his mother had a loving relationship, and because of that she did not object to reminding him of his mother.

It was most difficult for her to watch what

Daphne and Mr. Petworth were doing to her poor Mr. Maxwell, so she met his dark eyes and attempted to take his thoughts away from the pain he must be enduring.

Now that she knew Mr. Maxwell, she no longer noticed his spectacles. Just like with Daphne. For the first time, she actually looked into his eyes. His brown eyes had no honeyed flecks; they were almost black. "Do you know, Mr. Maxwell, your beard is already filling out, and I quite like the way it looks on you."

"I thought you didn't like men with facial hair," Daphne said.

"I must have meant fair-haired men. I believe it suits Mr. Maxwell with his dark colouring."

Her comments had him completely clamming up. He wouldn't even meet her gaze. She must have embarrassed him.

"Now that I am assured your terrible wound is being seen to, I must express to you my profound gratitude. You risked your life to save mine. I will never be able to repay so great a debt."

"There's no debt, my lady. I was happy to be useful."

"Useful! You were heroic! I've never witnessed such bravery."

"It was nothing, and I beg that you not speak of it again."

He was grimacing from the pain, and sweat beaded on his forehead. She had to restrain herself from stroking his brow. Really, she did not know what had come over her! She had never been particularly demonstrative. Until today.

Her first two ploys to distract his thoughts had obviously embarrassed him. Perhaps she should stick with Orientology. "Tell me, Mr. Maxwell, have you ever been in a mestaba?"

He nodded, then chuckled.

"What's funny about that?"

"We left behind seven of the Egyptians, four soldiers, Mr. Arbuthnot, and Lord Beddington with his army of servants to search every mestaba in Gizeh for you."

"I do wish Jack and our four soldiers would return," Daphne said. "We need to dispatch a soldier to Gizeh to call off the search."

Rosemary could tell Daphne was worried about Jack.

Footsteps on the stairs alerted them, and all eyes went to the door. A bearded, turbaned European stood at the doorway and in French introduced himself as the surgeon.

Daphne sighed. "Now that I know Mr. Maxwell will be in the surgeon's capable hands, I shall borrow Mr. Petworth to accompany me to where my husband is.

* * *

Once more, he had failed to capture that damned Williams. He must have seen them in close proximity to his lodgings and fled. Nothing could be more conspicuous than soldiers with fair skin, bright red jackets, white breeches, and towering beaver hats.

They had not seen Williams. But he wore black robes, and could go almost undetected in shadowy doorways.

Jack had gone back to Williams' dark room and waited, his pistol aimed at the door he had hoped Williams would enter. He waited and waited until well after the streets filled with Egyptians going about their day's work. Then his wife came scurrying up the stairs, accompanied by Petworth, thank goodness.

"Are you here, dearest?" she called.

"Yes," he grumbled.

"I've been so worried about you." She entered Williams' room, satisfied herself that Jack was unharmed, then allowed her gaze to fan over the chamber. "It's apparent that he was a military man at one time. His chambers are relatively tidy for a bachelor."

"He saves his nastiness for murder," Petworth said, snarling.

Jack couldn't agree more.

"I hate to think that a man who was unfit for the military has gotten the best of me," Jack said.

Daphne came to his side and set a gentle hand on his shoulder. "Not for long, love. With Mr. Petworth's able assistance, you'll find the evil man and bring him to justice."

"Where do you think he might have gone?" Petworth asked.

"My guess is that he's reporting to the man from whom he takes orders."

"If only we knew who that was," Daphne said wistfully. "Do you think it could be Ahmed Hassein? I can't help but think he's got something to do with all this. I saw his two guards in the European quarter this morning. Why do you suppose they were there?"

Jack's brows elevated. "It's very likely he wished for them to spy on us."

"They would have been much more inconspicuous had they dressed as native Egyptians," she said.

"Native dress reminds me of Maxwell," Jack said, moving to the door. "The last time I saw him, I caught sight of blood. Is he all right?"

"I think he'll be all right," Petworth said.

"But he's got a ghastly knife wound to his arm."

"Laid it wide open," Petworth added.

"We left him in the hands of a French surgeon. I was terribly worried about you."

He took her hand and pressed a kiss to it. "As you can see, I am fine—but feeling defeated." They began to walk down the stairs.

"I have no doubts you'll get your man. It's just taking longer than you're accustomed to," she said.

"We need to send a pair of soldiers to Gizeh."

They continued to hold hands as they descended the staircase. "Allow the men to eat something first, then dispatch a pair," she said.

Jack chuckled to himself. "I wonder if Arbuthnot's clothes have gotten dirtied."

She smiled. "I doubt it. He will find a way to avoid such unpleasantness."

As they rode back to the hotel, Daphne said, "You know, dearest, I'm not perceptive about these things, but I believe Rosemary has taken a fancy to Mr. Maxwell."

"She could not do better."

"You'll get no argument from me."

"You know, do you not," Jack said, "that even were Maxwell to return her affection, he would never act upon it?"

She nodded solemnly. "Because of the disparity in their stations."

He remembered how he had once resisted his acute attraction to Daphne for the very same reasons. He wondered if anything other than their near-death experience would ever have forced them to admit their love for one another.

Chapter 14

Jack felt guilty for ordering a pair of soldiers back to Gizeh when he and the rest of their exhausted party were planning to collapse in their beds. "I vow that you will have the next two days duty free," Jack had told the soldiers.

There was much to discuss when Jack and Daphne got to their bedchamber. "What did you think of Lord Beddington?" she asked.

"His answers to our questions seemed honest. He seemed amiable."

"You don't sound terribly convincing."

"That's because it's suspicious to me that he and his army of servants were already at Gizeh when we arrived—and somebody during that time prior to our arrival set the trap that could have killed Maxwell or your sister."

"There is that." She allowed her robes to fall to the floor, and she stepped out of them. "But I cannot believe Lord Beddington would try to kill the daughter of his old school friend. He and Papa were exceedingly fond of one another. I also have difficulty believing that one of the wealthiest men in all of Europe would have to resort to murder to obtain a coveted antiquity."

"I'm inclined to agree with you on that." He swept aside the mosquito netting and sat on the edge of the bed to remove his boots.

"Allow me to assist." She went to her knees in front of him and helped yank them off.

"Perhaps we could get Habeeb to question his servants. If his underlings were ordered to rig up the stones, do you not think others would know that?"

"It's possible." His brows lowered. "Speaking of Habeeb, I wonder if he's been able to locate the women."

She lowered herself on to the bed. "If he had, he'd be sitting on that bench in front of our hotel."

"He does seem to be reliable." Jack fell back on the mattress.

"Another thing about Lord Beddington . . . how would he even have known we were in Cairo? It's been over half a year since he left for Thebes."

He rolled over to face her. "There is the fact these wealthy men with villas keep a staff here even when they're elsewhere. He could have sent a messenger to his staff in Cairo to alert them that he was not much more than an hour away. Perhaps one of his loyal retainers reported to him about our presence. Did he even say how long he'd been at Gizeh?"

"No, he didn't. I had the impression he may have been there a few days."

"Enough time to communicate with his agents in Cairo. Enough time to plan attacks on Amal and on Rosemary."

"But we have no reason to believe Lord Beddington's staff would be up to sinister activities. I do believe we should consider everyone until we find the guilty person or persons, but I'm more suspicious than ever of Ahmed Hassein after seeing his soldiers in the European quarter."

"That does arouse suspicion, though we aren't the only Europeans staying here."

"But I'm almost sure we are the most recently

arrived."

"What's that supposed to mean?"

She pouted. "I'm not exactly sure, but I'm sure it's important."

"We have nothing on which to base our assumption that Hassein's behind all these incidents."

"Nothing except his reputation for dishonesty and dastardly deeds."

"But our only source for the revelations about Hassein was Arbuthnot. How reliable is his information?"

"I will concede to you on that point. Sounds like another bit of poking needed for Habeeb."

"I'd rather not vest too much faith in Habeeb's abilities. I expect a few questions addressed to Briggs should give us the confirmation we need."

"That would be simpler." Her lips pressed against his cheek. "My husband is so brilliant."

"Daphne . . ." he growled.

She ignored his chastisement. "That Williams is tied up in all of this does point to a British connection."

"But he is said to speak fluent Arabic. I think he's for hire to anyone who will pay for his filthy services."

Daphne sighed. "He would have killed Rosemary, wouldn't he?"

"It's very likely."

"Oh, dearest, I forgot to tell you! Rosemary said Williams told her he killed Amal."

Jack winced. "No surprise there, but what kind of cold-blooded killer admits to so horrendous a crime?"

Her hand cupped his face. "I'm just grateful he didn't kill you."

He pressed a kiss into one of her hands. "You had no worries. I'm taller, stronger, and more well trained than he." He frowned. "How in the bloody hell did he get the best of me?"

"He did not get the best of you. He merely got away from you like the coward he is."

There was that. His eyelids began to drift downward.

"Dearest?"

"Yes?"

"What about Mr. Arbuthnot?"

"What about him?"

"We've never considered that he—or even Mr. Briggs—could be the guilty party."

"I will own Arbuthnot is conceited, annoying, and pretentious, but I can hardly believe him a murderer. And he says he's never heard of or met Williams."

"I don't care how big Cairo is. After all the time Mr. Arbuthnot's been here, surely he would at least have seen a fellow countryman."

"But as I understand it, Williams often dresses like a native."

The oddly melodic tones of the mid-afternoon Call to Prayer wafted into their chamber through the open window. They were both silent for a moment, even though they did not understand Arabic. His glance fell to Daphne. This daily Muslim ritual always transported her to a mystical place. A smile would lift her face as a dreamy expression would come over it and stay there until the muezzin was finished.

After a relative silence fell over the city, she continued. "I was rather shocked that Lord Beddington took to his native dress so thoroughly that he actually wore a turban."

"Frankly, I was too."

"I suppose it must be what one does when one lives in the Orient. The French surgeon had also grown a beard and wore a turban—with trousers."

"Speaking of the surgeon reminds me of how pleasantly surprised I was at how tenderly Rosemary treated poor Maxwell."

"It was especially commendable, given her aversion to blood. You know she fainted?"

"I did not."

Daphne nodded. "When he lifted his sleeve away. Thankfully, she pitched forward—right into Mr. Maxwell's arms. After she regained consciousness, she vowed to be brave and begged admittance into the man's sick chamber. I thought she was wonderfully brave, and her presence there was most comforting. She feels dreadfully guilty that he jeopardized his life to save hers."

"I will own I was astonished at the man's bravery. How deceiving appearances can be!"

"He was terribly heroic. I daresay Rosemary's in awe of him."

Daphne's lids kept closing, her honey-colored lashes sweeping down on her lightly freckled cheek. She'd force them open, but seconds later, they would close again. Soon she was in a deep sleep.

* * *

Rosemary was able to sleep just long enough to refresh herself before she awakened. She snapped up and surveyed her chambers to assure herself no intruders were lurking. Would she do this the rest of her life as a result of her harrowing experience the night before? She should feel secure. Daphne and Jack and Mr. Maxwell were all on her floor, and soldiers were guarding the exterior. Exactly like last night, yet they still got her.

The very idea sent pricks of goose bumps to her upper torso.

She was unable to shake a deep sense of foreboding. It took her a moment to understand this worry that gripped her wasn't fear for herself. She was concerned about Mr. Maxwell. His wound was so horrendous. She'd known people who died after sustaining wounds much less severe than his.

She left her bed and attempted to arrange her hair in a flattering fashion.

Then she went to his chamber and softly tapped at the door.

"Come in."

He was just as he'd been when she had left, fully dressed, stretched out on his bed. The dear man—as a gentleman—went to get up as she strolled into the chamber.

"Please, stay down. I wish for you to conserve your strength after your ordeal of earlier today."

He lowered himself back to the bed and frowned. "Perhaps you ought not to be here, my lady."

He was concerned about her reputation. "Did we not decide earlier when I was not even half clothed that we would dispense with English standards of propriety?"

The very idea of standing in front of him half clothed was not nearly as humiliating as she would have thought even a week ago. Now, such a memory unleashed a feminine power she'd been unaware she possessed. She found herself wondering if a man like Mr. Maxwell found her alluring.

A week ago, she would never have considered that Mr. Maxwell had any interests outside of Orientology. Were scholars not stuffy persons who lived for their research to exclusion of all frivolous pursuits—including romance? There was the fact his scholarly father had wed and sired at least one child.

Something inside her melted at the notion of this Mr. Maxwell siring a child, at the notion of Mr. Maxwell kissing a woman, the notion of him falling in love.

A week ago, she'd thought of him rather as one thinks of an object. Like a stuffy tome. Or something that conveys one to its destination. But she'd never thought of him as a flesh and blood man. (And she really didn't like to be reminded of just how much blood the man had to spare.)

She no longer thought of him in such inhuman terms. He had shown himself not only to be extremely intelligent but also the bravest man she'd ever known.

He nodded solemnly.

"I can abandon those strictures of Society when I am with you because I know you are a gentleman. You would neither attempt to take liberties with me nor would you ever reveal my indiscretions to another person once we return to England."

His dark eyes softened. She noted that his spectacles lay on the table closest to his bed. "You, my lady, have not committed any indiscretions. You adapted to your environment—something intrepid travelers often do. And I beg that you never chastise yourself over the unthinkable offense that was committed against you last night. You are as blameless as a newborn babe."

In that moment she thought she had never been so close to another person. Her thoughts kept flitting to the long spell when they had held hands—something she had never before done with any man. She had initiated the hand holding to sooth him during the painful treatment to his arm, but it was she who was soothed by the comforting warmth that spread within her as his hand clasped hers with gentle firmness.

She would like nothing more at this moment than to sit by his bed and hold his hand again, but she was cognizant of the vast impropriety of even being in a man's bedchamber without benefit of a chaperon. There could not be any physical contact between them.

She pulled the room's only chair up to his bed and sat in it. "I know it's not proper to be here, but we are both proper people who will not do improper things." The mention of improper things sent heat rushing to her cheeks. And to other parts. "Because of all we've been through together, we must consider ourselves as family."

A serious expression swept across his pensive face. "While I do feel protective toward you, I cannot think of you as . . . a sister or as a father thinks of his child. I'm not of your class."

She nearly giggled at the idea he could think of her as his child. He was only a handful of years older than she. For some odd reason, she would rather he had considered her like . . . well, like Jack considered Daphne. "Jack's not of Daphne's class, but have you ever seen a more perfectly suited couple?"

"They do seem perfectly matched."

She laughed. "I don't know how we got off into this discussion. I came here because I'm concerned over you. I had to reassure myself that you're all right."

"And now you should be satisfied." He sounded as if he wished to be rid of her.

"The surgeon did say not to move that arm for several days. I'm here to fetch and carry and do everything I can to ease your discomfort."

"That's unnecessary."

"It's necessary for my peace of mind. It's my fault you were so badly injured. You could have been killed because you were rescuing me."

"I will happily exonerate you from any blame in my little cut."

"Little cut! How can you act as if it's insignificant? It's not, and I mean to see that you don't trivialize so serious an injury." Anger had crept into her voice. She stood and peered down at him, then spoke softly. "Forgive my outburst. It's just that after all the turmoil of last night, I'm on edge. I beg that you humor me and allow me to coddle you a bit. After all, you coddled me a great deal."

"It's very kind of you, my lady, but your attentions have coddled me quite enough. A professor is not accustomed to coddlement. Is that a word?"

She sat back down. "It sounds like a very good word to me. I think I shall be into coddlement fulfillment."

He chuckled. He was handsome when he chuckled. Without his spectacles. With his dark beard.

"Do you know what I've been wanting to ask

you?"

He looked apprehensive. "What?"

"Is it correct to call you Mr. Maxwell? Are you not Dr. Maxwell?"

A faint smile played at his lips. "I am Dr. Maxwell, but outside of Cambridge, I prefer not to use that title."

She pouted. "Would you object terribly if I referred to you as Dr. Maxwell? I adore the way it sounds."

"Far be it from me to object to anything you do, my lady."

The two of them sat conversing agreeably until dinner was served. She discovered that he was an only child, which reinforced her opinion that his mother was into serious coddlement of her only child but which distressed her about his father's lack of interest in . . . the softer side of life. Were scholars so wrapped up in their study they neglected . . . the softer side of life?

* * *

Just before she and Jack were to go downstairs for dinner, Daphne peered from her bedchamber window. There on the bench sat Habeeb. And beside him, an Arabic woman. Had he found Amal's servant?

Daphne nearly flew down the stairs.

$\mathcal{C}$hapter 15

Habeeb and the woman stood as Daphne approached. As small a man as Habeeb was, he looked tall next to the petite woman dressed in black veils and robes. The woman Habeeb introduced as Amal's maid wasn't much more than a girl.

Daphne expressed her condolences and asked that the woman come inside out of the heat. "I have a few questions I should like to ask her."

On the sofa in the hotel's parlor, Daphne sat on one side of the lady, Habeeb on the other, and Jack stood by the room's closed door.

"Please tell her," Daphne began, "that I believe the disappearance of Prince Singh is connected to her employer's murder. I hope she may know – through her mistress – something about Prince Singh's last hours in Cairo."

Habeeb translated to the young woman, who nodded solemnly as he spoke. Then her black eyes met Daphne's. She could not be a day older than Rosemary. Daphne was gratified that this young girl had moved home where her father could help protect her against the evil that had taken the life of her employer.

"Ask her if she may have overheard her mistress and Prince Singh speaking about why he couldn't see her on the night he disappeared."

Daphne watched expectantly as Habeeb conveyed her question to the youthful servant.

The girl nodded. Then she said something, something which brought a smile to Habeeb's face.

Habeeb eyed Daphne. "She says her mistress explained to her the reason Prince Singh could not come to her that night."

Excitement coursed through Daphne's veins. "And what was that?"

"The Prince told her mistress that he had the opportunity to make many times more on a pharaoh's mask than the English king had agreed to pay. A man who was even more important than the English ruler was coming to his house that night to take possession. The man was so important, and the sale so secretive, that Prince Singh was told to dismiss his servants that night."

"Was he not suspicious?" Jack asked.

Habeeb asked the former maid.

She shook her head and explained.

"She said that this man was known to Prince Singh."

Daphne's heartbeat accelerated. "And does she know his name?"

Habeeb questioned her.

"She does not know his name, but he was an Englishman."

* * *

At the dinner table, Rosemary insisted on feeding Maxwell. Jack could have laughed out loud. This man who in the presence of men was so bloody proud—and brave, too—was emasculated by a woman who'd not yet reached twenty.

"The surgeon said you're not to use your right arm, and I mean to see that his instructions are followed," Rosemary had insisted in a most commanding manner. "You know your arm will not mend if you keep moving it." Then her voice softened. "I owe you so much, my dear Mr. Maxwell. Please allow me this one little indulgence."

Maxwell was entirely too respectful of Rosemary. Jack understood. He'd once been rather the same with Daphne. Because of the disparity in their rank. But as they became closer to one another in the course of their inquiries, he learned to stand up to Daphne.

He hoped Maxwell would grow a spine where Lady Rosemary was concerned.

Once they were all situated at the table, and Rosemary was feeding Maxwell a spoonful of dates, Daphne lowered her voice. "We've had a breakthrough in our investigation."

The others' attentions whipped to her.

"Our dragoman has found Amal's personal maid. Apparently her mistress confided in her." Daphne said turned to Jack. "Did you not think the maid awfully young?"

He shrugged. "She was likely the same age as Rosemary."

Rosemary bristled. "I am certainly not young. I do hope before the year is out I will be a married woman."

"Pray, Lady Daphne," Maxwell said, "is the maid's age relevant to our inquiries?"

Now Jack did burst out laughing. "Leave it to Maxwell to bring logic to our investigation."

Daphne smiled at the scholar. "Do forgive me, Mr. Maxwell, for getting off topic in a truly feminine way. Now where were we?"

"You were telling us that the dead mistress confided in her maid."

"Indeed she did. She told the maid Prince Singh

was not coming to her that last night because he had an assignation with a man more important than the British ruler, a man who would pay many times more than the Regent for the Amun-re mask."

"Did she know his name?" Rosemary asked.

"No, but . . ." Daphne paused for dramatic effect. "He was an Englishman."

For several seconds, a chilling silence hung in the air.

"It's got to be Beddington," Maxwell finally said. "Did you not think it suspicious that two attempts were made on Lady Rosemary's life the first time we ever came into contact with him and his virtual caravan of servants?"

Jack nodded. "I was thinking along the same trajectory."

"That is why," Daphne said, unable to stifle the smugness that crept into her voice, "I've sent Habeeb to Lord Beddington's."

"Beddington's returned from Gizeh?" Maxwell asked.

Jack nodded. "When we were speaking to Habeeb, our soldiers returned."

"What, pray tell, is Habeeb to do at Lord Beddington's?" Rosemary asked.

"He's to mingle with Lord Beddington's servants," Daphne said. "Specifically, I wished for him to discover if any of them have knowledge of that stone rigging in the Great Pyramid either the day before we arrived or the morning of our arrival."

"I say, that's rather clever, my lady," Maxwell said.

"He's also to verify Lord Beddington's journey and to find out how long they'd been in Gizeh."

Daphne sent a wan smile to Maxwell. "Habeeb has proven to be exceedingly useful."

"You're quite turning him into another Andy," Rosemary said. "Truth be told, I'm shocked you were able to leave him behind in London."

Daphne sighed. "I wanted to bring him. He would have loved it, but the ship captain strictly limited the number of passengers he could bring."

"Poor Andy," Rosemary said. "I daresay the lad will never be content to just be a coachman after all the exciting inquiries you've put him through."

Maxwell eyed Jack. "I expect Habeeb's life will seem most dull after we leave."

Daphne rolled her eyes. "I daresay poor Habeeb will be much safer. Conceive if you will, in the past four days we've seen one woman murdered, another woman's life threatened, and one blackguard Egyptian slain. Add to that, it is very likely that Prince Singh was slain."

"We'd all be much safer if we'd pile into a boat and return to England." Jack might sound flippant, but nothing would please him more than to put these three on a sailing vessel. Either Rosemary or Maxwell could easily have been killed. Would Daphne be the next target?

"You know, my darling," Daphne said to Jack, "that neither of us could ever let down our dear Regent."

Oh, but Jack could. His allegiance to the Regent would crumble if it interfered with Jack's ability to protect his wife. Jack's first concern was and always would be Daphne. He glowered at her.

"Really, Lady Rosemary," Maxwell protested, "I'm sure I could feed myself with my left hand."

Her brows elevated. "I'm sure you could, but I hate to think of the damage to your white cravat."

Daphne giggled. "My sister's right, Mr. Maxwell."

He possessed enough good humor to chuckle along with them.

"I believe after dinner I shall read to you," Rosemary informed Maxwell. "It's awfully difficult to read with the use of only one hand."

After dinner, the four of them gathered in the drawing room, with Rosemary quietly reading a book on the Koran to Maxwell while Jack and Daphne played chess. Jack would bet a pony Maxwell would rather be playing chess, but the man was too bloody polite to Daf's manipulative sister.

Daphne kept watching Rosemary and whispering to Jack how profoundly grateful she was that her sister had been rescued. Her divided concentration helped Jack to victory. With an unprecedented lack of disappointment in her defeat, Daphne quickly turned her attention to her sister. "Rosemary, I'm sure that book is fascinating, but you really must go to bed now. You couldn't have slept much last night, and I can tell by your eyes that you're tired. You mustn't ruin your eyes as I did mine."

"Forgive me," Maxwell said to Rosemary. "I had almost forgotten about your ordeal of last night. You really must get a good night's rest."

"And please realize, dearest love, that you will truly be safe tonight," Daphne told her.

Jack thought of the previous night's drugged soldier. Who could have been responsible for adding laudanum to the port? Lord Beddington, to Jack's knowledge, hadn't been by the soldier's campfire. Arbuthnot had, but he could not have known which of the soldiers would be on duty that night, and none of the other soldiers had been drugged.

There was also the fact that Beddington'd had nearly a hundred men to do his bidding—just in Gizeh. Could he not have had one of his servants administer the opiate?

This damned investigation was proving to be as fruitless as a eunuch.

* * *

At breakfast the following morning—much to Maxwell's consternation—Rosemary insisted on feeding him.

"I assure you, my lady, I'm capable of holding the coffee cup up to my lips with my left hand."

She nodded. "You may drink your coffee without my assistance, but I'll be right here to cut up your eggs and to assist you in any way I can."

He rolled his eyes. "You really mustn't feel as if you're indebted to me."

Daphne's eyes sparkled. "Being one's savior is a heavy burden, to be sure, Mr. Maxwell. I daresay my sister will spend the rest of her days following you around like a lap dog."

"I hope you jest, my lady," Maxwell said.

"My wife jests."

There was a knock upon the breakfast room door, and Jack bade the person enter.

A middle-aged British man dressed in lime-green livery came into the chamber and stood just inside the door. "I've brought a note from me master, Lord Beddington, to Lady Daffie Dryden." His brow hiked, he looked from Daphne to Rosemary.

"I'm Lady Daphne."

He crossed the room and handed it to her. The note was written on very high quality paper bearing the Beddington crest of a lion's head shield. She broke the seal, unfolded it and read. Then she looked up at Jack. "His lordship has invited us to dinner."

"We shall be delighted to attend," he said to the servant.

"Does we include me and Mr. Maxwell?" Rosemary asked.

"Indeed it does." Daphne turned back to the servant. "Thank his lordship for extending the invitation. We look forward to seeing him this evening."

Once the servant was gone, Daphne turned to her husband. "We must think of something we can do tonight to draw out the truth."

His lips formed a tight line. "A man who has already murdered twice will evade the truth to his dying breath."

Daphne brightened. "Perhaps one of us—after eating—can use the pretext of visiting the necessary room to search his lordship's house for the Amun-re mask or for something that connects him with Prince Singh."

"Mr. Maxwell certainly will not!" Rosemary said. "He's already endangered his life once—and besides, he's not to move his arm."

Daphne could barely suppress a grin as her amused gaze met Jack's. "And I shan't allow Rosemary to, either. She's been through far too much."

Jack scowled. "Your plan, my dearest, has as much merit as a lunatic's ravings. Do you know how bloody many servants Beddington has?"

"You're not to curse in front of my maiden sister."

"Forgive me, Lady Rosemary." Jack had a

difficult time remembering to censor his use of bloody. Too many years living among men.

"Our Papa uses that word all the time," Rosemary said. "And Mama is forever chastising him in the exact same manner as Daphne just chastised you."

Jack folded his arms across his chest and drew a breath. "One woman's already been murdered, and Rosemary almost killed. I'll not have any of us exposing ourselves to such potential danger."

Daphne pouted. "You're not going to be the one searching his house, either."

"I keep thinking about what the Pasha told us about the Amun-re mask ending up in Constantinople," Jack said.

Maxwell nodded. "Where it was said to sell for a very great price."

Jack's gaze locked with Maxwell's. "The Pasha doesn't strike me as a man who would make up such a story."

"I have read that the Orientals don't have the same reverence for truth as there is in Western culture," Rosemary said.

"But I daresay Jack's right about the Pasha," Daphne said. "Remember, the Pasha was the first to point to an Englishman."

A puzzled look crossed Jack's face. "I admit, right now, no one appears guiltier than Lord Beddington, but I'm still having the devil of a time believing the man capable of such evil—especially given his vast wealth."

"Perhaps the source of his wealth has been depleted," Daphne suggested. "If only Papa were here. He would know."

There was another tapping at the chamber door, and once again Jack bade the person to enter.

At first Jack thought the uniformed newcomer was one of their nine soldiers still in British military regimentals. Then he realized the man standing before them was considerably more handsome than any of the men who had accompanied them on this trip, and his uniform was not that of a House Guard. Tall and well-muscled, the youthful officer's uniform was spotless. His Hessians were so well polished he could have seen his face in them. His white gloves were immaculate.

Jack had met this man before. In London.

It was Captain Cooper, Rosemary's idol.

$\mathcal{C}$hapter 16

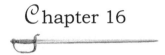

The spoon Rosemary was holding in her hand dropped midway to Maxwell's mouth. Her eyes widened. Her heartbeat roared. This was a dream come true. From the moment she'd set foot on Egyptian soil she had fantasized about Captain Cooper being stationed in Egypt.

And now here he was in the flesh.

Her admiring gaze traveled the glorious length of him in his military splendor. Her profound admiration of him remained unchanged. No man had ever worn a uniform better. He was as tall as Jack and built rather in the same exceedingly masculine manner. But where Jack was dark, Captain Cooper's hair was blond, and his eyes were blue.

"My dear Captain Cooper," Daphne exclaimed. "What brings you to Cairo?"

He moved into the room. "My regiment's been at Fort Rached these six months past, and several of the fellows I serve with had an urge to see the pyramids."

Jack offered him a chair, and Daphne offered food. He took the former and refused the latter.

"Then you'll be going to Gizeh today?" Daphne asked.

He shook his head. "I've no desire to see the pyramids. I'm sick to death of Egypt and its heat and its silly clothing and those annoying Calls to Prayer. I cannot wait to return to good old

England."

"You mustn't speak ill of Egypt, Captain," Daphne said, her eyes sparkling with mirth. "My sister, Lady Rosemary, is enamored of all things Oriental."

It was then that his eyes met Rosemary's. "Then I daresay I shall have to alter my opinion."

Her heartbeat fluttered. There was no mistaking it. He had flirted with her. It was actually—she hated to admit—the first time he had ever flirted with her. She lowered her lashes bashfully as a gentle smile lifted her mouth.

"Captain," Jack said, "I should like to make you known to our traveling companion, Stanton Maxwell, who is England's most eminent expert on Orientology."

The two men stiffly greeted one another. "Pray, pay no attention to Dryden," Mr. Maxwell said. "I'm merely a student of the Orient who has much more to learn."

Rosemary admired Mr. Maxwell's humility. She knew without a doubt that in spite of his youth, Mr. Maxwell was the most well-informed man in England on all things Oriental.

"You may have read Mr. Maxwell's book, *Travels Through the Levant*," Daphne said. She could not have seemed more proud had she been Mr. Maxwell's doting mother.

Captain Cooper's brows scrunched. "I'm not precisely sure where the Levant is. How fortunate you all are to have so knowledgeable a man in your company." His head turned toward the entrance. "Why in the devil are there British soldiers in tents in front of your hotel?"

"There wasn't enough room in the European hotel for them," Daphne said.

Jack nodded. "Lady Daphne and I were charged by the Regent to undertake a commission for him, and he insisted that a small detail of House Guards accompany us to ensure our safety. I daresay that decision was made to alleviate Lord Sidworth's fears for his daughters in exotic foreign lands."

Captain Cooper's gaze met Rosemary's again. "And I suppose—being enamored of all things Oriental—Lady Rosemary had to join your traveling party?"

She smiled at him. "How clever you are, Captain." Though, deep down, she did not think him very clever. Who did not know where the Levant was? And how could an Englishman pass up the opportunity to see the pyramids in person? Had he taken leave of his senses?

Nevertheless, his desire to see her as well as his magnificent presence made her feel like a princess.

"So what do you plan to do in Cairo?" Daphne asked him.

"I confess, I'd heard of your party, and I said to myself, by Jove, you've got to sail down—or up, whatever the case may be—to Cairo and pop in to see Lady Rosemary Chalmers."

He remembered me! Truth be told, Captain Cooper had never given Rosemary much indication that he was anything more than minimally aware of her existence, which was understandable, given his supreme popularity with all the maidens at Almack's.

And now she had a clear field! To think, he'd traveled at least five days down the Nile just to see her!

"Should you like to procure a room here at our

hotel?" Jack asked.

"By Jove, I would."

"If there are no vacancies," Daphne said, "I suppose you could double up with Mr. Maxwell—if that is agreeable to you, Mr. Maxwell?"

Mr. Maxwell set down his coffee cup. "Quite," he said, nodding.

Rosemary had been unable to remove her gaze from Captain Cooper's physical perfection. "This is a wonderful surprise, Captain. We must take you to the bazaar. You can procure perfumes and silks and any manner of things to take home to your mother and sisters at a fraction of the cost they'd be in England."

"I expect one would have to have a dragoman present to barter for one," the Captain said.

"Our dragoman is on another commission at present," Rosemary said, "but since Mr. Maxwell speaks Arabic, he can converse with the shopkeepers for us."

Captain Cooper eyed Mr. Maxwell. "I say, old fellow, what have you done to your arm?"

Mr. Maxwell shrugged. "A little cut."

"It most certainly was not a little cut!" Rosemary protested. "A dagger nearly severed his arm."

"Mr. Maxwell sustained his near-mortal injuries," Daphne said, "rescuing my sister after she was abducted by . . . white slavers."

Captain Cooper's brows shot up, his mouth gaped open. Mr. Maxwell spit out his coffee. Jack glared at Daphne.

Why had Daphne gone and fibbed about white slavery? Rosemary supposed she did so to mask the truth about their clandestine investigation. But why slavery? No one would ever want an earl's daughter for a maid. She was indolent, untidy, and had not the least notion of how one would go about cleaning anything.

Jack coughed. "My wife has a fanciful imagination."

"Was Lady Rosemary abducted?"

"Oh, yes," Rosemary answered. "The two men were beasts." She turned to Mr. Maxwell. "Mr. Maxwell had to kill one of them whilst rescuing me."

His mouth still gaping open, Captain Cooper addressed Mr. Maxwell. "You own a sword?"

Mr. Maxwell nodded. "When one travels in the Orient, one must be armed."

"He has a pistol, too," Rosemary said. "That's what killed the vile man who abducted me."

Captain Cooper turned to Jack. "And where were you, sir, while Maxwell was saving your sister?"

"I was with him—fighting off the other man."

"Did you kill him, too?"

Jack frowned. "No. In fact, he got away."

"It's disgusting how these Arabs have no respect for women," said Captain Cooper, avoiding eye contact with both Daphne and Rosemary.

"Unfortunately, the man who got away was British. A deserter who'd once served under me," Jack said.

Captain Cooper scowled. "Pity you didn't kill him."

Because of the captain's presence, Rosemary allowed Mr. Maxwell to feed himself—provided he use only his left hand. She did so for two reasons. First, she did not want to diminish Mr. Maxwell's masculinity in front of the supremely masculine Captain. Secondly, she did not want the

supremely handsome Captain Cooper to think Mr.
Maxwell had captured her affections. Nothing
could be further from the truth. He was merely
her rescuer. Certainly not her lover.

Captain Cooper cleared his throat. "I say, would
it not be better that you don't go about telling
people about Lady Rosemary's brush with . . .
white slavery?"

"It's not like I actually had to mop floors or iron
petticoats."

Captain Cooper's eyes narrowed, a questioning
look on his flawless face. Mr. Maxwell coughed.
Jack glared at Daphne.

"We do hope we can rely on your discretion,
Captain," Daphne said.

Why was her sister beaming so?

"Oh, yes, quite so."

* * *

How proud Rosemary was to walk through the
bazaar on the arm of Captain Cooper. All eyes
went to the handsome officer in his well-fitted red
coat adorned with gold medals and epaulets. How
she wished her friends back in London could see
her with last Season's most sought-after man.

She took care that Mr. Maxwell was on her
other side so that he could interpret for them with
the various shopkeepers. "I am fairly adept at
translating," he told them, "but I daresay I know
nothing about the value of the merchandise—or
about bargaining."

She sighed. "That was one area in which
Habeeb earned his salary."

"Would you object if we went to the antiquities
bazaar?" asked Daphne, who, along with her
husband, trailed behind the trio, followed by half
a dozen House Guards.

"I should be most interested in going there again," Rosemary said. She would never tire of looking at old papyrus scrolls or brightly painted sarcophaguses—or was that sarcophagi? "Tell me, Mr. Maxwell, which is correct—sarcophaguses sarcophagi?" She had yet to ask the man a question he could not answer.

"While you will hear both, I believe the correct form for the singular is sarcophagi."

"What in the devil is a sarcophagi?" Captain Cooper asked.

"It's a rather fancy word for a rather fancy coffin," she replied.

"You have likely seen hundreds in English churches," Mr. Maxwell told the Captain. "Any stone coffin-sized box that has a person's effigy on top is a sarcophagus. In Egypt, the sarcophagi can be highly ornamental."

"How I dislike it when spellings change—words like fungus becoming fungi," Captain Cooper said. "It's enough to make one wish to strangle the person who came up with all the ridiculousness, is it not?"

"It certainly can be perplexing," she agreed.

"Not so perplexing when one has Mr. Maxwell at the ready. The man is a walking library," said Daphne.

Rosemary turned back to watch her trailing sister and nodded. "He is indeed."

"Never heard of someone being a walking library," Captain Cooper said. Under his breath he muttered, "What man would want to be a bloody library?"

Rosemary elbowed him for his insensitive remark.

On the way to the antiquities bazaar, they

stopped at the same stall where Rosemary had previously purchased perfume. Captain Cooper was interested in procuring two bottles.

"If you like the fragrances I purchased, I can tell you what we paid for them. I thought it was exceedingly fair, but I can take no credit for it. I owe my satisfaction to our dragoman's bartering," Rosemary said.

"If Lady Rosemary vouches for their quality, I know my mother will be ecstatic with them." Their eyes met. Her heartbeat accelerated.

It took all three of them to negotiate the sale with the perfume seller, but in the end, Captain Cooper happily walked away with two bottles of Rosemary's favorite perfume.

Ten minutes later, their group strolled along the most opulent street in all of the bazaar, their destination the gold-pillared shop at the end of the lane. Ahmed Hassein's establishment.

The two huge sentries wearing fez hats stood on either side of the entrance, but their master was not within. An assistant rushed to greet them in French. While he was speaking with Jack and Daphne, Captain Cooper whispered to Rosemary, "Just another reason why I hate Egyptians. They must revere the foul Frenchies for it's the only other language they're willing to speak."

"You speak French, do you not, Captain?" she asked.

He frowned. "I do not, nor will I ever. I hate the French even more than I hate the Egyptians."

"It would seem a soldier who must represent the empire all over the globe should be more tolerant, my dear Captain," Rosemary said. She was afraid Mr. Hassein's assistant may have heard the officer's disparaging remarks.

Like all the Egyptians they had met, the assistant wore a turban, flowing robes, and sported a bushy beard. "You are the Englishmen who visited with Ahmed Hassein before?" he asked in French.

"Yes," Jack replied.

"My employer said that if you returned I was to tell you there is information he wants to impart to you. If you come back in the morning, he will be here."

"We will be back in the morning," Jack said.

The rest of the group gathered around a heavily gilded vertical sarcophagus that depicted an ancient kohl-eyed man whose heavy gold necklace indicated he was of high rank. It had not been there the last time they were in this shop. Rosemary turned to the shopkeeper. "Did this belong to a pharaoh?"

"Indeed, it did, madam," he answered in French.

"Which pharaoh would that be?" Mr. Maxwell asked.

The man cleared his throat. "It is believed to have been the coffin of Khufu."

"That would be impossible," Mr. Maxwell answered.

She was waiting for Mr. Maxwell to elaborate, but he was not one to flaunt his vast knowledge.

The assistant shrugged. "I may have it wrong. My employer will be able to provide more thorough information, but alas, he is not here at present."

"When does this date to?" she asked.

"I believe it dates to the Middle Kingdom," the shop assistant said.

The nonconfrontational Mr. Maxwell only slightly shook his head in denial.

"Can you ask the bloke how much one of these will set a fellow back?" Captain Cooper asked.

Rosemary had never known anyone who could not converse in French. Except for the lower classes, of course.

Jack asked.

"This is the most rare and finest example of royal sarcophagi we have ever received, and its value is nearly without price. Alas, my employer has other financial obligations that compel him to seek a buyer for the crown in his possession. Since he needs a speedy sale, he has consented to allow this incredibly rare piece to sell for only ten thousand British guineas."

"Our ruler would be thrilled to have it in his collection," Daphne said. "A pity we cannot convey that information to him at present."

Since Ahmed Hassein was known to be disreputable, Rosemary found herself wondering if this was even an authentic antiquity. She suspected Mr. Maxwell would know.

After they left the shop, she asked Mr. Maxwell if he could determine the authenticity of the sarcophagus.

"I expect it's genuine, but I'm no expert. It is only with papyri that I am competent to judge."

She was quite certain he was merely being modest. Not even an antiquities dealer like Ahmed Hassein was as knowledgeable of his ancestors as was the Cambridge scholar.

As they returned to their hotel, Jack and Daphne received a letter. It wasn't really her concern, but Rosemary was consumed with curiosity about who had sent it.

Daphne peered over her husband's shoulder as he read. It took just seconds to read, and then he looked up. "Lord Beddington has offered to send his carriage for us tonight."

Rosemary's heart sank. "What about Captain Cooper?"

"Lord Beddington shouldn't mind one extra. I'll send around a note informing him that our party has grown by one." She smiled up at Captain Cooper. "His lordship has been away from England for many years and welcomes the opportunity to mingle with Englishmen."

* * *

As Jack was fastening Daphne's pearls for the evening's dinner, he said, "You really shouldn't have said what you said to Captain Cooper about Rosemary being abducted by white slavers."

She looked up at him, a black expression on her face. "Why ever not?"

"Something like that could ruin her reputation. I didn't want to go into specific detail with you back in Gizeh, but white slavers traffic in women's bodies."

Daphne's stomach plummeted. "Thank God she was rescued!"

"First off, Madam Devious, you know very well she was not abducted by white slavers."

"Oh, dear, I almost forgot."

He glared at her. "You never forget anything, Madam Schemer. At what game are you playing?"

She sighed. "I never have cared for Captain Cooper, and now that I've spent an entire afternoon with the man, I am more convinced than ever of his unworthiness of my sister's affections."

"I cannot disagree with you."

"I would not be averse to him thinking of Rosemary as damaged goods. I trust that as a gentleman he would never repeat such a confidence."

"I think you've had other schemes in operation regarding that particular triangle."

"Thou doth knowest me too well." She sighed again. "I confess that I hope that the more she is with the Captain, the more she will come to realize how ineligible he is."

"And there's something else . . ."

She nodded. "Yes, the more opportunities she has to compare him to Mr. Maxwell, the greater the likelihood she will come to understand which man is the worthier."

He dropped a kiss into her hair. "What if Maxwell isn't interested in your sister?"

She harrumphed. "He was willing to give his life for her! That's quite enough to convince me of his high regard for her. You attempted to give your life to save me, did you not, that night in Hampstead?"

He nodded. "But you were my wife. That's what a husband does."

"There is that."

Seconds later she looked up at him. "Have you any particular inquiries we should make of Lord Beddington tonight?"

"First, we must find out why he wants us so soon after his return to Cairo. Does he feel our investigation is too close?" He shook his head ruefully. "God, I wished I knew something. Anything! We've not learned a damned thing."

"Yes, you have, my darling. You know Gareth Williams is involved. You know Gareth Williams murdered Amal. You know that an Englishman is responsible for Prince Singh's . . . almost-certain murder."

"There is that." He proffered his arm. "Is my lady ready for the waiting carriage?"

$\mathcal{C}$hapter 17

As Daphne had expected, Lord Beddington's house was a mixture of East and West. Unlike many of the villas they'd seen here that were built around central courtyards, this one was built much in the English manner with a corridor from which all the ground-floor rooms could be entered. This corridor was constructed of the local tile. Their footsteps clanged against the floors as they followed Lord Beddington's very English butler from the front entry hall to his lordship's drawing room.

That chamber was nothing like an English drawing room. The former ambassador was obviously influenced by the Pasha, for the floor here was covered with opulent silken pillows of every colour.

When they entered, Lord Beddington, dressed in the Oriental style, rose from his seated position on one of these pillows. He went straight to Rosemary and took her hand. "Permit me to say how very happy I am that you have been restored to us, Lady Rosemary." His eyes traveled the length of her. "I am gratified that you appear to have suffered no ill consequences from the shabby deed."

"I am more gratified than you can know," she answered. "I shall forever be indebted to Mr. Maxwell and Captain Dryden for my heroic rescue." She cast a shimmering gaze at Mr.

Maxwell with his arm in a sling. "Mr. Maxwell could have suffered a mortal injury during my rescue."

All eyes darted to Maxwell. "'Twas nothing," the embarrassed scholar said.

Rosemary's attention returned to their host. "And I thank you too, my lord, for so kindly offering your assistance in the search for me."

"There's nothing I wouldn't have done to restore you to your dear father," the earl said. "Though I haven't seen Lord Sidworth in a great many years, I count him as one of my dearest friends." He turned to Jack. "May I hope the culprits have been apprehended?"

A dejected look swept across Jack's face. "The Egyptian who abducted Lady Rosemary was slain during the rescue. The other man got away."

"Another Egyptian?" Lord Beddington asked.

Though Jack had heretofore been opposed to acknowledging Williams' presence in Cairo, that was no longer the case since the two had so openly confronted one another and since Jack might have been seen at Williams' residence. The person who employed Williams would now know all of this.

Was Lord Beddington that man? Daphne had a hard time believing it. Papa wouldn't have a friend who was a greedy murderer. Though she supposed few schoolboys were actually murderers. And he and Papa had become great friends at school. Perhaps Lord Beddington grew corrupted later.

She truly did not think he had.

Jack still scowled. "The second man, I am ashamed to say, was one of our own countrymen, a deserter who served under me in Spain."

Lord Beddington frowned. "A bloody traitor, then." Shrugging, he continued, "I daresay once he caught sight of the lovely English lady, his more vile instincts took over. How fortunate that she was rescued before the wicked man could . . . carry out his intentions with Lady Rosemary."

Mr. Maxwell winced. Captain Cooper stared at the floor.

Daphne was trying to determine if their host truly believed Rosemary's abduction was motivated by a single British man's baser instincts, or if his lordship was throwing that out to camouflage Williams' true motivation—which is something the vile mastermind of these sinister occurrences would do. Surely that man was not Lord Beddington.

She stepped forward and offered her hand to their host, and after they exchanged greetings, said, "My lord, I should like to present to you Captain Cooper, who is staying in Cairo for a few days."

Even though the captain had not been in the original invitation, Lord Beddington could not have been more amiable to the young officer, asking him about his posting and his regiment.

Once all the salutations were complete, Lord Beddington offered Rosemary his arm. "Shall we go into the dinner room?"

On the way to that chamber, they passed a smaller eating room where it was obvious the diners ate on the floor.

The large dinner room they came to was much in the English style, but instead of crystal chandeliers, this chamber was illuminated by hanging lanterns that looked like something the Prince Regent would have at the Royal Pavilion.

The high-back chairs around a long table were upholstered in intricately designed damask, a blend of rich red and gold silk. A starched white cotton damask cloth covered the table which was already set with a vast array of foods in silver bowls and platters. European food.

Though Daphne prided herself on her ability to adapt to various cultures, she had to own that she preferred European foods. How she had missed these dishes the past several days! There was a tureen of soup, meat pies, leg of mutton, fish with a buttery sauce, and an assortment of colourful vegetables.

"I hope you don't mind that the meal's not entirely English," Lord Beddington said. "My chef, after all, is French, and I thought his very fine creations would be welcome among this gathering."

"Indeed they are," Daphne said, bestowing a smile upon their host.

They all proceeded to pass around plates and bowls and fill their dishes while a pair of footman dressed in the Turkish style poured wine for each diner.

She glanced across the table as the footman was pouring wine in Jack's glass and recognized him as Habeeb. How resourceful the dragoman was! He looked up, met Daphne's stare, and winked before moving to the next diner.

She wondered how she or Jack could contrive to steal a moment with him. Had he learned anything yet? Because of the almost cocky expression on his face, she had hope that he had indeed found out something.

Under the table, she kicked Jack. He glared at her, brows hiked. She ticked her head in Habeeb's direction.

Instead of looking at Habeeb, Jack's gaze whipped to Mr. Maxwell, whose glass Habeeb was filling. Jack's gaze swung back to her, a puzzled look on his face.

She jerked her head up in the hopes he would look above Mr. Maxwell's head.

Jack began to leap from his chair. "Daphne, are you unwell?" Concern made his voice uneven.

Now she glared. "I. Am. Very. Well."

He sighed and sat back down.

How could she get him to look at Habeeb? One did not normally notice footmen. Such a pity.

Thankfully, Lord Beddington—as well as Rosemary—was fascinated with whatever it was Mr. Maxwell was discussing. She drew a breath and spoke to her husband in a low voice. "I was in hopes you could communicate with the man who I said had a great many wives." She prayed he would not blurt out Habeeb's name. "He's very much like Jonathan at Papa's." Would Jack remember that Jonathan was her parents' longest-serving footman?

The puzzled look on Jack's face soon cleared, his gaze darted to the footmen, and a smile of recognition lifted his mouth. "I will oblige my lady."

Reassured that Jack would prevail, Daphne turned her full attention to the delicious food. She showed great restraint by not ooing and aaing with each morsel. "My lord, I don't think I've ever—not even at the Regent's—tasted food superior to this. The French sauce is heavenly."

"As proud as I am of my chef, my lady," Lord Beddington said, "I can't help but to believe your praise may be coloured by the comparison to simple Egyptian fare."

They all chuckled.

"My chef will be inordinately pleased to be told you find his cooking superior to that which you've enjoyed at the Regent's, for everyone knows of our Prince Regent's epicurean prowess."

"I did not think any food could ever compare to his," Jack said. "Until tonight."

"Tell me, my lord," Captain Cooper said, "why is it that you wear a turban and dress in the Oriental style?"

"When I was British ambassador to the Ottoman Empire I began to dress thusly for special occasions—to show my respect for their customs and practices. I believe an ambassador, while representing his own country, must also serve as a bridge between the two countries."

"But you're no long ambassador," Captain Cooper said.

A dead silence fell over the table. Daphne cringed. She prayed Rosemary did not marry this man.

"Quite so," his lordship said with a cheerful smile. "I have found—much to my wife's consternation—that I am enamored of all things Oriental."

Rosemary nodded. "As am I."

"Are you even enamored of the summer heat?" Captain Cooper asked their host.

"You've got me there," Lord Beddington responded. "I do dislike the heat when it's intense as it is now. However, were I to have the choice between living in dreary, wet England or in the Arabian desert, I would not hesitate to choose the desert."

Mr. Maxwell shrugged. "I feel the very same,

but I have duties at Cambridge."

Jack eyed the scholar. "You are fortunate that your calling allows you the opportunity to enjoy both the East and the West."

"I vastly prefer my native land," Captain Cooper said, "but my calling keeps me from my homeland."

Daphne could not control her tongue. "Perhaps, Captain, you should seek another calling." She'd bet a monkey he chose to be a soldier because he was possessed of the kind of manly physique which so splendidly filled out a uniform. Vain creature.

"Can't quit during wartime. Not the thing at all."

"I agree," Jack said.

Somehow, Captain Cooper had contrived to sit beside Rosemary, and he made a great show of being solicitous of her. Rosemary herself—much to Daphne's consternation—happily basked beneath his attentions, subtly glowing like a votive candle in a dark church.

At Rosemary's other side was Mr. Maxwell, whom she assisted by cutting up his mutton. Prior to leaving their hotel he had extracted a promise from her that she refrain from trying to actually feed him. He and their host got into a discussion of their Arabian travels.

Daphne found herself analyzing Lord Beddington's behavior. It did not appear that he had asked them here to query them about their activities in Cairo.

His questions about Rosemary's abduction were those which anyone would have been curious about. Failure to ask about it would have been exceedingly odd. It might even have pointed to potential guilt.

The longer she sat there—gorging on meat pies and local fish smothered in the chef's special buttery sauce—the more convinced she was of his lordship's innocence. Were he the guilty party, would he not have been directing the conversation to questions about the reason for their presence in Cairo? She would have to share with Jack all her reasons for believing Lord Beddington innocent.

Though she could not remember a time in any of their investigations when she and Jack had not held identical beliefs.

* * *

After the men had enjoyed their port, Jack excused himself. His nose easily guided him to the kitchen where he asked to speak to the footmen regarding the wine they had served. A moment later, Habeeb appeared.

"Do you speak English?" he asked for the benefit of onlookers.

"I do."

"Very good, old boy." Jack put an arm around him and walked away from the kitchen. "There are some questions I'd like to ask about the wine."

Once in a dimly lit section of the corridor, the two men huddled.

"Have you learned anything helpful?" Jack asked.

Habeeb nodded. "I was going to come to you in the morning—after I disappeared from this post. I have learned that the English lord has been in Thebes since a few weeks after the time of your Christmas and only came to Gizeh three days ago."

"Do you know if his lordship communicated

with another Englishman? A Welshman?"

"I asked if while they were in Gizeh any other Englishmen visited with Lord Beddington and was told that your party was the only one."

"Did anyone know of any prank being rigged in the Great Pyramid?"

Habeeb shook his head.

"One last question. Had any of the servants heard that Lord Beddington might have run into financial troubles?"

"No. They all say he very rich man."

Jack thanked him and made his way back to the others, anxious to tell his clever wife what he'd found out.

* * *

Two hours later, they were in their bedchamber, stripped of most of their clothing, and sitting against the head of the bed. He was able to share with his wife all that Habeeb had told him.

"I just knew that Lord Beddington was not evil," she said triumphantly.

His shoulders sagged. "That puts us back to where we were before he came into the picture. A huge blank."

"I think a private visit with Mr. Briggs is in order tomorrow."

Jack moved to her, brushed her golden curls from her face, and settled his lips on hers. "A most agreeable plan, my love. And now I have another most agreeable plan . . ."

* * *

In the middle of the night Daphne awakened. She sat up in bed, her heart pounding. What had so suddenly awakened her? Then she felt something odd. As if something was crawling on her legs. Or on the sheet which covered her legs.

There was just enough moonlight for her to see. The sight was enough to stop her heartbeat. She flung back the sheets as if they were aflame. A shrill, alien-sounding scream broke from her throat. Her chest felt as if it were exploding.

Jack surged up. "Daphne! What's wrong?"

"A snake! A huge snake was crawling on our bed."

$\mathcal{C}$hapter 18

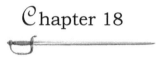

"Good lord!"

He leapt from the bed and fetched his sword.

If the snake were poisonous, it could kill Daphne. "Get the hell out of here! I'm going to kill the damned thing."

She was standing on the mattress at the head of the bead, whimpering. "I'm too scared."

He moved closer to the bed. Thank God for the night's full moon. He saw movement. "It's on the floor now—at the foot of the bed. Stay where you are."

"I-I-I won't budge."

Jack prided himself on his bravery, but he had to own that staring down a venomous snake was more frightening than facing cannon fire. He still remembered those deadly cobras from his days in India. A subaltern in his camp was killed by one. While he slept.

A menacing chill inched down Jack's spine.

He wished to God he was wearing his boots.

Suddenly, the viper's head rose, and its hood fanned out, shimmery under the moonlight. Jack would swear the damned thing was watching him.

His heart thundering, Jack lunged toward the cobra and with all his strength swung his sword at the snake before he quickly retreated.

Success! He'd managed to sever the head from the rest of the body. From a distance of several feet away, Jack watched its pale, coiled body squirm for several seconds before the movements slowed, and it finally died.

Jack moved to Daphne. "It's dead."

She dropped down and collapsed in his arms, hysterically crying. "I w-w-w-ant to go home. I ca-a-a-an't sleep in a place where vile vipers slither upon a sleeping person."

He stroked her back and murmured in her ear. "Snakes don't climb to second stories."

She drew away from him, lowering her brows. "What are you saying?"

"Someone put that snake in our room, probably while we were dining at Lord Beddington's."

"Now see here, Jack, you can't suspect my father's friend of such wickedness."

"I'm not. The truth is I don't know who wants us dead."

"Why did we not see the snake when we first returned home and lighted a candle here?"

He shrugged. "My guess is that the snake was put under the bed. I learned a bit about cobras when I lived in India. They're not aggressive. It probably chose to stay in hiding as long as our candle burned. It only began to explore the chamber once the room fell into silence."

She shivered. "A cobra? Are they not terribly poisonous?"

"They are."

"You know, dearest, it's not inconceivable that someone might have put the snake in after we were asleep."

"But our door was locked." As soon as he spoke, he gave her a knowing nod. "We do leave our window open, and someone with a ladder could have done the deed."

"But toting a tall ladder about the city makes

that option less credible."

He nodded. "First thing in the morning, we ask everyone who was here in the hotel last night if they saw anyone who did not belong here, ask if anyone saw someone near our chamber. And . . . we'll see if anyone saw someone carrying a ladder." He sighed. "I shouldn't have brought you to Egypt."

"You know very well I would not have let you come without me."

"I honestly didn't think your life would be in danger."

"Our lives, dearest."

He drew her to him and held her close for a very long time.

* * *

They were rather late getting off to speak to Mr. Briggs the next morning. As soon as he was dressed, Jack walked the outer perimeter of the hotel, stopping beneath their window, his head bent as he examined the earth. He was looking for signs that someone might have been there once the city had gone to sleep. But the dirt had not been disturbed. Since even his boots left indentations, he was sure the person who wanted them dead had come from the inside while they had dined at Lord Beddington's.

Once Daphne came down for breakfast, they questioned the other guests. All three of them: two German university students and a middle-aged Dane. They conversed in French. No one saw anyone who did not belong there the previous night. No one saw anyone near Jack and Daphne's chamber. No one saw someone with a ladder. The three other guests each said they had retired to their rooms after dinner, not to come out again.

When it was just three of them in the breakfast room, Rosemary raised her brows and addressed them. "Why are you asking all these questions?"

Since Captain Cooper had not yet come down, Daphne could speak openly. "We believe someone tried to kill us last night."

Rosemary gasped. "How?"

"A cobra was put into our bedchamber."

At that moment Maxwell strode into the breakfast room. "What's this about a cobra?"

Rosemary whirled to him. "My sister says someone put a cobra in their bedchamber last night whilst they were sleeping." An exaggerated shiver convulsed her upper torso.

Maxwell winced.

Rosemary faced Daphne. "It's a very great thing that you discovered it before it killed you. Pray, how did you discover it?"

"I'd been asleep probably three hours when I awakened, feeling something crawling on me."

Rosemary shrieked and clutched at her heart. "Dear Almighty Savior, you could have been killed!"

Jack put an arm around his wife. "Yes, we know."

Daphne peered lovingly into her husband's face. "Thank God Jack's sword was close! He was able to cut the beastly thing's head off."

Rosemary was still cringing.

Maxwell's voice softened when he spoke to her. "Look on the brighter side, Lady Rosemary. You were not the intended victim this time."

Rosemary looked up at him, eyes shimmering. "Thank God! I should have died of fright."

Daphne sighed, meeting Maxwell's gaze. "I'm

still very concerned about her. I want her to sleep in our room tonight."

Rosemary's brows still lowered, she offered her sister a feeble smile. "It will take no further persuasion. I'll be there!"

"I am most relieved to hear that," Maxwell said.

"Where's your Captain Cooper?" Jack asked his sister-in-law.

At the mention of Captain Cooper, all expression drained from Maxwell's face. Bloody bad form for Jack to have spoken as he had about that damned Captain.

"I believe he said something about indulging his natural inclination to sleep late," she replied.

"What will you be doing this morning while we go to the Consulate?" Daphne asked.

"Mr. Maxwell has offered to lead us on a tour of Cairo," Rosemary said. "I'd thought to meet you later at the bazaar. I'm eager to know what it is Mr. Hassein has to say to you."

Jack nodded and lowered his voice. "So long as you guard our inquiries from Captain Cooper."

Rosemary and Mr. Maxwell agreed at the same time.

When Jack and Daphne left their hotel for the old town, they exchanged brief greetings with Captain Cooper as he came down the stairs, his sword banging against the wall.

Even though it was just nine in the morning, the heat was hard to tolerate, and dust stirred up from each of their steps. A short time after Jack and Daphne began to walk, Jack said, "A pity we have no horse upon which to ride into town."

"It most certainly is not a pity. Walking is excessively good for one."

"That may be the case in England, but it's too

bloody hot here to walk about." He swatted flies from his face.

She sighed. "It's quite disheartening to realize this is the coolest part of the day, is it not?"

He agreed.

"I daresay later in the day I will long for a horse."

They were finally getting proficient at finding the Consulate amongst the labyrinth of narrow streets in Old Cairo. Fifteen minutes after they left their lodgings, they found themselves being ushered into Mr. Briggs' office. It was several degrees cooler inside the building than it was outside.

The Consul stood to greet them. "Beastly business about your sister, Lady Daphne. Beastly." He kissed her proffered hand and begged that they sit before his desk.

"Are you aware," Jack asked, "that a British subject—likely a traitor—played a role in my sister-in-law's abduction?"

The Consul's eyes widened. "Who?"

"A Welshman named Gareth Williams. Ever heard of him?" Jack asked.

"Can't say that I have."

"Because of his dodgy background, it's possible he's using another name," Jack said. "The man—I can't in good conscience call him a soldier—served under me in Spain. He deserted at Badajoz."

"Sounds to be a thoroughly unpleasant character."

They had decided not to divulge that he was Amal's killer. Not now. Justice for her murder could wait until the murder or murderers were caught.

"Speaking   of   thoroughly   unpleasant

characters," Daphne said, "Can you verify that
Ahmed Hassein is disreputable?"

The Consul puckered his lips in thought. "That
is difficult to answer because there are different
levels of corruption. I believe there may have been
times when Mr. Hassein has allowed forgeries to
be passed off as authentic antiquities. That is not
to say that he doesn't sell some demmed fine
stuff. Some very valuable pieces. It's the smaller
things like amulets and papyrus that he may be
dishonest about.

"I would say, though, that I've never heard
anything else that might impugn his character.
He's said to be a fair and benevolent master to his
servants. In the years I've been here, I've not
heard anything disparaging about him."

Daphne was most perplexed. This was an
entirely different tale than what Mr. Arbuthnot
had told them. Which man was lying? How
reliable was this man's information?

"Changing the subject," the Consul said with a
smile, "I understand you've had the pleasure of
meeting Lord Beddington."

"Indeed we have," Jack said.

"He and my Papa were school friends."

"A fine gentleman, that one." He leaned back in
his chair, as if the contemplation of his wealthy,
titled friend transported him to some celestial
place. "You, if my information is correct, had the
honor of dining with him last night, did you not?"

Jack's spine stiffened. "How did you know?"

"His man came around to our office to get your
address."

So both Mr. Arbuthnot and Mr. Briggs as well
as others here at the Consulate yesterday knew
that they were not going to be at their hotel last

night.

Had one of them been responsible for placing the cobra in their bedchamber?

* * *

Despite all the horrendous things that had happened since she'd arrived in Egypt, Rosemary had never enjoyed anything more. So many new and exciting experiences! From her first morning sailing down the Nile to the day she'd climbed atop a dromedary and ridden across a desert unchanged since biblical times, each new experience made her feel more alive than she'd ever felt. She would never forget the sound of the muezzin's hauntingly lyrical Call to Prayer, even though she understood not a word of Arabic.

She was even becoming accustomed to the heat. She rather thought she was like Mr. Maxwell and Lord Beddington, who had come to prefer the heat—even intense heat like today's—over England's frequent gray, rainy days.

As she strolled through the narrow streets of the old town with her two favorite gentlemen, she found herself wishing again that all the debutantes in London could see her now. How jealous they would be that it was she who had captured the Captain's affections. For she now had no doubts that he was showering his attentions on her.

There was the fact she was likely the only unwed English lady in all of Egypt. He had little choice. Even though her rational side told her he would have been equally attentive to any English girl here in this exotic land, her romantic side told her he was finally at liberty to reveal his long-held affection for her. In London, he had known—she tried to assure herself—that he would be going to foreign lands. It would not have been right to engage a young lady's affections only to leave her for a considerable period of time.

But so long away from his homeland had most certainly sharpened Captain Cooper's desire to . . . perhaps unite himself with her? Her heart fluttered. Would he ask for her hand? This is what she had craved for the past year and a half.

She peered up at his aquiline profile. How handsome he was! How liberating it was to be in Cairo! In London she would never be permitted to stroll without a chaperon through the streets with two gentlemen—neither of which was a relation or a chaperon.

She swatted a fly from her face. Flies and snakes were definitely two things she would never miss about Egypt. Did one ever become accustomed to these horrid pests? "Tell me, Mr. Maxwell, did you learn to tolerate the flies as well as you learned to tolerate the heat?"

Chuckling as he brushed flies from his mouth, he shook his head. "I don't think even the natives grow accustomed to them."

"Just one more thing I hate about the country," the Captain said, then smiling at her whilst patting her hand that rested on his proffered sleeve, his voice gentled. "But if the lovely Lady Rosemary fancies this forsaken place, then I shall endeavor not to abuse it."

Wafting into the street was a fluted tune which caught their attention. She turned toward the establishment from which it came and could see three dancing girls. She slowed as she watched them, and the gentlemen at either side of her slowed too. Rosemary was mesmerized by the women (as were the profoundly silent, boldly staring men with her—and the string of soldiers which followed her everywhere).

The dancing girls were very handsome. Their movements as they swayed to the music were unlike anything she had ever seen, and their dresses were more European than Oriental. The necklines plunged to a V, revealing the valley between their breasts—much larger breasts than Rosemary possessed.

None of the dancers exceeded the age of five and twenty, and all of them had raven hair adorned with gilded headdresses. It was a rare sight to see a woman's hair in this part of the world.

As she and her companions stood there watching, she said in a low voice, "They're beautiful."

"Indeed they are," Captain Cooper agreed, "but I daresay you shouldn't be here, my lady. They're not the sort of women with whom you should be this close." He offered his arm and began to stroll away.

"Then why was my sister so insistent that Mr. Maxwell should make himself known to one?" As soon as she said the words, she realized what Daphne must have been trying to convey to Mr. Maxwell. And she felt the heat rise into her cheeks.

Captain Cooper coughed.

She eyed Mr. Maxwell. He shrugged. "I told your sister I don't dance."

Captain Cooper coughed again.

"Oblige me, Mr. Maxwell," she said, "by directing us to Mr. Hassein's establishment in the bazaar. Do you not think that Jack and Daphne will have concluded their business at the

Consulate by now?"

"I do."

* * *

Just seeing the tall sentries in front of Mr. Hassein's shop gave Daphne goose bumps. Why had these fez-wearing men been in the European quarter the previous morning? The only Egyptians normally seen there were the most menial of laborers, not tall, handsome men dressed in a curious mixture of Egyptian and Turkish.

She had a mind to ask them, but she doubted if they spoke a word of English. Or French.

Just as she was about to enter the shop, she caught sight of her sister ambling down the lane between her two admirers and followed by four of the Regent's House Guards.

"What perfect timing!" Daphne remarked. She waited to enter the establishment with her sister, while the gentlemen followed. She rather liked demonstrating to these Muslims that in her culture, women could go first, that women were respected, that women's presence in public was desired.

Upon entering the shop, her gaze connected with Hassein's. "You have returned," he said in French. "My man told me he gave you a message from me."

Jack came to stand beside her, and they both nodded. "What is it you wanted to tell us?" Jack asked.

Hassein's intense gaze met Jack's. "You know of a Frenchman who is called the duc d'Arblier?"

Daphne felt as if her heart could explode. Her limbs began to tremble.

Jack nodded.

"I believe you are at war with the French, is that not so?" Hassein asked.

"That is so," Jack said.

"You might wish to ask Ralph Arbuthnot what he was doing with the Frenchman."

$\mathcal{C}$hapter 19

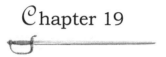

The duc d'Arblier was in Cairo? Her pulse pounded. The very notion made Daphne ill. Many times, d'Arblier had tried to kill Jack. She had no doubts last night's cobra was meant to kill Jack, and she had no doubts d'Arblier was responsible for the evil deed whether he physically put it there or not.

For a few seconds back in Mr. Hassein's shop at the bazaar, Daphne had thought she was going to snap her record as the only Chalmers sister never to have fainted. After Mr. Hassein disclosed the connection between that vile duc and Mr. Arbuthnot, she somehow managed to thank the proprietor and beg to take her leave. Without fainting.

As she reached the gilded pillars at the shop's entrance and saw the fez-wearing sentries, she stopped and turned back to face Hassein. "Was it not your guards whom I saw in the European Quarter recently?"

He nodded. "Indeed it was. A Frenchman sold me this extraordinary scarab." He opened a silken box and moved across the shop to show them a scarab of a beetle. It was of gold and encrusted with emeralds, rubies and sapphires. "My guards went to collect it. It is just the sort of item which thieves would be most interested in. I need not tell you, those two men have never once been threatened."

"I confess I feel threatened by them," Daphne said good naturedly. "They're rather ferocious looking."

"Exactly why I hired them."

After they left the bazaar, they needed a place where they could converse without being heard. They had much to discuss. Their heretofore slow progress had finally yielded fruit. Not only fruit, but she was quite certain they possessed enough information to solve the crimes.

Mr. Arbuthnot was not the kindly fellow countryman he tried to portray. He was evil. He had to be evil if he was in league with d'Arblier.

As they walked, she thought of things Arbuthnot had said and done since they'd arrived, things that might indicate his guilt. It had been his dragoman who'd procured the services of the Egyptians for their expedition to Gizeh. Either *Arbuth-knows-it-all* or his man must be responsible for enlisting the scoundrel who'd abducted Rosemary. Now Daphne was certain he was the one who had put the laudanum into Rosemary's guard's port. She also recalled that Arbuthnot boasted of buying his house. Few civil servants could afford to purchase property.

"I have an idea," Mr. Maxwell said. Then he turned to Rosemary. "Why don't you show Captain Cooper the docks at Bulak? There's much of interest."

She glared at him and lowered her voice so the Captain wouldn't hear. "While you stay and have all the excitement?"

He shrugged. "It's obvious the Captain wishes to be alone with you."

Her eyes rounded. "Do you really think so?"

He nodded solemnly.

She sighed. "Very well, but you must vow to tell me all when I return." She moved back to the Captain and tucked her arm to his as they strode away.

* * *

How she wanted to stay with the others. Rosemary was exceedingly curious to see how they would proceed. She did not know anything about the duc d'Arblier, but she did know Mr. Arbuthnot, and now she highly suspected he was in some way to blame for all these terrible things that had happened.

His culpability made her shiver. To think, a British public servant—a man they had trusted since the moment they'd set foot in Egypt—was acting against them. He could be responsible for the threats against her life.

It was difficult for her to be a gracious, informative guide to Captain Cooper when her thoughts were elsewhere.

The sun was now high in the sky—the hottest part of the day. She vowed not to complain. At least she was at liberty to wear a light muslin morning dress. Poor Captain Cooper must wear his heavy woolen jacket.

"I have found, Captain, that when the heat is at its most unbearable . . ." She stopped to swat at several flies which had landed upon her face. "I try to remember a dreary day in London that is so cold I feel like ice water is in my veins, like my bones have frozen. I think of a day so cold that the only thing I could want was to swath myself in blankets and sit in front of a fire. I remember when the fog is so thick I cannot see the house across the street." She looked up at him and smiled. "Then I don't so terribly object to the

Egyptian heat."

"How clever you are, my lady. I shall have to try your little trick."

With the four soldiers trotting behind them, they began to stroll toward Bulak, few words exchanged between them.

He patted her hand. "I cannot tell you how happy I am to finally be alone with the loveliest lady I know."

She felt the heat climb into her cheeks as she peered up at him, shyly lowering her lashes as a gentle smile settled on her mouth.

"I rather fancy you and me stopping at a coffee house. If my memory serves me correctly, it's right up here."

The strong coffee they served at these places wasn't to her liking, but she wanted to be amiable. "Yes, I believe you're right."

Because it was the hottest part of the day, no others were in the dark little shop when they entered and sat at a small table.

It was impossible to communicate with the server when neither of them spoke Arabic. She wished Mr. Maxwell were here.

Smiling broadly, the server, who had a massive black beard, finally brought them two small cups of the strong brew, and then disappeared behind a curtain to give them privacy.

Captain Cooper settled his hand over hers. "I don't have to tell you, Rosemary, how profound are my feelings for you."

How improper! No man had ever called her by her first name. "I- I –I am most flattered."

"It's I who am flattered just to be in your company."

"Amazing, is it not, that we are permitted to do

in Cairo what would never be acceptable in London?"

He drew her hand to his lips and softly kissed it. "Indeed it is." His voice was low and husky, and the glittering in his blue eyes was unlike anything she'd seen before. Unless such a glittering came from a person rendered senseless from laudanum. She felt uneasy.

"There's a question I've wanted to ask you, my lady."

She smiled up at him. "What question?"

"I would be the most fortunate man in his majesty's army if you would do me the goodness of consenting to become my wife."

She felt as if she'd been struck in the chest with a cricket bat. Was there any air left in her lungs? She was completely stunned by the Captain's declaration. She'd known he was attracted to her, but she also knew he had no intentions of leaving his position while his country was at war.

Before she could respond, he continued. "I know I'm not worthy of an earl's daughter, but your father has already consented to have one army officer as a son-in-law. I know it's a lot to ask you to give up your luxurious manner of living to follow the drum with me to God-only-knows where. But I will say there are presently three officers' wives in our camp, and they all seem to vastly enjoy such a life."

She felt rather as if she were in a dream. Her dreams were coming true! For one-and-a-half years she had longed to hear such a declaration from the handsome Captain. She was the one who felt honored. Quite honestly, when she'd embarked on this Egyptian journey she had no hope that the Captain would ever be attracted to her.

A smile lifting her lips, she met his gaze. "I think following the drum sounds exceedingly exciting. I shall be honored to become your wife."

His gaze darted from her to the curtain, then to the soldiers waiting in the street, their backs to them. He stood and pulled her to him, his strong arms closing around her while he hungrily kissed her.

This was her first kiss. It wasn't as magical as she had imagined. For one thing, he was so tall that she had to tilt her head into a most awkward position. For another, his breath smelled of garlic. She was now thankful she abhorred garlic. She wouldn't want to carry such an odor on her person.

She supposed kissing was an acquired skill, clearly an acquired taste.

When the kiss terminated, she realized she was embarrassed. She looked at the floor, and then scooted back into her chair to finish her coffee.

She could not wait to tell Miss Elephantine. The two ladies, who were the best of friends, together had ogled the handsome Captain whenever he entered a ball.

They finished their coffee and once more began to walk to Bulak. "I shall take a leave and travel back to England with you to seek your father's approval. That given, I shall need to procure a special license so we can speedily marry and return to Fort Rached."

"It all sounds so terribly romantic."

* * *

After Rosemary and Captain Cooper left them, Mr. Maxwell faced Jack and Daphne. "No one will be in the Coptic church this time of day. We'll be able to speak in private there."

She and Jack followed Mr. Maxwell. "Did you not say the Coptics are Christians?" she asked.

"Yes. They're very much like the Greek Orthodox Church, which both have origins in the 1st century AD," Mr. Maxwell said.

The crosses that topped the church's twin mini-domed bell towers could be seen from several hundred yards away. When they got closer, Daphne asked Mr. Maxwell what the church's name was.

"It's call the Hanging Church, but not for reasons you might suspect. It's more to do with how it's situated."

They climbed up twenty-nine steps to enter the church, which Mr. Maxwell said was many hundreds of years old. The church was in the Christian basilica style, but its brightly coloured mosaic arches in the Moorish style clearly bespoke the Egyptian heritage.

No one else was there. The three of them marched down the nave and sat in the first row pew. Jack sketched out enough information about his arch nemesis to give Mr. Maxwell some idea of what they were up against with the cunning duc d'Arblier.

"It seems plausible that his desire to possess the Amun-re mask was motivated by his hatred of the Regent," Maxwell said.

"And he's such a thoroughly despicable person that he'd rather murder for it than to diminish his own wealth," Daphne said.

"You're likely right, love." Jack's brows lowered. "I don't understand how someone could be so cold-blooded a killer. It's not as if the duc isn't one of the wealthiest men in all of France. Why did he not just pay for the mask?"

"Perhaps Prince Singh decided not to sell it to him," Mr. Maxwell suggested.

Jack nodded. "The duc is not accustomed to being thwarted. In anything."

Daphne's eyes narrowed. "How does that vile Mr. Arbuthnot play into all of this?"

"I'm not sure," Jack said. "But I know he has to."

"I agree," Daphne said "Now that I've thought about it, there are several things that point to his guilt."

Jack nodded. "Things like him adding the laudanum to the guard's port back in Gizeh?"

"Yes," she said. "And it was him and his dragomen who secured the services of the Egyptians for that expedition."

"And one of them clearly was instructed to capture poor Lady Rosemary," Maxwell added.

"There's also the lies he's told," Daphne said. "He told us he didn't know Prince Singh, told us Ahmed Hassein was a murderer." She drew a breath. "Also, he told me he'd begun to acquire property." She shrugged. "Of course, that was not a lie."

"On a civil servant's salary?" Maxwell asked, grinning.

"Also," Daphne said, "he's English. We've been told since early on that it was an Englishman who was to meet with Prince Singh that night."

"Remember, too, he chose not to go in the pyramid that day," Jack said, shaking his head. "I can't believe I didn't give him serious consideration. I wonder if I'd ever have unraveled this without Hassein's helpful tip."

"Yes, you would have." Daphne glared at him. "Hassein wouldn't have had any connection with us had our inquiries not taken us to his shop. We were thorough, and it's those types of inquiries which have proven to unearth the truth."

"I think it's time the three of us pay a not-so-friendly call upon the man," Mr. Maxwell said.

* * *

They found Arbuthnot in his office at the Consulate. When they entered the chamber, he stood, smiling at them and issuing pleasant greetings, but when he saw the somber expression on each of their faces, his clouded. "Pray, is something wrong?" His gaze flicked to the door which Maxwell was closing. Once the door was closed, Maxwell stood in front of it, his arms folded across his chest as he glared at the attaché.

Jack knew a few things about interrogating the enemy. "Indeed there is," Jack said. "You're a bloody traitor. How much did d'Arblier pay you?"

Arbuthnot's face blanched. "I don't know what you're talking about."

"A very reliable source has told us of your close relationship with the Frenchman," Daphne said.

Arbuthnot finally shrugged. "So what if I do know him? He's not here in any official capacity. Is it a crime to share a hookah with the fellow?"

"As it happens, my hostile relationship with the duc goes back a long way. Nothing he does is innocuous," Jack said.

"He's evil," Daphne said venomously. "He hates both my husband and our ruler."

Jack moved to him. His sheer size advantage should intimidate Arbuthnot. "You lied to us about knowing Prince Singh. You lied to us about knowing Gareth Williams. You lied to us about

Ahmed Hassein being a murderer." Jack came even closer, sneering. He grabbed Arbuthnot's fine woolen jacket and twisted it. "You better tell the truth now, or I'll see you hanged for murder."

Arbuthnot collapsed into his chair. "I'm not a murderer. I was just a very small part of his foul deeds." He sighed, and a moment later started at the beginning. "Knowing that I was acquainted with Prince Singh, d'Arblier asked me to be an intermediary with the Indian. D'Arblier was determined to get the mask. He told me to tell the prince that I was brokering a deal with an anonymous collector who was willing to double what the Regent was paying for the mask."

"Did you go to Singh's house with d'Arblier that night?" Jack asked.

His eyes filling with tears, he nodded. "I had no idea what his true reason was for insisting that the servants be given the night off, no idea he meant to murder Singh in order to possess the mask." His voice began to crack.

Even though Jack had known in his bones that Singh had been murdered, he'd foolishly clung to the hope that he had not.

"Once he plunged his dagger into Prince Singh," Arbuthnot continued, "I was certain he was going to murder me too. It would make sense for him to make it look as if I had killed Singh. But to my profound surprise, he smiled at me. He said he needed a man inside the British government. He said he would pay handsomely. He asked what my salary was and promised to match it.

"I didn't believe him. Not after what he'd done to Singh, but I would have promised anything that night to save myself from that murderer." He sighed. "He left Egypt then, but true to his word, each quarter the funds he'd promised were deposited in my bank.

"Things went on smoothly for several months. I heard nothing from the Frenchman, but I was well paid. Once he knew you'd be coming . . ." He peered at Jack. "He called in his vouchers, so to speak. Had he known before you landed in Alexandria, I'd have put in a d'Arblier puppet for your dragoman, but I'd already engaged Habeeb."

"So d'Arblier didn't know we were coming until after the Consul learned?" Daphne asked.

"Yes."

"Did he try to order you to kill me?"

"No. I gathered he wanted that pleasure himself. He did make it clear that he wanted to inject chaos into your party so that you would return to England for fear of the ladies' safety."

"That day you showed up as we were going to Gizeh, it wasn't the Consul who asked you to come, was it?" Jack asked.

Arbuthnot shook his head. "D'Arblier insisted I come. He'd already dispatched Williams. Something about rigging some stones to fall on your party when they entered the burial chamber in the Great Pyramid."

Daphne glared at Arbuthnot. "Did you select the Egyptian who abducted my sister? You knew she was going to be taken, did you not?"

He avoided making eye contact. Hanging his head, he nodded. "He made me put the laudanum in the guard's glass. He assured me he wouldn't kill your sister, that he merely needed to extract whatever information he could about your investigation on behalf of the Regent. He also wanted to frighten you into returning to England."

Daphne's voice cracked. "You had to know that

when they were finished interrogating her, they would kill her."

He looked up at them, remorseful. "I would not have let that happen."

Jack gave an insincere chuckle. "Keep telling yourself that, Arbuthnot. The truth is you're frightened of d'Arblier. You're a coward."

"We know that Williams killed Singh's mistress," Daphne said. "Was it because the duc feared she might know something about that fateful night her lover died?"

Arbuthnot nodded ruefully.

"Pray, Mr. Arbuthnot," Daphne continued, "how was Prince Singh's body disposed of?"

The carpet! That's why it was missing, Jack thought.

Arbuthnot drew another deep breath. "There was no bloody mess, except on the carpet. We rolled his body in the carpet." He stopped, as if he could not go on.

"Where'd you put the body?" Jack asked.

"You've seen the Indian prince's final resting place."

"In the desert," Daphne whispered.

His eyes met hers, and he nodded.

"If you hope to keep that no-good neck of yours out of the noose, you better tell me where I can find d'Arblier."

Arbuthnot's eyes closed. "He's gone. He boarded a boat for Alexandria this morning. That's the truth. Since I've lost mine, I swear it on my father's honor."

Jack cursed.

"Late yesterday, the duc, Williams and I met and shared information. As we were seeing him off on the *felucca* he said he would get you yet,

Dryden."

"Williams never came back to his lodgings. Do you know where we can find him?"

"He's at my house."

"And the Amun Re mask?"

"Williams—at the behest of the duc—sold it in Constantinople. It fetched a great deal of money for the duc, and that degenerate Williams made a tidy bonus."

So the Pasha had been right about that.

Finally Maxwell spoke. "Should you like me to ask Mr. Briggs to send around for the Turkish authorities to arrest this man?"

Arbuthnot squeezed his eyes shut.

Jack nodded grimly. "Yes."

$\mathcal{C}$hapter 20

Jack felt lower than an adder's belly. The mystery was solved, but there was no jubilation. Prince Singh was dead. The Regent would not get his Amun-re mask. Ralph Arbuthnot was likely going to hang. And the duc d'Arblier was on his way back to France.

Their only success was seeing Williams apprehended and charged with murder. The authorities took a statement from Rosemary that he'd confessed to her. They planned to take custody of the hair Jack had found on the murdered woman. Habeeb was bringing Amal's maid to the jail so she could identify Williams. All in all, there was a tight case against the Welshman.

It wasn't until late that afternoon they got away from the Consulate and made it back to their hotel, sadly flat as he, Daphne, and Maxwell gathered in the hotel's drawing room. They were soon joined by Rosemary and her Captain. Since there was no longer a need for secrecy, they were free to disclose in front of Captain Cooper the reason for their presence in Egypt. This they did as they told Rosemary all that had transpired in their confrontation with Arbuthnot.

"I never cared for Mr. Arbuthnot," Rosemary said, "but I hate to see him hang."

"Mr. Briggs said that the fact he accepted money from a French agent was enough to charge him with treason," Daphne said.

Captain Cooper winced. "The penalty for which is hanging."

"It's too late for Arbuthnot to learn that he who lies with dogs riseth with fleas," Jack said. There was no greater dog than d'Arblier.

Rosemary had not taken a seat but had continued to stand next to the Captain. "I have an announcement to make."

All eyes went to her.

"I have given Captain Cooper permission to ask Papa for my hand in marriage."

If the poor girl had been expecting a gushing of congratulations, she had miscalculated. Several seconds of complete silence followed her announcement. They were all stunned.

Maxwell was the first to respond. He stood, crossed the floor, and offered to shake Cooper's hand. "Felicitations, Captain. You are a most fortunate man."

Then he moved to Rosemary and bowed. "I hope you will be very happy, my lady."

Drawing his breath, he said, "I shall take my leave. I have correspondence that demands my attention."

Poor fellow. Maxwell may have turned in a commendable performance, but there was no doubt he was gravely wounded by the announcement.

Daphne was quick to follow suit, offering her congratulations, but Jack could tell she did so only for politeness. Her voice lacked the warmth such an occasion would normally elicit in her.

Begrudgingly, he offered the ill-suited couple his best wishes.

Before an awkward silence could ensue, they

were called to the dinner room. Maxwell never showed. Daphne picked at her food. Jack knew she was anxious to be alone with him to discuss this proposed addition to her family.

Half way through the meal, she rose, saying that she'd lost her appetite. "I know you and Captain Cooper have much to discuss. I think, too, you'll be safe in your chamber tonight and won't have to come to our room—unless, of course, it would please you to do so."

"I believe the threats to my safety are now gone," Rosemary said.

Jack stood, claiming his appetite had deserted him also. "It's been a wretched couple of days."

In their chamber, Daphne collapsed on the bed, fully clothed. Her voice was incredibly somber when she spoke. "My sister has made a grave mistake."

"I know. It's not a good match. Except for Cooper."

"I really thought she and Mr. Maxwell were perfect for each other."

Jack shrugged. "It's hard to compete with one who's the epitome of masculine physical perfection." Not that Jack normally noticed another man's appearance. It was just that he'd heard so much praise heaped upon Cooper that he'd taken notice of the man's height and build and realized that few men were in possession of such attributes. A pity. Maxwell, though small, was twice the man.

"I'm just so beastly blue-deviled. I had loved coming here, and now as we're about to leave, I realize nothing has worked out well. The crowning blow is that my sister is throwing her life away on an unworthy suitor."

"It's Rosemary's decision. We must accept it."

"I was disappointed when Cornelia told us she was going to marry Lankersham, but at least Lankersham was a duke. Captain Cooper is beneath Rosemary on every count—most especially in intelligence."

He came to sit beside her, taking her hand in his. "It's Rosemary's life."

She sighed. "I suppose we'll see about returning home tomorrow."

"I thought you wanted to go to Thebes."

Her face brightened. "You'd take us?"

"With Maxwell." He frowned. "But I don't suppose Cooper could take that long of a leave."

She turned up her nose. "He wouldn't even have the slightest desire to see the antiquities there. He's so utterly unsuitable for Rosemary."

"We'll discuss all this tomorrow. I can tell you're exhausted."

* * *

Rosemary came to her chamber and closed the door behind her. How she missed her maid! Since she had come out of the school room, she'd had a personal maid who saw that her clothes were cleaned and ironed, who styled her hair, and who assisted her in dressing. It was a luxury Daphne, who was impervious to fashion, could not understand. With a sigh, Rosemary began to strip off her dress and prepare for bed.

On this, the night of her engagement, she should be ecstatically happy. But she was not. She supposed adjusting to the idea of being betrothed was rather like adjusting to kissing. It would take time.

As she doused her candle and fell onto her bed, she thought of all that had transpired in that one single day. The whole course of her life was altered. It was a long time before she fell to sleep, and not terribly long after she did, she awakened from a curious dream.

In her dream, she was kissing. And she was vastly enjoying the kissing. When she looked up at her lover, she saw spectacles. It was not the man to whom she was betrothed! It was Mr. Maxwell.

The very thought of kissing Mr. Maxwell sent her heartbeat roaring. She suddenly recalled that this was not the first time she'd had so profound a physical reaction to him. She remembered how she'd felt two days previously when he'd opened his eyes and slowly swept his gaze down her body. Every cell in her body had tingled. She'd felt womanly for the first time in her life.

Today, when Captain Cooper's lazy gaze had moved from her head to her toes, she'd felt nothing. Nothing except uncomfortable.

She lay in her bed for a long time, pondering this strangely intoxicating feeling that had come over her. Isn't marrying Captain Cooper what she'd wanted since the day of her debut? Now that she had captured his affections, she felt neither victory nor joy.

All she could think of was Mr. Maxwell. How lucky was the woman who engaged his affections. Would they spend half the year in Arabian countries and half at Cambridge as he'd done as a bachelor? What an exciting life they would have.

More than that, she thought of kissing Mr. Maxwell. She wondered if in reality his kisses would elicit no more passion than those of Captain Cooper. Or would they be the blissful kisses of her dream?

She felt traitorous. Here she was, engaged to

the Captain and dreaming about Mr. Maxwell. Something was grossly wrong with all this. A woman should not be feeling remorse on the night of her betrothal.

She had done the wrong thing.

The very contemplation of kissing Mr. Maxwell caused her breath to grow short.

"That settles it," she told herself. "There's no way to know if I'm in error until I kiss Mr. Maxwell." If his kisses left her as dissatisfied as Captain Cooper's, then she would know that kissing was an activity that must be cultivated over time, rather like the trial and error involved in botanical studies.

She sat up in her bed. She was about to do something she would never contemplate were she in her homeland, but here in Egypt she could indulge in acts that would never be sanctioned in London.

Besides, Mr. Maxwell was an honorable man.

She got up and moved to the small mirror over the wash basin and brushed out her hair. Next, she dabbed rosewater on her neck. Then she left her room and padded down the corridor to Mr. Maxwell's chamber and knocked softly.

Footsteps answered. "Who's there?" he asked.

"It's Lady Rosemary."

"Is something wrong?"

"Please, allow me to come into your chamber."

"Give me a moment." More footsteps.

Daphne had told her it was not uncommon for men, especially in these climates, to sleep naked. The idea of Mr. Maxwell stretched naked on a bed caused her to throb in places she'd previously been unaware of.

A moment later, he swept open the door. He

was barefoot but had managed to slip on trousers and a shirt that he hadn't bothered to tuck in. He still had not shaved, and his beard was quite masculine looking. He'd left off his spectacles.

He let her in and softly shut the door. "You shouldn't be here."

"I know, but I also know that you're a gentleman who would not take liberties and would not ever disclose that I came to your chamber in the middle of the night."

"Of course I wouldn't." He moved backward, away from her encroachment. "Pray, my lady, why have you come?"

She never removed her heated gaze from his. "I have come to ask something of you."

"Anything."

She moved to him, her breath ragged. When there were just inches between them, she looked up at him and spoke in a husky purr. "I should like for you to kiss me."

Before he could protest, she stood on her toes and leaned into him, pressing her lips against his. His breath hitched for only a second, and then he gathered her close and gave in to the maddening, dizzying, thoroughly delightful intoxication of this kiss.

It was nothing like the Captain's. This was the most pleasurable thing she'd ever done! She did not know who'd initiated it, but their mouths opened to each other's exploration, and she was quite sure she could swoon from utter joy.

In that moment, the veil of melancholy lifted from her. She may have done the wrong thing with Captain Cooper, but she was definitely doing the right thing with Mr. Maxwell. This is the man she was meant to spend her life with.

This was the man she loved.

He finally forced himself to break the kiss, and when he spoke, there was a breathlessness in his voice. "Forgive me. I shouldn't have."

Her index finger lightly touched the mouth that had given her such pleasure. "Don't say that. I'm so happy you did."

"You are?"

She nodded.

"Why did you want me to kiss you?"

"For a very good reason, a reason that could profoundly affect the rest of my life."

His brows lowered. "I don't understand."

"I felt nothing other than possible repugnance when Captain Cooper kissed me for the first time today. I knew in my heart that wasn't how one was supposed to feel with the man one is supposed to marry."

She drew a deep breath, then continued. "Tonight I dreamed I was kissing you, and it wasn't at all repugnant. That's why I came. I had to know if your kisses would accelerate my pulse, if your kisses would ignite my passion, if your kisses would steal away my breath."

He was silent for a moment, as if he were afraid to ask. "That's an extraordinarily lofty expectation."

She couldn't dispel the memory of that wonderful kiss. "Oh, but you are an extraordinary kisser, Stanton." She had never before called a man by his Christian name.

"Do you really think so? I have no expertise in such matters."

"Today I've learned that kissing is not about expertise. It's about the love between two people. I've come to realize that I cannot marry the

Captain when my heart belongs to you." She knew that because of the disparity in their rank, she had to be the first to make a declaration.

"Oh, God," he growled as he moved to her and drew her into his arms. "You really aren't going to marry him?"

"No, my dearest Stanton." How she adored calling him by his first name!

His hands sifted through her long tresses. "I'm very happy to hear that."

"Now that I've made a cake of myself over you, I was hoping you might say something romantic to me. Do you think you could ever fall in love with me?"

"I know nothing of love, but I know yours is the first face I've pictured every morning, the last every night. I know that the anticipation of being with you each day made me happy, that when you were with Captain Cooper I was sad. I know that I would lay down my life to preserve yours. For I cannot imagine a world without beautiful Rose."

She kissed his cheek "I am your Rose, my love."

He drew back, lifted her right hand, and softly kissed it. "Come, let's go to the window seat and plan our future."

"I do hope you're going to offer for me."

"You possess everything I could ever want in a wife. Could you—once you sever your ties with the Captain, that is—consent to marry me?"

"Nothing could make me happier."

Hand in hand, they strode to the window seat. He threw open the window just as the first Call to Prayer of the day rang out from the minaret and wafted through the smoky-coloured predawn skies.

* * *

Daphne had grown so accustomed to the Calls to Prayer that she'd been sleeping through the predawn Fajr. But not today. She had a feeling something had happened to Rosemary, and she leapt from her bed to rush to her sister's chamber. *I just need to know she's all right.* Daphne knocked on Rosemary's door, but there was no answer. She tried the knob, and her heart thudded. It was open! After all her sister had been through, there was no way she would be so careless.

That had to mean she was not in her chamber.

Daphne threw open the door and moved to Rosemary's bed. It was empty. There was no sign of her in the chamber. Good, lord! She'd been abducted again.

Her heartbeat thundering, she raced back to her own bedchamber and awakened Jack. "Rosemary's gone!"

He bolted up. "That can't be!"

"But she is!"

"You're overreacting. You know as well as I that there are no longer any threats to her safety." He drew a breath. "Has it occurred to you that she and her intended might be . . . having a little cuddle?"

"That scoundrel! How could he take advantage of Rosemary's innocence? Come, you and I are going to his room."

"I'll do no such thing! He's done the honorable thing by offering for her."

"If he's having a cuddle with my maiden sister, that is not at all the honorable thing!" She stomped her foot. "I'll go without you."

When she got to the door of their bedchamber, she turned back. "He is on the third floor, is he not?"

"Daf, you can't run about the hotel in your night shift."

"I'm not taking the time to get dressed." She stalked off.

Cursing, he threw his legs over the bed to go after her (once he dressed).

When she got to the third floor, she wasn't precisely sure which chamber was Captain Conceited's. She recalled that he'd gotten the last available chamber. She'd been told it was the smallest and was at the back of the building. Deciding that the third floor plan must be identical to her floor, she knew which was the smallest chamber. It would be the one above Mr. Maxwell's.

She went to that door and softly knocked. Nothing. Good lord, what if the Captain had abducted Rosemary? She knocked louder. This time she heard a man's grumble, then heavy footsteps. "Who's there at this ungodly hour?" he demanded.

"It's Lady Daphne. I'm looking for my sister."

The door whipped open.

Oh, dear. The captain didn't appear to be wearing . . . anything. He did show her a modicum of respect by standing *behind* the door. "Lady Rosemary's not in her chamber?" He sounded truly distressed.

"Are you sure she's not with you?"

"I'd bloody well know it if my betrothed was with me! And I resent that you'd think a fine lady like Rosemary would be coming to the room of a man to whom she was not married."

"I was only hoping, for I fear the white slavers have taken her."

"Dear God."

Jack walked up. "Now see here, Daphne. No white slavers got your sister."

"Not last time, but they must have this time."

"Allow me to get dressed," Captain Cooper said. "We must begin searching for her."

"Dearest, go awaken Mr. Maxwell. We'll need his help."

Jack nodded, squeezed her hand sympathetically and began to descend the stairs. She solemnly followed. What had begun as a journey of a lifetime for her sister had resulted in one's worst nightmare. She prayed Rosemary would not be harmed, prayed that she wasn't being sold into some sultan's harem.

What she saw when she reached their corridor gladdened her heart. Mr. Maxwell's doorway framed Rosemary in her night shift standing exceedingly close to Mr. Maxwell, whose arm was around her. They looked like a couple who'd long been happily married.

Daphne raced to her sister and hugged her. "I was so worried about you!"

"I have an announcement to make," Rosemary said, tilting her head to bestow a loving smile on Stanton Maxwell.

"Dearest," Daphne said, "if you're going to announce you intentions of marrying Mr. Maxwell, you simply cannot do that until you terminate your betrothal with Captain Cooper."

Heavy footsteps hurried down the stairs, two stairs at a time. When Captain Conceited met them and ran his eye over Rosemary and Mr. Maxwell, he exploded. "What the devil's going on? What have you done to my intended?" The Captain lunged at Mr. Maxwell, swinging a fist at his face.

But Mr. Maxwell ducked, then shoved away the other man, who was twice his size.

When the Captain started back, Jack interceded, standing between the two men. "I think Lady Rosemary and Captain Cooper may need a few minutes together."

"I'll not speak to her, not when she's so improperly dressed," the Captain said.

"Then allow me to tell you," Rosemary began, "that despite that you did me a great honor by asking me to be your wife, I have decided we will not suit."

"It's just as well," Captain Cooper hissed. "I won't have a wife who's been sullied by white slavers."

Mr. Maxwell was so enraged, he shoved Jack aside and assaulted the captain, crashing a fist into his face.

To all of their astonishment, the huge Captain fell to the ground.

All was silent.

The Captain nursed his bruised pride for a moment before he got to his feet and began to mount the stairs. "I'll return to Rached this morning."

Jack and Daphne joined the happy couple in Mr. Maxwell's chamber. By now the sun was rising, and she could clearly see their faces. A happier couple she had never seen. How perfect they were for each other!

"I would say, my dear sister, that the past day has been momentous for you."

Rosemary's adoring gaze lifted to Mr. Maxwell, then to her sister. "Indeed it has. I have never been possessed of a stronger conviction than this: there's only one man in the world with whom I would want to spend my life."

"And has Mr. Maxwell gone down on bended knee?"

A look of distress came over his face. "I've erred. I was supposed to go to my knees and beg for your hand?"

"No, you goose," Rosemary said. "You've done everything perfectly." She turned to Daphne. "I'm not precisely sure which of us did the asking. I knew Stanton would need a bit of a nudge from me."

How naturally her lover's name rolled off her tongue, Daphne thought.

"I would never have been so presumptuous," Mr. Maxwell declared.

"I am sure our Papa will love you, Mr. Maxwell," Daphne said.

Rosemary regarded her sister. "I know you're disappointed in the outcome of your inquiries, but this expedition has been the greatest, most exciting thing that's ever happened to me."

Daphne nodded. "In spite of the fact we weren't terribly successful and in spite of the fact you were almost killed, and in spite of the fact that murdering Frenchman got away, I have to say I've loved every moment—save the in-spite-of moments, that is."

"I must offer you felicitations, Maxwell. My wife and I have known for some time that you two were perfect for one another."

Mr. Maxwell meekly thanked him.

"Oh, I've just thought of the most wonderful thing!" Daphne said. "When we were at the consulate today, a traveling English clergyman stopped by. We can get him to marry you!"

Rosemary threw her arms around the second

man she'd become betrothed to. "Oh, Stanton, would that not be wonderful? We could share a cabin on the ship back to England!"

Jack cleared his throat. "I was thinking about an expedition to Thebes."

Rosemary squealed like an ecstatic child. "Oh, Stanton, is that not wonderful?"

Maxwell nodded and eyed Jack. "I'm delighted you will be able to manage the journey to Thebes."

"If you're married, the two of you will be able to share a tent," Daphne said. Her shimmering gaze met Jack's as she looked forward to more moonlit desert lovemaking with her own husband.

The End

Author's Biography

A former journalist and English teacher, Cheryl Bolen sold her first book to Harlequin Historical in 1997. That book, *A Duke Deceived*, was a finalist for the Holt Medallion for Best First Book, and it netted her the title Notable New Author. Since then she has published more than 20 books with Kensington/Zebra, Love Inspired Historical and was Montlake launch author for Kindle Serials. As an independent author, she has broken into the top 5 on the *New York Times* and top 20 on the *USA Today* bestseller lists.

Her 2005 book *One Golden Ring* won the Holt Medallion for Best Historical, and her 2011 gothic historical *My Lord Wicked* was awarded Best Historical in the International Digital Awards, the same year one of her Christmas novellas was chosen as Best Historical Novella by Hearts Through History. Her books have been finalists for other awards, including the Daphne du Maurier, and have been translated into eight languages.

She invites readers to www.CherylBolen.com, or her blog, www.cherylsregencyramblings.wordpress.co or Facebook at https://www.facebook.com/pages/Cheryl-Bolen-Books/146842652076424.

CPSIA information can be obtained
at www.ICGtesting.com
Printed in the USA
LVHW031503270222
712137LV00018B/114